BAM! BAM! BAM!

It sounded like som
sledgehammer. I r
bloodshot eye.

Bam! Bam! Bam!

I have a little trouble with my temper, especially
when I have a hangover. I yanked the door
open.

Invaded by dwarves.

For a minute I didn't see the woman. She barely
came up to my chest. I eyeballed the three guys
behind her. They were lugging enough steel to
outfit their own army, but I wouldn't have been
shy about wading in. Two of them were about
fifteen years old and the other was about a
hundred and five.

"I don't make a habit of busting female heads,"
I said, "but in your case I think I can make an
exception."

She was not impressed. . . .

SWEET SILVER
BLUES

SWEET SILVER BLUES

Glen Cook

A SIGNET BOOK

NEW AMERICAN LIBRARY

PUBLISHED BY
THE NEW AMERICAN LIBRARY
OF CANADA LIMITED

NAL BOOKS ARE AVAILABLE AT QUANTITY DISCOUNTS
WHEN USED TO PROMOTE PRODUCTS OR SERVICES.
FOR INFORMATION PLEASE WRITE TO PREMIUM MARKETING DIVISION,
NEW AMERICAN LIBRARY, 1633 BROADWAY,
NEW YORK, NEW YORK 10019.

First Printing, August, 1987

2 3 4 5 6 7 8 9

SIGNET TRADEMARK REG. U.S. PAT OFF AND FOREIGN COUNTRIES
REGISTERED TRADEMARK — MARCA REGISTRADA
HECHO EN WINNIPEG, CANADA

SIGNET, SIGNET CLASSIC, MENTOR, ONYX, PLUME, MERIDIAN
AND NAL BOOKS are published in Canada by The New American
Library of Canada, Limited, 81 Mack Avenue, Scarborough,
Ontario, Canada M1L 1M8
PRINTED IN CANADA
COVER PRINTED IN U.S.A.

1

Bam! Bam! Bam!

It sounded like someone was knocking with a sledge-hammer. I rolled over and cracked a bloodshot eye. I couldn't see a figure through the window, but that wasn't surprising. I could barely make out the lettering on the grimy glass:

GARRETT

INVESTIGATOR

CONFIDENTIAL AGENT

I had blown my wad buying the glass and wound up being my own painter.

The window was as dirty as last week's dishwater, but not filthy enough to block out the piercing morning light. The damned sun wasn't up yet! And I'd been out till the second watch barhopping while I followed a guy who might lead me to a guy who might know where I could find a guy. All this led to was a pounding headache.

"Go away!" I growled. "Not available."

Bam! Bam! Bam!

"Go to hell away!" I yelled. It left my head feeling like an egg that had just bounced off the edge of a frying pan. I wondered if I ought to feel the back to see if the yolk was leaking, but it seemed like too much work. I'd just go ahead and die.

Bam! Bam! Bam!

I have a little trouble with my temper, especially

when I have a hangover. I was halfway to the door with two feet of lead-weighted truncheon before sense penetrated the scrambled yolk.

When they are that insistent, it's somebody from up the hill with a summons to do work too sticky to lay on their own boys. Or it's somebody from down the hill with the word that you're stepping on the wrong toes.

In the latter case the truncheon might be useful.

I yanked the door open.

For a moment I didn't see the woman. She barely came up to my chest. I eyeballed the three guys behind her. They were lugging enough steel to outfit their own army, but I wouldn't have been shy about wading in. Two of them were about fifteen years old and the other was about a hundred and five.

"We're invaded by dwarfs," I moaned. None of them was taller than the woman.

"Are you Garrett?" She looked disappointed in what she saw.

"No. Two doors down. Good-bye." *Slam!* Two doors down was a night-working ratman who made a hobby of getting on my nerves. I figured it was his turn in the barrel.

I stumbled toward bed with the vague suspicion that I had seen those people before.

I wriggled around like an old dog. When you're hung over there is no way to get comfortable, feather bed or creek bed. Just as I was getting reacquainted with being horizontal again, *Bam! Bam! Bam!*

I told myself I wouldn't move. They would take the hint.

They didn't. It sounded like the entire room was about to cave in. I was not going to get any more sleep.

I got up again—gingerly—and drank a quart of water. I chased it with skunky beer and clung to my temper precariously.

Bam! Bam! Bam!

"I don't make a habit of busting female heads," I

told the tiny woman when I opened the door again. "But in your case I think I can make an exception."

She was not impressed. "Dad wants to see you, Garrett."

"Say, that's wonderful. That explains a gang of runts trying to break my door down. What does the gnome king want?"

The old codger said, "Rose, it's obvious this isn't a convenient time for Mr. Garrett. We've waited three days. A few more hours won't make any difference."

Rose? I should know a Rose from somewhere. But where?

"Mr. Garrett, I'm Lester Tate. And I want to apologize—on Rose's behalf—for bothering you at this hour. She's a headstrong child, and having been overindulged by my brother all her life, she's blind to any desires but her own." He spoke in the soft, tired voice of a man who spends a lot of time arguing with a whirlwind.

"Lester Tate?" I asked. "Like in Denny Tate's uncle Lester?"

"Yes."

"It's beginning to come back. The family picnic at Elephant Rocks three years ago. I came with Denny." Maybe I had laundered my memory because Rose had been an unspeakably nasty wench that day. "Maybe it was all the hardware that made me forget your faces." Denny Tate and I went back about eight years, but I hadn't seen him in months. "So how is Denny?" I asked, maybe a little guilty.

"Dead!" barked sweet sister Rose.

Denny Tate and I were heroes of the Cantard Wars. That means we did our five years and got out alive. A lot of guys don't.

We went in about the same time, were barracked less than twenty miles apart, but never met till later, here in TunFaire, eight hundred miles from the fighting. He was light cavalry out of Fort Must. I was Fleet Marines, mostly aboard the *Imperial Kimmswick* out of Full Harbor. I fought in the islands. Denny rode

over most of the Cantard, chasing or running away
from the Venageti. We both made sergeant before we
got out.

It was a nasty war. It still is. I like it better now that
it's much farther away.

Denny saw more of the worst than I did. The fighting at sea and in the islands was sideshow stuff. Neither we nor the Venageti wasted wizards on it. All the
flash and fury of sorcery got saved for the struggle on
the mainland.

Anyway, we'd both survived our five, and had done
part of them in the same general area, and that had
given us something in common when we met. It was
good enough till we got to know one another.

"So that's why you're a walking arsenal. What is it?
A vendetta? Maybe you'd better get inside."

Rose cackled like a hen laying a square egg.

Uncle Lester laughed too, but it was a laugh of a
different breed. "Shut up, Rosie. I'm sorry, Mr. Garrett. The weapons are here to feed Rosie's hunger for
drama. She believes we don't dare enter this neighborhood unarmed lest the local thugs ravish her."

It was not a good dawn for me. Few of them are.
Without thinking, I cracked, "The thugs in my neigh-
borhood have some taste. She doesn't have to worry."
Blame it on the hangover.

Uncle Lester grinned. Rose looked at me like I was
dog flop she wanted off her shoe.

I tried to gloss over with business. "Who did it?
What can I do about it?"

"Nobody did it," Rose told me. "He fell off a horse
and busted his head, his neck, and about ten other
bones."

"Hard to believe a skilled horseman could go that
way."

"It happened in broad daylight on a busy street.
There's no doubt that it was an accident."

"Then what do you need me for? Especially before
the sun is up?"

"That's for Dad to tell," Rose said. The shrew had

a lot of anger in her, anger that was there before I gave her cause. "Bringing you in on it was his idea, not mine."

I knew Denny's old man modestly. Well enough to use his first name if I was the kind of snotnose who calls his friends' parent by name instead of Mister. He ran a very successful cobbler's business. He, Denny, and two journeyman handled the custom and commercial trade. Uncle Lester and a dozen apprentices made boots under an open-end deal with the army. The war had been good to Denny's dad.

They do say it is an ill wind indeed that blows no one any good

Well, I was awake. Hair of the dog and scintillating conversation had reduced the pounding in my head to the tramp of ten thousand legions. Still there was a nagging guilt about not having made time to see Denny before the old gal in black climbed on his back. I decided to find out why the old man needed somebody in my line of work when there wasn't a doubt about how Denny checked out.

"Let me get myself put together and we'll be on our way."

Rose grinned wickedly. I realized I'd fed her a murderous straight line.

I didn't stick around to hear her pounce on it.

2

Willard Tate was no bigger than the rest of his tribe. A gnome. He was bald on top with tasseled gray hair to his shoulders on the sides and longer in the back. He was bent over his workbench, tapping tiny brass nails into the heel of a woman's shoe. Clearly he was at the top of his trade. He wore square TanHageen spectacles and they don't come cheap.

He was engrossed in his work. Recalling his state since his wife died, I figured he was working off grief.

"Mr. Tate?" He knew I was there. I had cooled my heels for twenty minutes while they told him.

He drove one more nail with a single perfect tap, looked at me over his cheaters. "Mr. Garrett. They tell me you made mock of our size."

"I get nasty when somebody drags me out before the sun comes up."

"That's Rose. If she has to see you in, she'll see you in the hard way. I made a bad job of her. Keep her in mind as you rear your own children."

I said nothing. You tell somebody you look forward to blindness more eagerly than to having kids, you don't win any friends. Those that don't think you're lying think you're crazy.

"Do you have a problem with short people, Mr. Garrett?"

About six flip answers never saw the air. He was dead serious. "Not really. Denny wouldn't have been my buddy if I did. Why? Is it important?"

"In a sideways sort of way. Did you ever wonder why the Tates are so small?"

I had never dwelled on it. "No."

"It's the blood. The taint of elvish. On both sides, several generations before my time. Keep that in mind. It will help you understand later."

I wasn't surprised. I'd suspected it before, the way Denny got along with animals. Plenty of people have the taint, yet most cover it up. There is a lot of prejudice against the half elfin.

My hangover had improved, but not much. I had no patience. "Can we get to the point, Mr. Tate? You want me to do a job, or what?"

"I want you to find someone." He rose from his bench and shed his leather apron. "Come with me."

I went. He took me into the Tate secret world, the compound behind the manufactory. Denny never did that.

"You've been doing all right for yourself," I said. We entered a formal garden, the existence of which I'd never suspected.

"We manage."

I should manage so good. "Where are we headed?"

"Denny's apartment."

Buildings stood shoulder to shoulder around the garden. From the street they looked like one continuous featureless warehouse. From the garden I could not imagine how I'd ever thought that. These houses were as fine as anything up the hill. They simply didn't face the street and make temptingly dangerous statements.

I wondered if they killed the workmen when the job was done. "The whole Tate tribe lives here?"

"Yes."

"Not much privacy."

"Too much, I think. We all have our own apartments. Some have street-side doors. Denny's does." Tate's tone said "This is a Significant Fact."

My curiosity was definitely growing. Tate's whole attitude indicated indignation at Denny's having had secrets from his old man.

He took me to Denny's place. The air inside was stuffy and warm, the way closed places get in summer. Nothing had changed since the one time Denny had invited me in—through the street-side door—except that Denny wasn't there. That made a lot of difference.

The place was as plain and neat as a new cheap coffin. Denny had been a man of ascetic habits. He'd never hinted at the comforts enjoyed by his family.

"It's in the basement."

"What is?"

"What I want you to see before I start explaining." He collected a lantern and lit it with a long match, which he kept burning.

Moments later we were in a basement as spotless as the ground floor. Old Man Tate and his match went around lighting lamps. I made like a cat too lazy to lick his own paws and just hung around with my mouth open.

Tate wore a small, smug smile when he faced me again. "Well?"

The cat that had my tongue could have fought a couple weights heavier than a snow leopard.

The only place you even hear about that much precious metal lying around is in stories about dragon hoards.

Actually, when my mind started working, I saw it wasn't so much after all. Just more than I'd ever imagined I would see in one place. A few hundred robbers working double shifts for four or five years might pile up as much.

"Where . . . ? How . . . ?"

"I don't know most of the answers myself, Mr. Garrett. My knowledge is limited to the notes Denny left. They were all written to himself. He knew what he was talking about. There is enough to fill in the outlines, though. I expect you'll want to read everything before you start."

I nodded but did not hear him. My friend Denny, the shoemaker. With a basement full of silver. Denny, whose only mention of money had been about the share he had taken when his regiment had overwhelmed a Venageti treasure caravan fleeing the defeat at Jordan Wells.

"How much?" I croaked. I was not getting any

better. The little guy that sits in the back row inside my head started catcalling me. I never thought wealth could have so much impact upon me.

"Sixty thousand marks in Karentine coined silver. The equivalent of eighteen thousand marks in coined silver of other states. Eight hundred four-ounce bars. Six hundred twenty-three eight-ounce bars. Forty-four one-pound bars. One hundred ten pounds in larger bars. Just under one thousand coined goldmarks. There's some billet tin and copper, too. A nice amount, but it doesn't count for much compared with the silver."

"Not unless a couple copper sceats would make the difference between eating and starvation. How did he do it? Don't tell me making ballroom slippers for fat duchesses. Nobody gets rich . . . working." I almost said "honestly."

"Trading in metals." Tate gave me a don't-be-stupid look. "Playing the changes in the shifting exchange rate between gold and silver. Buying silver when it was cheap against gold, selling it when gold was cheap against silver. He started with his prize money from the army. He switched back and forth at the best points in the cycle. That's what I meant when I said keep the elvish blood in mind. We people of elvish ancestry have a feel for silver."

"You're stereotyping yourself, Pop."

"You understand what I've said? How he came by it? I don't want you to think it's dishonest wealth."

"I understand." That did not make me think it was necessarily honest.

Anyone with a knack for reading the shifts could get rich the same way. Silver goes up and down violently according to the army's fortunes in the Cantard. As long as we are plagued by sorcerers, there will be an incredible demand for the metal.

Ninety percent of the world's silver is mined in the Cantard. Under all the excuses and historical claims, the mines are what the war is all about. Maybe if we could rid the world of magicians and their hunger for the mystic metal, peace and prosperity· would break out all over.

"Well?" Tate asked.

"Well what?"

"Will you do the job for us?"

Good question, I thought.

3

I looked at Tate and saw a momentary idiot, a fool
trying to twist me into doing something he feared I'd
turn my back on if I knew the whole story. "Pop,
would you make shoes if you didn't know the size? If
you hadn't even seen the person who was going to
wear them? Without knowing anything about getting
paid? I've been real patient on account of you being
Denny's old man. But I'm not going to play games."

He hemmed and hawed.

"Come on, Pop. Open the poke. Shake it out. Let's
see if the little porker oinks or meows."

His expression became pained, almost pleading. "I'm
just trying to do right by my son. Trying to carry out
his last wishes."

"We'll put up a statue. When does the clam open
up? Or do I go home and finish sleeping off this
hangover?" Why do they always do this? They bring
you in to handle a problem, then lie about it or hide it
from you. But they never stop screaming for results.

"You've got to understand—"

"Mr. Tate, I don't have to understand anything
except exactly what is going on. Why don't you start
from the beginning, tell me what you know, what you
want, and why you need me. And don't leave anything
out. If I take the job and find out you have, I'll get
extremely angry. I'm not a very nice man when I get
angry."

"Have you had your breakfast, Mr. Garrett? Of
course not. Rose wakened you and brought you straight
here. Why don't we do that while I order my thoughts?"

15

"Because there's nothing guaranteed to make me madder quicker than a stall."

He went red in the face. He was not used to backtalk.

"You talk or I walk. This is my life you're wasting."

"Damn it, a man can't . . ."

I started toward the stairs.

"All right. Stop."

I paused, waited.

"After Denny died, I came here and found all this," Tate said. "And I found a will. A *registered* will."

Most people don't bother to register, but that didn't amount to anything remarkable. "So?"

"So in the will he names you and me his executors."

"That damned sawed-off little runt! I'd break his neck for him if he hadn't already done it himself. That's it? All the shuffle-footing and coy looks is because he rung in an outsider?"

"Hardly. It's the terms of the will that are embarrassing."

"Yeah? He tell everybody what he thought of them?"

"In a way. He left everything but our executor's fees to someone none of us ever heard of."

I laughed. That was Denny. "So? He made the money. It's his to give away."

"I don't deny that. And I don't mind, believe it or not. But for Rose's sake . . ."

"You know what he thought about her? Want me to tell you?"

"She is his sister."

"Not that he had any choice about it. The nicest thing he ever said about her was, 'She's a useless, lazy, whining, conniving freeloader.' The word *bitch* came up a few times, too."

"But—"

"Never mind. I don't want to hear it. So what you want is for me to find this mysterious heir, eh? And then what?" They want you to do some crazy things sometimes. I could guess why Denny registered his will. A Rose with thorns.

"Just tell her the bequest is here for the claiming. Get a statement of intent we can file with the registry

SWEET SILVER BLUES 17

probate. Already they're harassing us about showing them that we're doing something to execute the terms of the will."

That figured. I knew those jackasses. Before the brewery gave me the consulting job, I did investigations for them, free-lance, to make ends meet. "You said 'her.' This heir is a woman?" Denny never mentioned knowing any women all the time I knew him. I had him figured for a complete asexual.

"Yes. An old girlfriend, from when he was in the army. He never fell out of love, it seems, and they never stopped writing letters, even though she married somebody else. You'll find your best leads in those letters. You were in the Cantard, too, so you'll know the places she talks about."

"The Cantard?"

"That's where she is, yes. Where are you going?"

"I've been to the Cantard once. I didn't get a choice that time. This time I do. Find yourself another patsy, Mr. Tate."

"Mr. Garrett, you're one of the executors. And I'm too old to make that trip."

"Won't hold a shot of legal water, Pop. An executor don't have to do squat if he didn't say he would and sign to do it up front. Good-bye."

"Mr. Garrett, the law allows the executors to draw up to ten percent of the value of an estate to recompense themselves and to cover their expenses. Denny's estate will go on the up side of a hundred thousand marks."

That was a stopper. Something to make me think. For about two winks. "Five thousand ain't to die for, Pop. And I don't have anybody to leave it to."

"Ten thousand, Mr. Garrett. I'll leave you my side. I don't want it."

I admit I hesitated first. "No."

"I'll pay your expenses out of my own purse. That makes it ten thousand clear."

I stayed clammed. Was the old coot in training for a devil's job?

"What will it take, Mr. Garrett?"

"How come you're so hot to find this frail?"

"I want to meet her, Mr. Garrett. I want to see the sort of woman capable of making a monkey of my son. Name your price."

"Even rich don't do you any good if the wild dogs of the Cantard are cracking your bones to get at the marrow."

"Name your price, Mr. Garrett. I am an old man who has lost the son he expected to follow him. I am a wealthy man with no more need to cling to wealth. I am a determined man. I will see this woman. So again I say, name your price."

I should have known better. Hell, I *did* know better. I'd been saying so for ten minutes. "Give me a thousand on account. I'll look over the stuff Denny left and do some poking around at this end, just to see if it's feasible. I'll let you know what I decide."

I went back down the stairs and pulled up a chair behind the desk where Denny's letters and notes were piled.

"I have to get back to work," Tate called. "I'll have Rose bring you some breakfast."

As I listened to Tate's tiny footsteps fade away, I couldn't help but weigh the possibility of dear Rose slipping something poisonous into my food. I sighed and turned to my work, hoping this next meal wouldn't be my last.

4

The first thing I did was look for the stuff Denny's family had missed. Misers always have something they think they have to hide. A basement like that, plain as it looked, had a thousand crannies where things could be squirreled away.

Just as I spotted it a little dirt fell from the under-flooring overhead. I cocked an ear. Not a sound. Somebody was doing a passable job of cat-footing around up there.

I had my feet on Denny's desk and was expanding my literary horizons when Rose and my griddle cakes sneaked on stage. I checked her over the top of the first page of a letter that somehow had a quality of *déjà vu*. But I didn't pay much attention. The smell of griddle cakes with wild honey, tea, hen's eggs, hot buttered bread, and steamed boodleberry preserves was a bit distracting to a man in my condition.

Rose was distracting, too. She was smiling.

Snakes smile that way before they strike.

When her sort smile you had better check over your shoulder for a guy with a knife.

She placed the tray before me, still smiling. "Here's a little of everything we had in the kitchen. I hope you'll find something to suit."

When they're nice to you, you had better get your back against a wall.

"Your feet hurt?"

"No." She gave me a puzzled look. "What makes you ask that?"

"The look on your face. It has to be pain."

19

Not a flicker of response, except, "So the old man talked you into it, did he?"

I raised an eyebrow. "Into what?"

"Finding that woman of Denny's." Plenty of vitriol pent up behind that smile.

"Nope. I told him I'd go over Denny's papers and look around town a little. I would tell him what I thought. That's all."

"You're going to do it. How much did he offer you to find her?"

I put my best blank cardplaying face and stared into the starved ice marbles of her eyes. I don't believe that stuff about windows of the soul. I've seen too many lying eyes. But beyond hers lay nothing but shatter-sharp flint and frosty iron.

"I'll give you twenty percent if you don't find her. Twenty-five if you find her dead."

Blank-faced, I started on my breakfast. There was ham and sausage, too. The tea was so good I drained half the pot before I touched anything else.

"I could be very generous," she said, turning sideways, posing to show what she had.

She had the equipment. All of it, and plenty of it. A prime little package, but a package filled with rot. "Denny said that you like small women."

Some better than others, I thought. "I make a point of trying not to be cruel to people, Rose. The best I can do here is speak plain and say I'm not interested."

She took rejection well. She ignored it. "I'm going with you, you know."

"With me? Where?"

"To the Cantard."

"I've got a flash for you, lady. I'm not doing any dirty work for you, and you aren't crossing the street with me. I do thank you for bringing breakfast. I need it, and appreciate it. Now go away and let me see if there's any reason I should be fool enough to get into this at all."

"I'm a stubborn woman, Garrett. I usually get what I want. If you won't help me, you'd better walk away from the whole thing. People who get in my way get hurt."

"Unless you're out of here by the time I finish this cup of tea you're going over my knee and getting what your old man should have given you while you were still young enough to have some sense pounded into you."

She retreated to the stairway. "I'll claim you raped me."

I grinned. Last refuge of the female scoundrel. "I'm not rich like you, but I can afford a truthsayer. Go ahead. Let's see how your dad takes losing two kids in one week."

She started upstairs. End of that game.

I went back and dug the dark package from the shadow between two floor joists anchored on the outside foundation. It was not hidden. Every space along that wall was stuffed. But the wrapping of this bundle was a cavalry saddle blanket. Denny's service meant a lot to him. He kept every memento. What he would wrap in his saddle blanket would be important too.

I dropped my seabag into the harbor as I strutted down the gangway the day I mustered out. Tells you how thrilled I was with the life of a Royal Marine.

The bundle contained a stack of military maps of the Cantard, most ours, a few Venageti. Both kinds are dangerous to have. You could get arrested for spying. The people who ask questions for the court don't stop till you confess.

With the maps were overlays of skin scraped transparently thin and several slim, expensive, bound journals.

I took the lot to Denny's desk.

Each of the overlays examined a critical battle of the past six years. The names of captains, commanders, and outfits were noted. One journal examined each battle commander by commander and unit by unit.

What the hell? Denny wasn't any war buff.

Reading gave me a glimmer, though. For instance, the table of royal officers:

1: Count Agar: Impulsive. Overly aggressive. Prone to act on inadequate intelligence.

9: Margrave Leon: Timid. Wants sure thing before offering battle. Easily rattled during engagement.

14: Viscount Noah: Vacillator. Excessively ferocious when engaged. A spendthrift of men and matériel.

22: Glory Mooncalled: Best all-around commander under Karentine colors. Excellent tactician. Able to train slowest and most uninspired men. Handicapped by low birth, mercenary status, and role in Seigod Mutiny while serving Venageti side. Weakness is a consuming hatred of Venageti warlords.

There was a Venageti list, too, and an analysis of potential matches and mismatches. If you were in the business of shuffling gold and silver, it would be handy to know who would control the silver mines a few months down the road. Denny had been serious about trying to outguess fortune.

I smelled an old dead carp, though. Denny drew forty-eight marks prize money and mustering-out pay. You don't turn forty-eight marks into a hundred thousand without cutting corners.

Denny's business log contained some hints.

Note from V: An agent of Stormlord Atto inquired the cost of 50 pd silver. First tremor of preparation for new offensive?

Z reported verbally: Harrow made port with 200 pd silver in ballast. Must sell before Mooncalled takes Freemantle.

Harrow southbound with 1000 pd granulated inside hollowed ballast billets. Biggest deal yet. Pray for fair weather.

Letter from K. Warlord Ironlock, 20,000 men, 3 firelords of the Eastern Circle, Third Rite, ordered to Lare. Attack through the Bled? Viscount Blush defending. Buy coined silver.

V, Z, and several others could be the cavalry cronies Denny hung out with. There were hints it was a tight group operation. But K was no old army buddy.

I turned to the heir and lover's letters last, about the time a cousin dropped in to ask what I wanted for lunch.

"Whatever the rest of you are having. With a quart of beer. And tell old man Tate I need him."

That was when I started the letters. That's when the guy in the cheap seats decided I was going back to the Cantard. The rest of me fought the valiant fight for a long time.

5

"You look like you saw a ghost," Tate said.

I looked up from the letter I'd been staring at for five minutes. "What? Oh. Yeah. Almost. Mr. Tate, you told me it was honest money."

He did not say anything. He had suspected it was something shady.

"You had any unusual visitors? Sudden old friends of Denny's asking questions?"

"No."

"You will. Soon. There's too much here for them to let it go. Be careful."

"What do you mean?"

It seemed an honest question. So maybe he did not know the world well enough to read what Denny had written. I laid it out for him.

He did not believe me.

"Doesn't matter what either of us thinks. The point is, so far I'm interested enough to keep on. I'll need that thousand. There are going to be heavy expenses from the start. And a box. I need a big box."

"I'll have Lester bring the money from the office. Why do you want a box?"

"To pack all this stuff."

"No."

"Say what?"

"You're not taking it out of here."

"I'm taking it or I'm taking me away. You want me to do a job, you let me do it. My way."

"Mr. Garrett . . ."

"Pop, you're paying for results, not the right to mess

with me. Get me a box, then go pound nails in a shoe. I don't have time for whining and games."

He hadn't recovered from what I had said about Denny. He did not have any fight left. He took off.

The funny thing was he left me feeling guilty, like I had been giving him a hard time just to puff up my own ego. I didn't need that guilt. So I ended up giving in and just letting everything go the way Tate wanted.

Strange how you can manipulate yourself when somebody outside can't.

I leaned back and watched dust fall from the underflooring as a pair of sneaky feet stole after Tate.

I was still that way when the cousin brought lunch and beer. I was busy inhaling that when Uncle Lester appeared with a fat moneybag and a big wicker chest. I finished my beer in one long draft, belched against the back of my wrist, asked, "What do you think about all this, Uncle Lester?"

He shrugged. "Ain't my place to say."

"How's that?"

"Eh?"

It began to sound like hogs-at-the-trough time—all grunts and snorts. "Did you read any of this stuff?" I asked.

"Yes."

"Care to comment?"

"Looked like Denny was dipping his toes in the shadows. You could tell that better than me."

"He was. And he was an amateur. A damned lucky amateur. You ever have any hints that he was into anything?"

"Nope. Unless you count that woman's letters. Them writing back and forth like that all this time seemed a mite odd to me. Ain't natural."

"Yes?"

"The boy was kin, and he's dead, and you don't want to speak ill of either one. But he was a bit strange, that boy. Always a loner 'fore he went off to the war. I'd bet that woman is the only one he ever had. If he had her. He didn't look at one after he got back."

"Maybe he crossed?"

Lester snorted and gave me his best look of disgust, like I didn't know about the Tates and the elves back when—though the cartha are the interspecies rage these days.

"Just asking. I didn't think so. He seemed to be a guy who just wasn't interested. I've been in brag sessions when he was around. He never had a story to tell."

Lester smirked. "Listened polite like, way you might if'n I started telling stories about when I was a kid."

He had me.

It is not often Garrett gets caught with nothing to say.

He grinned. "On that note I'll be goin'."

I grunted at his stern. Then I leaned back and closed my eyes and surrendered to the haunt that had me so distracted. To the coincidence so long the devils themselves must have pulled it in.

Kayean Kronk.

Maybe Denny *could* spend all those years in love with a memory. I gave it three hard ones before I broke the spell.

There was only one thing to do. Go see the Dead Man.

6

He's called the Dead Man because they killed him four hundred years ago. But he is neither dead nor a man. He is a Loghyr, and they don't die just because somebody sticks a bunch of knives into them. Their bodies go through the motions—cooling out, rigor mortis, lividity—but they do not corrupt. Not at any rate mere humans can detect. Loghyr bones have been found in the ruins on Khatar Island; they are very similar to a human's when they are dry.

"Hey, Old Bones. Don't look like the diet is working." The Dead Man is four hundred fifty pounds of mean, a little ragged around the edges, where the moths and mice and ants have gotten to him. He was parked in a chair in a dark room in a house that pretended to be both abandoned and haunted. He smelled. The corruption process is slow, but it goes on. "You need a bath, too."

A psychic chill set me shivering. He was sleeping. He isn't easy to get along with at his best, and he's at his worst when newly awakened.

I am not sleeping. I am meditating.

The thoughts hammered at my brain.

"Guess it's all a matter of perspective."

The psychic chill became physical. My breath clouded and my shoe buckles frosted over. I hurried with a little propitiations that are necessary when dealing with the Dead Man. The freshly cut flowers went into the big crystal bowl on the filthy old table before him. Then I lit candles. His sense of humor insists there be thirteen of them, all black, burning while he is in consultation.

To my knowledge he is the only Loghyr ever to allow his genius to be commercialized.

He does not need the candlelight to see visitors or flowers. But he likes to pretend that he does.

Aha! I see you now. Garrett. You pestilence. Can't you leave me alone? Every other day you're in here, worse than the moths and mice.

"It's been five months, Chuckles. And from the looks of this place you've been meditating the whole time."

A mouse that had been hiding beneath his oversized chair made a break for it. The Dead Man snatched it with his mind and sent it flying out of the house. Moths exploded away from him. He was incapable of doing malicious harm to bugs, who wanted to eat him, but could make life unholy hell for people with the effrontery to ask him to work.

"You have to work sometime," I told him. "Even a dead man has to pay the rent. And you need somebody to give you a bath and clean the place up. Not to mention getting the vermin out again."

A big, shiny black spider crawled out of one piglike nostril on the end of his ten-inch trunk. It did not like my looks. It ducked back inside.

Cheap flowers.

They were not. I had given him absolutely no legitimate cause for complaint. He couldn't banish me because he didn't want to work. I knew the state of his finances. His landlord had come to me about his last month's rent.

Must not be much of a client you have, Garrett. You sneaking around after cheating wives again?

"You know better." I was out of all that, thanks to him.

How much?

"You owe me for a month's rent already."

You have the smug, content look of a man whose expenses have been guaranteed.

"So?"

How much can you soak your client before he squawks?

"I don't know."

Enough, I think, the way you look. Which is like a man who has a good fix on the pot at the end of the rainbow. Start reading.

"What?"

Stop playing the idiot, Garrett. You're too old. You dragged that crate of stuff here so you could bore me. That is the worst of being dead, Garrett. It is damned boring. You cannot do anything.

"Loghyr don't do anything when they're *alive*."

Read, Garrett. Your welcome is wearing thin.

I won. Sort of. He listened while I gave him every word, showed him every map. A smooth, professional report. I stumbled only twice, once over the name Kayean, once when he set a squeaking mouse whizzing playfully around my head. It took a couple of hours and I got very dry. But I'd prepared for that, having been through it before.

As I downed a long draft of beer, my head rang to, *Very thorough. As far as it goes. What did you leave out?*

"Nothing. You got the whole show."

You are lying, Garrett. And not very convincingly. Though perhaps you are lying more to yourself than to me. You tripped on the woman's name. It has meaning to you.

Well, if you will lie to your best friend, you will lie to yourself. The Dead Man doesn't tell any tales. "It has meaning."

Continue.

"I knew a Kayean Kronk when I was in the Cantard. Her father was one of the Syndics of Port Fell. I was nineteen when I met her. She was seventeen. I fell hard. I thought she did too. But the campaign in the islands came up and I only got to see her maybe two days a month because we spent most of our time at sea. After about six months of that she started getting cool. Then I came in and there was a very kind letter asking me not to come see her, she was in love, the usual sort of thing. I never saw her again. I heard she was going with a cavalryman, and her father disliked

him even more than he had disliked me. That was the
last I heard of her till today.

"I had a rocky few years after that. It hit me pretty
hard."

End of confession.

A long silence.

Your friend never mentioned that woman's name?

"He never mentioned a woman."

*An odd coincidence, and a long one, but not impos-
sible. It would be illuminating to know if he was aware
of the identity of the woman's previous lover. How did
you meet?*

"We met in a tavern where veterans hung out. We
had liked one another. Not one detail I could recall
implied that he had knowledge of me through a third
party. I don't think he was the kind of guy who could
stay around somebody who had been his lover's lover.
I'd bet his whole fortune that he didn't realize that I
was the Marine she'd been seeing."

*You may be betting it. You realize that the amount of
money involved is going to have a lot of people interested in this business?*

"That's why I came to you. I need your advice."

My main advice you would ignore.

"What's that?"

*Leave it alone. Stick with the brewery work. This
could get you killed. Especially on the Cantard end.
Some very dangerous people have to be involved there,
if only peripherally.*

"How so?"

Who did the woman marry? the Dead Man countered.

"I don't know. Why? Do you think it's important?"

*I will hazard to opine that it may become the crux of
the affair.*

"Why?"

*It is evident from the woman's letters that she has
access to information very restricted in nature and extremely dangerous to possess. She passed along data
not only on the present movements and future plans of
your armies, but on those of the Venageti as well. The
implication is that she is in a unique position. Among*

*you humans, females are not permitted to assume the
responsibilities of such a position as a career. Thus, the
further implication that she is mated to a man in such a
position.*

The Dead Man's mind speech has all the nuance of
verbal communication—once you learn to do without
gestures and facial expressions. He was crowing. "I
could have figured that out soon enough."

*About the time someone cut your throat. You count
upon your ability to bluff or battle your way through
obstacles, rather than thinking your way around them.
It is a failing common to your race. All of you seem to
believe that exercising your minds is shameful or pain-
ful, and prefer instead to snatch up a sword at the first
hint of . . .*

He was off on his favorite crusade. Soon he would
begin the paeans to the infinite superiority of Loghyr
reasoning and logic and wisdom. I shut him out.

That can be done if he is distracted by musing upon
his own magnificence, if you're subtle and don't draw
attention to what you're doing. I hid behind my beer
and counted silently. Having heard it all before, I
knew how long he needed to get it out of his system.

Garrett!

So I miscalculated by a few seconds. He probably
cheated. He knew me pretty well, too. But he was
abnormally mellow. He employed none of his usual
childish devices. Maybe I had given him enough to
crack the boredom of being dead.

"Yes?"

*Pay attention. I asked if you are determined to go
ahead with this.*

"I'm not sure."

*Your body calls your mouth a liar. I have this advice
for you, inasmuch as you mean to go ahead despite all
reason. Do not go this one alone. And do not permit
emotion to get in the way of your usually strong instinct
for your own best interest. Whatever else this woman
may be or may have been, she is not the girl you loved
when she was seventeen. No more are you that callow
Marine of nineteen. If ever, for a minute, you allow*

yourself to believe that those days can be restored, you are lost. They are dead. Take it from an expert on being dead. There is no way to get your health back. You live on memories of what was and fancies about what might have been. Both can be deadly to the man who loses sight of the demarcation between them and reality.

"End of speech?"

End of speech. Were you listening?

"I was listening."

Did you hear me?

"I heard."

It is well. You are a pestilence upon my waning centuries, Garrett, but you keep me amused. I do not want to lose you yet. Be careful in the Cantard. You will not have me there to lift you out of the consequences of your folly. It grates, but I fear I would miss you, insolence, disobedience, and all.

Which was about the nicest thing he ever said to me. I had to get out before we started getting maudlin.

I made a beer run before going back to give him his bath and his place a bit of cleanup.

7

It was past suppertime when I left the Dead Man's place. The shadows were long and indigo. The sky was turning colors you usually see only in elvish portraiture. It had been a long day, and there was a lot of it yet to go.

The first order of business would be to see the Dead Man's landlord and get him a few months ahead on his rent.

I'll buy the place for him if I ever make the big strike, though he could do that for himself if he wanted. It would, however, take several months of concentrated work for him to earn enough money. The very thought sends him into psychic spasms.

Next step would be to look up Morley Dotes, which I'd had in mind even before the Dead Man admonished me against following my usual lone-wolf course. He was right. The Cantard is no place to go alone.

A massive hand hurtled out of an alley mouth, snagged my arm, and yanked.

Sometimes the city isn't so safe either.

I slammed into a wall and slid away from a fist I sensed more than I saw. I threw a feeble right that was just a distractor while I unloaded a girlish shin kick. The mountain of muscle and gristle before me waltzed back far enough for me to take in its true dimensions. They were awesome.

"Saucerhead Tharpe."

"Hey, Garrett. Man. If I'd knowed it was you, I'd never have taken this job."

"Shucks. I bet you say that to all the boys."

"Aw. Don't be that way, Garrett. We all got to make it the best way we know how."

I caught a glimpse of a familiar short person watching from across the street.

I dragged out a fat purse containing part of the largesse her uncle had bestowed upon me earlier.

"Hey. Come on, Garrett. You know you can't bribe me to lay off. I'm really sorry this's got to be you and me. But I got paid for the job. Where would I be if it got around that I could be bought off? I'd be out of work. I'm very, very, sorry, Garrett. But I got to do what I got paid to do."

I had expected no luck, but it had seemed worth a try.

I said, "I'd be the last guy to ask you to welsh on a deal, Saucerhead."

"Gee. I'm glad. I was scared you wouldn't understand."

"I want you to do a job for me, Saucerhead. There's five marks in it."

"Yeah. I'd feel a whole lot better about this if I could do something for you. What is it?"

"That woman across the street. The one that sicced you onto me. When we're done here I want you to take her down to the Bazaar, strip her down naked, bend her over your lap, and give her thirty good whacks on the backside. Then turn her loose and let her walk home."

"Naked?"

"Naked."

"She wouldn't get out of the Bazaar, Garrett."

"There's another five in it if she gets home all right. But without finding out you're looking out for her."

Saucerhead grinned. "It's a deal, Garrett." He stuck out a palm the size of a snowshoe. I dropped five marks into it.

Saucerhead's hand dipped into a pocket.

I hit him up side the head with the purse. I put everything I had behind it. Then I ran like hell for two steps.

He gave Rose her money's worth, fulfilling his contract to the letter.

I tried to defend myself, of course, and actually did pretty well. Not many hang in there a whole minute against Saucerhead Tharpe. I even gave him one he might have remembered for the next ten minutes.

Always thoughtful, is Saucerhead Tharpe. After he put my lights out he tucked my purse underneath me, just in case somebody came along before I woke up. Then he went along to the next job on his agenda.

8

I hurt everywhere. I had about two acres of bruises. Saucerhead had found places to hit that I didn't know I had. All body and soul wanted was to go lay up for a week. But mind knew it was time to find Morley Dotes. Not even Saucerhead Tharpe would have messed with me if I'd had Morley Dotes along.

Morley is the best at rough and tumble. And, by his own admission, the best at most everything else. Some people would like him and Saucerhead to square off, just to see how it would come out. But neither of them will swat a fly without getting paid first. And Saucerhead isn't dumb enough to take a job on Morley. Nor is Morley vain enough to contract on Saucerhead. Neither cares much about who might come out best. Which says something about their professionalism.

The obvious place to look for Morley was a place called Morley's Joy House.

The name is one of his bad jokes. It is a hangout for the elfin, the cartha, and breeds. The fare is vegetarian and nonalcoholic. The entertainment is so impenetrable and dull that the existence of a dead Loghyr might be exciting by contrast. But Morley's kind of people enjoy it.

The place went silent when I stepped inside. I ignored an arsenal's worth of death-looks as I limped to the alleged bar. Morley's barman gave me the once-over. He grinned, revealing pointy darkelf teeth. "You have a knack for making people mad at you, Garrett."

"You ought to see the other guy."

"I did. He came in for some sprouts. Wasn't a scratch on him."

Conversations picked up behind me. The barman was being as friendly as darkelves ever are. That made me a marginally acceptable lower life-form, presence tolerated. Like that of a beer-drinking dog in a human tavern.

"Word's around already, huh?"

"Everybody who ever cared about you one way or the other already knows the whole story. Slick the way you evened things up."

"Yeah. That's out, too? How'd it go?"

"She made it home. I figure that's one quail that won't ever mess with you again, Garrett." He cackled in that way they have that gives you chills and makes you wonder if you will ever wake up from the nightmare. "Next time she'll get somebody to cut your throat."

The possibility had occurred to me. I'd made a mental note to rummage up some of my more interesting gimmicks and armaments. In the general course of business I find being fast on my feet protection enough, so I load myself down with hardware only in special cases.

This case looked like it was getting pretty special.

The Dead Man had warned me.

"Where's Morley?"

"Up." He pointed. "He's busy."

I headed for the stairs.

The barkeep opened his mouth to yell at me, then thought about it. That might start a riot. In his friendly voice he said, "Hey, Garrett, you owe us five marks."

I turned around and gave him the fisheye.

"Saucerhead said you'd knock it off his tab."

"A grin like that ought to be bronzed and saved for posterity."

It got bigger.

"That big goof isn't as dumb as he looks, is he?" I dug down carefully, my back to the crowd. No point in showing what I was carrying and having the boys who were high on lettuce getting fancy ideas.

"Nope."

I flipped the five coins and headed upstairs before he could get back to trying to stop me.

I hammered on Morley's private door. No response. I pounded again, rattling hinges.

"Go away, Garrett. I'm busy."

I shoved through the door, which was not locked. Somebody's wife squealed and dove into another room, a fistful of clothing trailing. Otherwise, I caught nothing but a flash of fancy tail. It was not one I recognized.

Morley did his best to look elf-haughty in nothing but his socks and a snarl. He could not bring it off, despite being half darkelf.

"Your timing is lousy as usual, Garrett. Not to mention your manners."

"How did you know it was me?"

"Magic."

"Magic, my ruddy red. You have trouble making food disappear. If you call that silage you eat food."

"Ah-ah. Watch your mouth. You owe me one apology already."

"I don't apologize. My mother makes excuses for me. How did you know it was me?"

"Voice tube from the bar. You look awful, boy. Saucerhead must have sold that gal his top of the line. What did you do to her?"

"Wouldn't lie, cheat, and steal for her. And turned her down when she tried to bribe me with the big bribe."

He laughed. "You never learn. Next time diddle the gal and walk. She'll sit around wondering what went wrong instead of sending cutthroats after you." His grin vanished. "What do you want, Garrett?"

"I've got a job offer for you."

"Not something foolish involving Saucerhead Tharpe, I hope."

"No. I've got a job I need some backup on. I can thank Saucerhead for reminding me that if I don't get it soon my health might suffer."

"What's in it?"

"For me, ten percent of a hundred thousand marks, plus expenses. You're expenses."

He whistled soundlessly, his pucker bringing his dark hatchet features to even more of a point. "What do we have to do? Take out one of the Venageti warlords?"

"You're closer than you think. I have to go into the Cantard and find a woman who just inherited on the up side of a hundred thou. I have to talk her into either coming here to claim it or waiving her claim in favor of whoever is next in line."

"That doesn't sound so tough. Except for the part about the Cantard."

"There are some people around who might feel that the money was not the deceased's to bequeath. There are some in the deceased's family who feel a strong reluctance to let so large a fortune go to a stranger. There is the possibility of similar difficulties on the legatee's end. It's possible her relationship with the legatee was, shall we say, imprudent."

"I love it when you talk dirty, Garrett. And I love what money does to you humans. It's the only thing that saves you from being totally tedious."

I did not have anything to say to that. People do get silly about money.

"I take it your principal has his own ax to grind in this, or he'd be with the keep-it-in-the-family faction."

"Could be."

"Is he as nebulous as you are?"

"Could be. You interested?"

"Could be."

I winced.

He grinned. "Suppose I just follow you around for a while? You're a chatty sort of fellow. I'll let you know when you've said enough to let me make up my mind."

"Oh, happy day! The pleasure of his company without having to pay for it. All right."

"Who said anything about not paying for it?"

"I did. No play, no pay."

"You got an attitude problem, Garrett. All right. What are you going to do now?"

"Go wrap myself around a couple of pounds of steak."

He turned up his nose. "All that red meat is why you people have such a peculiar odor. Where should I meet you?"

I raised an eyebrow.

"Matter of some unfinished business," he said evenly.

I glanced at the door to the other room. "I see. I'll be back."

9

Morley had pecked around the edges till I'd about lost the restored good humor brought on by beer and a fully belly. "You have a basic character flaw, Garrett. I think it's a self-image problem. Ninety-nine people out of a hundred will say any damned fool thing that pops into their heads and not worry about how other folks will see it. With you every damned word is a contract with the gods."

I scowled up the street. There were lights inside my place.

"You can talk without feeling you've committed something, Garrett. Hell, you should do like me. Believe every word you say like it was godsmouth when you say it, then forget it in the morning. The appearance of sincerity counts for more than actual truthfulness. People only need to believe for a few minutes at a time. They know the name of the game. You take that lady I was with tonight. Am I in love with her? Is she in love with me? Not bloody likely. She wouldn't be seen in public with me. But I still had to say all the words."

I don't know how he got onto that. He rambles. I ignored it, mostly. "You on the payroll or not?"

He looked at my place "Company?"

"Looks like."

"Could it be friendly?"

"My friends have better manners."

"I thought you'd admit you don't have any friends. Are you going in?"

"Yes. You behind me or not?"

"Temporarily, anyway. My cash position isn't what it should be. I've suffered several financial setbacks lately."

"D'Guni races again."

"You want to get rich quick, Garrett? Come down to the pond and see how I lay my bets. Then bet the other way. No matter what bug I pick, it zips out to the middle, then skitters in circles while the plodders head straight for the other bank. Either that or it gets eaten."

"The race is not always to the swift." Only elves would bet on the near-random results of water-spider races. "Ready?"

"Go ahead."

The door was unlocked. How thoughtful. There were four of them. Two sat on my bed. The other two occupied my only two chairs. I recognized three as cavalry veterans from Denny's crowd. The one called Vasco might be the V of Denny's notes. They were trying to look tough.

I guess they *were* tough, inside their heads. They had survived the Cantard. But they did not have the tough look that comes from growing up on the streets.

"Come on in, guys," I said. "Make yourselves at home. Fix yourselves a drink. My place is your place."

Vasco said, "See if he's armed, Quinn."

"He's armed," Morley said behind me. "Take my word for it."

One of my guests chuckled. "Look, Vee. A darko breed in man's clothing."

"Amateurs," Morley said.

"Amateurs," I agreed. "But the pros all start out as amateurs."

"Some have to learn their business the hard way."

What he meant was, anybody on the shady side of the law who knew what they were doing should know who he was.

Vasco made a gesture that restrained the character with the intemperate mouth. He said, "I figure you have some idea why we're here, Garrett. But there're a couple points I want to make sure you understand."

"Amateurs," I said again. "Pros know when to take their losses."

"That money didn't belong to Denny, Garrett. Not more than a third of it, anyway."

"Pros don't put all their eggs in one basket. And they don't put the basket where they can't get at it. If I was you boys I'd find a new line of business. Without Denny's contacts your old one is going to turn into a crapshoot."

Vasco winced. I knew too much. "We've got that angle covered, Garrett. All we need to do is get hold of Denny's papers and study up on his style. There weren't any secret codes or anything. The other end doesn't have to know that he's gone."

Might be workable at that. Maybe they were not so dumb after all.

Those records and notes and letters might be a silver mine.

"What did you do with them, Garrett?"

"So we get to the crux, eh?"

"Yes. I'll lay it out. We can take the loss on the silver if we get the papers and you stay away from the Cantard end. We ain't going to like it, but we can take it. My recommendation to you is, pocket your retainer and walk. Next best thing, if you think you have to make a show, is leave town for a while, then come back and say you couldn't find her. Or fake up a waiver and forge her chop."

"Sounds good," I said. "A practical solution to all our problems."

They looked relieved.

"Trouble is, when I got out of the Marines I decided I wasn't going to let anybody else run my life ever again. You guys were in the army. You know how it is."

It stunned them momentarily. Then Vasco said, "You look like you've had a bad day already, Garrett. I wouldn't want to give a man bruises on his bruises. Maybe you could reassess your position."

"You had your say. I made my position clear. You'd better be leaving. I'm not usually this tolerant of uninvited guests."

Vasco sighed. My old drill sergeant used to sigh that way when a recruit was particularly stubborn about learning. "Quinn, watch the breed."

I set myself. I'd picked my first move already.

"Stand aside, Garrett." That same sound of exasperation filled Morley's voice. "It's time for a little of that old elfin magic."

"Vee?"

"Take him, Quinn."

When Morley goes into action he seems to grow about six extra limbs. He uses them all so fast you hardly see them move. And when he isn't kicking or punching he's biting, head-butting, hip-jugging, or knee-dropping.

He opened by leaping up and giving Quinn the heels of both feet, *bap! bap!* right between the eyes. He flew to another victim without touching down. Quinn folded his cards and went to dreamland.

Vasco came after me.

I learned that you do not duke it out with a guy almost as good as you are when your whole body is stiff and sore from the last whipping you took.

He got me into a clinch that turned into a giant bear hug on the floor. He kept trying to bang his forehead off my temple. I got my teeth into his ear and chomped. That discouraged him. He threw himself away from me. From flat on my back I flicked out a heel and clipped him at the base of the skull. He went wobbly.

I jumped up, seized the moment by the scruff of the neck and seat of the pants, and ran him out the door to the accompaniment of appropriate old-time remarks about seedy little army types who failed to acknowledge the natural superiority of their overlords, the Marines.

A great glassy crash sent me hurtling back inside to help Morley.

He had polished off his share. He was eyeballing

Quinn. "Grab the other end and help me throw him out."

"You broke my window."

"I'm charging you double rate for this one, Garrett. You provoked them."

"I'm not paying you squat. You threw somebody out my window."

"You never heard a word I said about truth and sincerity. You had a perfect chance to close it all down when Vee suggested you take the retainer and run. But no! Bad Garrett has got Morley Dotes behind him. He can run his mouth like a fool and provoke them all to hell."

"I would have said the same thing if you weren't here."

He cocked his head and looked at me like a bird looking at a new kind of bug. "Death wish. Suicidal tendencies. Know what causes that, Garrett? Diet. That's right. Your meat-heavy human diet. You need more roughage. You don't get enough roughage, your bowels tighten up. When your bowels tighten up you get these dangerous, self-destructive mood swings . . ."

"Somebody is going to get his bowels loosened up. You had to go and throw somebody through my window, didn't you?"

"Will you quit with the damned window?"

"You know how much that window cost? You got any idea?"

"Not a candle to what this job is going to cost you if you don't stop complaining. All right! Next time I'll ask them pretty please to go out the door like nice little boys. Come on. Let's run it off."

"Run? Run where? Why?"

"To work off this nervous energy. To get rid of the combat juices flowing inside us. Five miles ought to do it."

"I'll tell you how far I'm running. I'm running all the way over there to my bed. Then I'm not moving except to breathe."

"You're kidding. The shape you're in? If you don't

stretch those muscles, then cool them out right, you're going to wake up so stiff you won't be able to move."

"Tell you what. You run my five miles for me. I'll consider forgiving you for the window." I crashed onto the bed. "I could use about a gallon of ice-cold beer."

Morley didn't answer me. He was gone.

10

Bam! Bam! Bam!

Morning is wonderful. Its only drawback is that it comes at such an inconvenient time of day. A time when the early birds of the world are aflame with their mission of bringing the joys of dawn-watching to the nations. And to me in particular.

Bam! Bam! Bam!

Two mornings running. I wondered if I had offered unwitting insult to the Seven Grand Devils of Modrel.

I went through all the usual cursing and threatening. None of it helped.

Morley would crow when he saw me. I was as stiff as he wanted. It took me three minutes to put my feet over the side and sit up.

The first thing I saw was a mottled green face half a yard wide staring through the broken window. I said something intelligent like, "Gleep!"

The face grinned.

It was a groll, a hybrid of human, troll, and the Beast That Talks that is never named in polite company. I grinned back. Grolls are slow of wit and often quick of temper.

Its giant toad mouth opened and spilled some of that hair-raising bass which is their excuse for speech. I did not catch what it said. It was not meant for me, anyway.

The banging on the door stopped.

"Hello yourself," I croaked, and dragged myself up onto my feet. I figured I'd better open up before his patience went and he let himself in through the wall.

There was another one outside the door. It looked

47

exactly like the other one—Big, wide, and ugly. I guessed it would stand twenty feet high in its socks—if it ever wore socks. It didn't wear much else, except a loincloth, a utility belt, and an empty pack harness.

The loincloth did not do much to preserve modesty.

So from here on I have to call them both He with a capital H. Mules would go gibbous with envy.

Both grolls noted my amazement and grinned. That's the sense of humor such creatures have.

"I'd invite you in if you'd fit," I said. One is polite to grolls at all times, irrespective of one's prejudices. Otherwise one finds oneself reassessing one's attitude while being squished between warty green toes.

A short one stepped around the big one. "I expect I'll fit," he said. "And I could use a drink, actually."

"Who the hell are you?"

"Dojango is the name, actually. These are my brothers, Marsha and Doris."

"Brothers?"

"We're triplets, actually." He responded to my unspoken question, "But with different mothers, actually."

Triplets with different mothers. Right. I didn't ask. Making sense out of the things human folks tell me is brain strain enough.

"What the hell are you doing here?"

"Morley Dotes sent us, actually."

"What the hell for? Actually?" One of the big grolls growled at me. I used my fingers to sculpt a friendly smile.

"To help in the Cantard."

The villain himself, Morley Dotes, had sneaked on stage. "So you decided you want the job, eh?"

"At the moment there are certain advantages, where my creditors are concerned, to my being both employed and being out of town," Morley replied.

"And you thought you'd gather all your friends under the umbrella of that advantage? Like maybe my principal wouldn't think of putting a bottom in my expense pot?"

"If you would use half that vaunted detective brain of yours, you would bless my vision."

"It's too early in the morning for me to remember my name. Enlighten me, O Illustrious One."

"Consider mules."

"Mules? What the hell do mules have to do with it?"

"We're going into the Cantard. No one will risk loaning or renting us mounts or pack animals. We'll have to buy. On the other hand, wages for Doris and Marsha will run about what it would cost for a brace of good mules. And they can carry twice the load twice as long. And they're a hell of a lot more use in a fight."

That made sense. Good sense. But . . . "What about friend Dojango?"

Morley sighed. "Yes. Dojango Roze. Well, Garrett, they won't break up the set."

I do believe I scowled. "You sticking me with deadwood?"

"Dojango can lift a blade. He can sniff out water and find firewood. He can understand Doris and Marsha. If you keep an eye on him, he can cook an edible meal without burning anything too badly."

"I'm trying not to slobber in anticipation." I scanned the triplets who had different mothers. They grinned groll good fellowship. They figured Morley had sold me.

Dotes said, "Keep Dojango away from the juice and he'll do all right."

Everyone knows breeds cannot handle their booze. Dojango's grin became apologetic.

"How much is this road show going to burn me?"

Morley tossed out an outrageous figure. I slammed the door and went back to bed. He had one of the big triplets lift him so he could yell numbers through the broken window. I faked a mean snore till some interesting integers began rattling around behind me. In fact, Morley was so pliable I began wondering how bad his creditor situation was. I did not need more complications than I already had.

"It's your diet that makes you so stubborn, you know that, don't you, Garrett? All that red meat filled with the juices stirred by the terror of the murdered beast, and you never exercising so you sweat them out of your own body."

"I figured it was something like that, Morley. That, too much beer, and not enough green, leafy veggies."

"Cattails, Garrett. The white hearts down near the roots of the young plant, diced into a tossed salad. Not only tasty, but informed with an almost mystical capacity for lightening the burden of guilt lying upon the carnivore's soul."

"Horsepucky." When I was in the Marines we raided an island where the Venageti promptly cut us off from our ships and drove us into a swamp. Cattails were a mainstay of our diet till the fortunes of war shifted. I don't recall them doing anything remarkable for the temperaments of our sergeants and corporals, who seemed carnivorous enough to eat their own young. Rather the opposite, in a geometric progression.

I know we all took it out on the Venageti when the time came.

Maybe I did not start eating cattails young enough. "Morley, I did a job for a professor at the university one time. He was always spouting who-cares facts. Like one time when he said there are two hundred forty-eight different kinds of fruits, vegetables, greens, and tubers that people eat. Hogs will only eat two hundred forty-six of those. They won't touch green peppers and they won't touch cattail hearts. Which goes to show you that hogs have more sense than people."

"No point trying to salvage you, is there? You're determined to suicide the slow way. Are the boys hired?"

"They're hired." I hoped I would not be sorry.

"How soon can we leave?"

"You in a hurry, Morley? You need to get out of town fast? That why you're being so agreeable about going into the Cantard?"

Dotes shrugged.

A shrug was answer enough.

Considering Morley's talents and reputation, it would

take somebody heavy to have enough clout to scare him. In my mind somebodies that heavy narrowed down to a crowd of one. The big guy himself. The kingpin. "Since when is Kolchak into bug racing, Morley?"

He popped down out of the window. His voice lingered behind him. "You're too damned smart for your own good, Garrett. It's going to catch up with you someday. I'll be in touch. Come on, you lummoxes. Dojango! Put that back. Doris!" He sounded like a muleteer trying to get a wagon started.

I went back to bed thinking I'd better use some of Tate's money to get a new window put in. Maybe a flashy piece with my name leaded in colors.

11

This old universe hasn't got one notion of the meaning of the word *mercy* where I'm concerned. I just got to snoozing when the door began shivering like a drumhead again.

"Going to have to do something about this," I muttered as I hit the floor. "Like maybe move and not tell anybody."

I opened up and found uncle Lester and the boys outside. "You guys decide to forget the whole thing, I hope?" I noticed that two of the kids had gotten into something rough. They showed plenty of bruises and bandages and one had an arm in a sling. "What happened?"

"Unfriendly visitors. Willard wants to talk to you about it."

"All right. I'm on my way." I took just long enough to make myself presentable, gulp some water, and pick up the lead-weighted head-thumper.

Willard Tate was in a state. He waited, wringing his hands. All my life I have heard that expression. Except for a maiden aunt whose every breath was an act of high drama, I'd never seen it before.

"What happened?" Uncle Lester was a clam. Maybe he was afraid if I knew too much I'd turn around.

Tate pumped my hand with both of his. "Thank you for coming. Thank you. I didn't know what else to do."

"What happened?" I asked again as he clung to my hand with one of his and dragged me like a stubborn child. Uncle Lester and the boys tagged along. I spotted a pale-faced Rose watching as we crossed the garden, headed for Denny's apartment.

Tate did not tell me. He showed me.

The place was a wreck. The apprentices were still cleaning up. Several of them wore bandages and bruises. Some wise soul had barred entry from the street by nailing boards across the doorframe.

Tate pointed.

The body lay in the middle of the room, belly down, one hand stretched toward the door.

"What happened?" I asked again.

Third time was a charm.

"It happened around midnight. I had the boys in watching, just in case, because you made me nervous the way you talked. Five men broke through the street door. The boys were smart. Odie came and woke everybody up. The others hid and let the burglars go downstairs. So we ambushed them when they tried to leave.

"We just wanted to capture them. But they panicked and started a fight, and they weren't shy about trying to hurt us. And now we're stuck with *that*."

I knelt to look at the dead man's face. He had started to puff up already. But I could still see the cuts and scrapes he had picked up flying through the window at my place.

"Did they get away with anything?"

"I did a count," Uncle Lester said. "The gold and silver is all there."

"They weren't after gold or silver."

"Huh?" All the Tates are brilliant. But they hide their light under a bushel. Maybe it's a business reflex.

"They were looking for Denny's papers. His letters to the woman. I took care of hiding most everything, but there could have been something I overlooked. Those papers might be worth more than any amount of metal they could haul out of here."

Old Man Tate looked dumbfounded, so I told him about my little chat with Denny's partners. He did not want to believe me. "But that's—"

"Trading with the enemy when you take the costume off it and look it straight in the face."

"I know my son, Mr. Garrett. Denny wouldn't betray Karenta."

"Did you hear me say anything about treason?" I thought it, though. Mainly in the context of what happened to folks foolish enough to get caught trading with the Venageti. I have no moral reservations about that. The war is a struggle between two gangs of nobles and wizards trying to grab control of mines likely to give their possessors near mastery of the world. Their motives are no higher than those displayed in squabbles between street gangs right here in TunFaire.

Being Karentine, I would prefer the gang running my country to win. I love being with a winner. Everybody does. But it doesn't hurt my feelings if somebody besides the lords makes a little profit from the squabble. I explained that to Tate.

"The problem is, the connection is still alive," I said. "And some pretty tough boys want to keep it that way. Meaning they don't want you and me meddling. Do you follow me?"

"And they want Denny's papers and letters and whatnots so they can keep contact with the woman?"

"You catch on fast, Pop. They'll let their claim to the metals go for the papers. And Denny will live on forever in letters he never wrote."

He thought about it. There was a part of him that wanted to grab the big score while it was there for the grabbing. But there was a part of him that was crazy stubborn, too. Maybe if he had been a little poorer . . . But somewhere along the way he had made up his mind and set it in concrete. Changed circumstances would not budge him. "I *will* meet this woman, Mr. Garrett."

"It's your neck," I said. And tried to time a meaningful pause. "And your family's. That could be one of the boys on the floor, attracting flies."

I got to him that time. He puffed up. His face got

red. His eyes bugged out, which is a sight in the half elfin. His mouth opened. He began to shake.

But he did not let it get hold of him. Somehow, he turned it off. After half a minute, he said, "You're right, Mr. Garrett. And it's a risk due more consideration than I have given it. If, as you say, those men were army friends of Denny's who survived the Cantard, it's damned lucky several of the boys weren't killed instead of that poor fellow."

"Like you said, they panicked. They just wanted to get away. But next time they'll be looking for trouble."

"You're sure there'll be a next time? Coming so close to getting caught already?"

"You don't seem to understand the stakes, Mr. Tate. In eight years Denny and those guys built a handful of prize money into a hundred thousand marks." Plus whatever fun they took along the way, but I did not mention that. The old boy did not need all his illusions stripped. "Think what they could have done with another eight years and that kind of capital."

Gotten into a crunch, probably. Too much wealth draws attention—though I suppose Denny knew that and planned accordingly.

"Perhaps I do not, Mr. Garrett. I'm only a shoemaker. My interest is fathers and sons and a family tradition that goes back more generations than can be counted. A tradition that died with Denny."

He was an exasperating old coot. I think he understood plenty. He just didn't give a damn anymore.

"You're certain they will return, then?"

"Breathing fire, Pop."

"Then it behooves me to take steps."

"The step you ought to take is to come to an accommodation."

"Not with those swine. They—and that woman—seduced my son away . . ."

I shut him out and gave my whole attention to the basement. As far as I could tell, nothing had changed. It seemed likely, then, that they had found nothing I might have missed. "Huh? I'm sorry. I missed that."

He gave me a look that said he knew why. But you could not get him to talk nasty at spear's point. "I asked if you knew someone I could retain as a guard for the premises."

"No." I did know someone. Me. But I was up to my nostrils with long cold lonely nights waiting for something that never happened, or that was really lethal when it did. "Wait." A thought. "Maybe I do. The people who are supposed to make the trip to the Cantard with me. I could do us both a favor by parking them here." Morley, too, if it put him out of the heat.

Tate looked startled. "You're going to go? You sounded so dead set against it."

"I'm still against it. I think it's about as smart as raiding a roc's nest. I don't even see any point to it. But I told you I'd look into it. I haven't really made up my mind yet either way."

He smiled. He grinned. I was afraid he would try to slap me on the back and maybe loosen one of my kidneys. But he restrained himself. A very restrained kind of guy, old man Tate.

He got very serious.

"What can you do about that man's body, Mr. Garrett?"

I figured we were going to get to that. "Nothing."

"What?"

"Nothing. He's not my problem."

The old boy gulped air. Then the sly merchant came tippy-toeing forward. "You want to hold me up for a bonus? All right. How much?"

"Don't bother. You don't have enough. I'm not putting a finger on that stiff. It's not my responsibility, and I don't do that kind of work. My advice is, call the magistrates and let them handle it. You'll be clear. He was killed during a break-in."

"No. I don't want anyone nosing into family business."

"Then have your boys take him and dump him in the river or an alley somewhere down the hill." There are bodies in the river most mornings. In the alleys, too. Unless they were someone important, they caused little comment.

Tate saw that he could not reach me through my lust for wealth. He gave that up. "You go ahead here, then. Send those men here as soon as you can. I have work to do. Keep me posted." He ducked out.

I poked around and wondered if the evil gleam in Tate's eye meant he thought he could put the corpse off on Morley and the triplets.

12

The flooring did its dust drop. I had noticed it several times before Tate left. I figured my sweetheart Rose was eavesdropping again. I ignored her.

Look as I might, I could not find anything missing. I settled back to give the whole business a think. It was obese with potential trouble. And I was getting near the point where I had to make a real decision.

The local end of it would take care of itself. There was nothing to investigate at this end. At the other end . . .

I did not want to think about that end yet. It would be unpleasant no matter how smooth it went. It would be unpleasant just traveling to and revisiting the Cantard.

A door opened and shut overhead. A moment later women began talking. The one with the quarrelsome voice had to be Rose. I wondered who the other one was.

A delightful aroma preceded her down the basement stairs. She proved to be a fiery little redhead with long straight hair, jade-green eyes, a few freckles, and high, firm breasts that thrust boldly against a ruffled silk blouse. There was nothing between that blouse and her but my daydreams.

"Where have they been hiding you?" I asked, jumping up to take the tray she carried. "Who are you?"

"I'm Tinnie. And you're Garrett. And the last time you saw me I was just a spindle-legged kid." She looked me right in the eye and grinned. Her teeth looked sharp and white. I wanted to stick out a hand and let her take a bite.

"Could still be on spindles for all a guy can tell from that skirt." It fell to her ankles.

Her grin got sassy. "You could get lucky and get a look sometime. You never know."

My kind of luck came down the stairs right then. "Tinnie! You've done your job. Get out."

We ignored Rose. I asked, "You're not Denny's sister, are you? He never mentioned you."

"Cousin. They don't talk about me. I'm the one who causes trouble."

"Oh? I thought Rose took care of that."

"Rose is just obnoxious. That doesn't bother them. I do things that embarrass them. Rose just makes people mad or disgusted. I make the neighbors whisper behind their hands."

Rose simmered and reddened. Tinnie winked at me. "See you later, Garrett."

Yeah. I wish. That little bit was enough woman to make a man sit up and howl at the moon. She had a sway as she sashayed past Rose and started up the stairs.

When you got down to it and ignored the personality of a black widow spider, Rose was not something the dogs barked at either. She was another small package with its contents all in the right places, and only prime materials had been used.

Rose could move with a sway that promised fireworks—if she wanted. But her fireworks were the kind that blow up in a man's face.

We eyed each other like a couple of tomcats about to square off. We both decided what she had in mind wouldn't work any better this time. She got flustered because she didn't know what else to do.

"Ought to have a backup plan when you jump in on something," I told her. "Like Saucerhead Tharpe."

"You're right, Garrett. Damn you, anyhow. How did you get so old being as stubborn as you are?"

"By guessing right most of the time. You wouldn't be a bad kid if there was room for anyone else in your world."

For a few seconds, there, I got the feeling she wished

there *was* someone else in her world. Then she said, "Too bad we couldn't have met under other circumstances."

"Yeah," I said, not feeling it. She would be trouble no matter what the circumstances. That was how she was made.

"We don't have any common ground at all, do we?"

"Not very much. Not unless you had some feeling for your brother. I was fond of Denny. How about you?"

I had touched something. At last.

"It isn't fair. Him dying like that. He was about the nicest guy I ever knew. Even if he was my brother. That Cantard bitch—"

"Easy!" I snapped it, which gave me away enough to make her gawk and wonder.

"What's in this for you, Garrett? Besides a chance to line your pockets? Nobody goes to the Cantard without more reason than money."

I thought about Morley Dotes when she said that. I thought about me. I wondered about me. Garrett, tough guy. Can't reach him. No emotional handles. But I was on the brink of doing something no moron in his right mind would do.

Like old man Tate, I wanted to see this woman who could put a halter on Denny.

Rose and I traded stares. She decided I wasn't going to give her a thing. "Be careful, Garrett. Don't get yourself hurt. Look me up when this is over."

"It wouldn't work, Rose."

"It could be fun giving it a look."

She sashayed up the stairs.

She did look good from that perspective. Maybe . . .

Seconds after the door slammed, while common sense was fighting for its life, a copper-wreathed face peeped at me from the head of the stairs. "Don't even think about it, Garrett. I wouldn't love you anymore."

Then Tinnie vanished, too.

I gulped some air and said "Duh!" a few times, then got my dogs under me and went galumphing off on the trail.

She was gone when I got upstairs. I was alone with the dead guy. Denny's friend. There was no sign of Rose or Tinnie when I looked into the garden. I closed the door and took a quick look through the dead guy's pockets.

Some vulture had beat me to it. There wasn't a thing left.

13

Old Man Tate got the body out somehow. Dropped it in the river, I guess. I didn't ask, and didn't hear a thing about it. A lot of people never heard from again take that one last swim.

I got Morley and the triplets installed at Denny's place. Morley thought it was a great idea. That being the case, I spent the evening hanging around his place, nicked by dagger looks from the breeds, hoping I would catch a flash to illuminate his eagerness to join a fool's quest.

I didn't catch anything brighter than candlelight.

All I found out was that I wasn't the only guy watching.

You get a sixth sense after enough years. Mine pegged two heavyweights in the first fifteen minutes. One was human and looked like he could give Saucer-head a fight. The other was so ugly, and stayed in his shadowed corner so deep, that I couldn't tell what he was. A breed for sure, probably with some troll and kobold in him, but more than that. He was as wide as he was tall. His face had been rearranged several times, probably for the better.

The bartender knew I had something going with Morley. He stayed civil. I asked about the men I had picked out.

"Don't know them. The ugly one was in here last night. First time. Sat in that corner all night nursing a beer he brought with him. I would've thrown him out if he hadn't bought a meal."

"That would've been a show to see." I took a pint of the water that passed for beer there and tipped him to take the sting out of the crack. "Think they're the kingpin's boys?"

"Not unless they're from out of town."

That was what I thought. I didn't recognize them either, but they looked like trouble on the hoof.

Well, no skin off my nose. As long as they were not interested in me.

I gave it up at Morley's place after the pint. There were better places to put an ear to the ground. I went and hung out in some of them. I didn't find out a thing.

Curious.

I headed for my place wondering if the glazier had gotten started yet. I felt no shame at all charging the replacement window to Tate.

The new window was in place and lettered as pretty as a blonde in her birthday suit. But I strolled by without admiring it, putting a slouch in my shoulders and a shuffle in my walk.

Maybe I wouldn't go home after all.

There were problems. One was that somebody was waiting in the breezeway beside the ratman's; even without seeing the glow of his pipe I could smell the weed he was smoking. The other was that there was somebody waiting inside. Whoever that was had all the lamps burning, using up oil at a rate to curdle my liver.

I knew a heavy weed smoker. Another friend of Denny's. Another old soldier, name of Barbera, who smoked so much that most of the time he didn't know if he was in this world or the next. A pathetic case, he was always in trouble because folks could talk him into anything. He had been one of Denny's charities.

No doubt Denny's other pals thought it would be a giggle to hop him up and sic him on me.

I faded into a shadow down the block and took a seat against a wall that needed tuckpointing. The view of my place was as scenic as a garbage dump.

A lot of nothing happened for a long time. Unless you count the flares as my lurker lighted up, or the passing of drunks so far gone they were unafraid of the nighted streets. Only after we started getting some

aromatic moonlight did anything interesting happen.
And that was just a couple guys checking in with the
weed man.

They passed me by without seeing me. But I got a
look at them.

Vasco and Quinn, my old pals.

So they meant to do me dirty, eh?

I didn't move, though I thought about knocking
some heads. I was beginning to wonder about that
lamplight. Vasco and Quinn had made no effort to
talk to whomever was inside. So maybe that whomever wasn't one of them.

Who, then?

My friend the ratman came home from his shift at
the graveyard, drunk as usual. In my less charitable
moments I've wished he would get lost in one of the
graves he digs.

He shuffled up to my new window, glanced inside.

Whatever he saw, it was interesting. He watched for
a minute. When he moved on he cast furtive looks
around. He didn't see anyone watching. That must
have given him courage. He slipped over and tried the
door.

It opened.

Barbera came blazing out of the shadows. He climbed
all over the ratman. When he had him pounded down
to about three feet high, he took off, headed my way.

A little message for me from Denny's pals. Mis-
delivered.

I reckoned they needed an answer.

I stepped out of the shadows as Barbera lumbered
past. He caught me from the corner of his eye. I said,
"Hi, there," and smacked his ear with my sap as his
eyes grew big and he tried to turn.

He did not go down. But his knees got wobbly and
his eyes glazed. I kicked him low, punched him high
with my left, bounced the sap off his forehead.

He wobbled a little more.

They need a lot of pounding when they're hopped.

I gave him all he needed, and then some, and when
he no longer knew what planet he was on, I snagged

the seat of his pants and walked him into an alley, where I gave him a few more taps with my sap. Then I took his pouch of weed. A while later I paid a half-dwarf half-goblin wino to deliver it to Vasco with the word that he had not gotten his money's worth.

That taken care of, it was time to see about my intruder.

I didn't do any seeing. When I got back to where I could see my place, a troop of Tates were going inside, stepping over the groaning ratman like he was something that fell behind the horse. In a moment they marched back out with an angry Tinnie.

So there you go. Exactly my kind of luck. If I found the pot of gold at the end of the rainbow, I'd break my leg running toward it and have to lie there watching some other clown walk away with it while I did my groaning.

I let the street clear. Then I went and got a bucket of beer and locked myself inside. Nobody disturbed me.

14

I'd planned to surprise everybody by showing up at the Tate place at the crack of dawn, ready to travel. But I had a dream about Loghyr bones.

Maybe it was the beer. That beer was green. But I knew better than to ignore it. It could be a summons from the Dead Man.

The worst thing about going out in the morning is that the sun is there. It slaps you right in the eyes. When you go back inside you can't see squat.

Squat was what I saw when I went into the Dead Man's place. It was as dark as a crypt in there.

About time, Garrett. Did you come via Khaphé?

"That wasn't a dream, eh?"

No.

"What do you want?"

I do not have the resources to follow all your adventures from afar. If you want my help and advice, you have to report to me occasionally.

I figured that was as near as he would get to saying he owed me. I would take what I was given. "What do you need?"

Details of what you have seen and learned since your last visit.

So I gave it to him, without leaving anything out.

He pondered awhile. *Buy yourself some poison rings, Garrett. Carry a boot knife.*

That was not the advice I expected. "Why?"

Are you known for such things?

"No."

Do the unexpected.

"I hiked all the way over here for that?"

It is the best I can do given the information you make available.

Make it my fault. Just like him. I did him a few odd jobs, cleaned the place up some, and burned some sulfur candles to make the vermin's lungs more robust. I wondered what Morley thought about breathing air. It's kind of hard to inhale green, leafy vegetables.

Then I took the Dead Man's advice. I stocked up on lethal hardware. I even picked up a few sneaky-petes I recalled from my Marine days. Let them come after me now, I thought. I'm ready for anything.

Horses. They are one of the little unpleasantnesses to be endured during any lengthy journey. Unless you want to walk. Morley Dotes had high praise for that sort of exercise, which meant it hurt. Personally, I have very little interest in voluntarily inflicting pain or discomfort upon myself.

I went to an outfitter I knew, a black giant they called Playmate. He was human, but must have had a little mixed blood somewhere. He stood nine feet tall. The color-impregnated clan scars on his cheeks gave him a ferocious look, but he was a sweetheart, as gentle as a human being could be.

Those gruesome features brightened when he spotted me crossing the yard of his place. He came at me with arms spread wide, grinning like I was going to rig out a battalion. I ducked his hug. He could crush you in his enthusiasm. Had he possessed the killer instinct, he would have made one hell of a professional wrestler.

I had done him some good on a skip trace awhile back. My getting the guy to pay up saved Playmate from bankruptcy. So he owed some good fortune to me, but this greeting was not that much more warm than what he gave strangers who wandered in off the street.

"What can we do for you, Garrett? Name it and it's yours. On me. Long as you need it."

"I need a couple of horses and camping gear for five for three or four months."

"You got it. Going out to try your hand at trapping? Business that bad?"

"I have a job. It's taking me out of town."

"Three, four months is a far piece out and back. Where you going?" He was headed for his stable, where a whole clan of four-legged assassins awaited my advent with malice bubbling in their blood.

"The Cantard."

Horses and I do not get along. I can ride, but just barely, when I have to. I'm a city boy and never saw much need to hang around with beasts that have it in for me.

Playmate slowed down. He gave me one of those looks you save for your crazy cousin when he says something totally stupid. "The Cantard? Garrett, you're a great man, and I have complete faith in you. If any civilian could get into and out of the Cantard alive, it would be you. But I'm not so confident of my animals."

"I don't want you to give me anything, Playmate. I'll buy what I need. No risk to you."

"Don't give me that tone of voice, Garrett."

What tone? I didn't intend the guy any grief.

We entered the digs of their satanic majesties the horses. Twenty pairs of big brown evil eyes turned my way. I could almost hear them sizing me up in their secret language, plotting misery.

"This is Thunderbolt," Playmate said, indicating a big black stallion with wicked teeth. "A spirited animal. Partly battle-trained."

"No."

Playmate shrugged, moved on to a roan. "How about Hurricane, here? Fast and smart and a little unpredictable. Like you. You should get along great. Complementary personalities."

"No. And no Storm, no Fury, no nothing with a fire-breathing name to live up to. I want an old mare on her last legs with a name like Daffodil and a temperament to match."

"That's disgusting, Garrett. Are you a man or a mouse?"

"Squeak. Me and horses don't get along. The last

time I rode one he tricked me by turning around while I was getting on. Then he stood there laughing at me behind my back."

"Horses don't laugh, Garrett. They're very serious creatures."

"You hang around me, you'll see them laugh."

"If you have a problem with animals, why make the trip overland? Catch a river barge down to Leifmold, then take a coaster south. It would save you six hundred hard miles."

Why not? It never occurred to me, that's why not. Sometimes you stumble into a rut so deep you can't see over the edges. I didn't want to go to the Cantard, really, so I'd developed the habit of thinking about getting in and out fast. The quickest way from one place to another is usually the shortest. The shortest haul from TunFaire to the Cantard is straight overland.

A ham of a hand slapped me on the back. "Garrett, you look like a man who's just had a religious revelation."

"I have. And the first saint of my new church is going to be Saint Playmate."

"As long as the job don't call for a martyr."

"Have faith, my friend. And make lots of donations. That's all this church will ask."

"Most of them only ask for the offerings. I tell you I almost started my own church once?"

"No."

"I was scoping it out when I thought I was going to lose the stable. I figure a man my size, tricked up in the right outfit, would make a hell of a prophet. And in a city as god-ridden as TunFaire, people are always looking for something novel."

"Wouldn't have thought you so cynical."

"Me? Cynical? Perish the thought. Come back when you need a horse, Garrett."

15

Morley and the triplets were sitting around looking smug when I showed up at the Tate place with my travel bag on my shoulder. "You guys earned your keep? Or are you just in practice for the next time the Grinning Death comes through?"

Morley stopped gnawing a carrot long enough to say, "We thumped some heads this morning, Garrett."

Doris bobbed his head and chortled something in dialect. Morley said, "He just claimed he broke twenty heads himself. He's exaggerating. There weren't more than fifteen guys involved. I recognized some of them. Second-raters. Whoever hired them was trying to get by on the cheap. He got what he paid for."

I wondered if any of them had recognized Morley. "Did they get away with anything?"

"A lot of bruises and a few fractures."

"I mean anything physical."

"That isn't physical enough for you?"

"Damn it, you know what I mean."

"Testy in the morning, aren't we? You didn't pay a bit of attention when I explained about fiber."

"Morley!"

"No. Nothing."

"Thank you."

"What's in the bag?"

"My travel gear. We're headed out."

"Today?"

"You have some reason to hang around?"

"Not really. You just caught me by surprise."

That was the idea. "The arrangements are made.

You guys are ready to go. We'll head for the boat from here and hide out there till we pull out."

"Boat? What are you talking, boat?"

Morley was ghost-spooked pale. The triplets looked green around the gills, which was something for Doris and Marsha, who were a lovely shade of pale lime to begin.

"Boat?" Morley croaked again.

"Boat. We'll barge down to Leifmold, then catch a coaster headed south. We'll stay with it as far as we can. Then we'll put ashore and finish what we have to overland."

"We mix with water worse than oil does, Garrett."

"Nonsense. All the great navigators were elvish."

"All the great navigators were crazy. I get seasick watching the water-spider races. Which may explain why I can't bet them worth squat."

"Probably not enough starch in your diet."

He looked at me with hurt puppy eyes. "Let's take it overland, Garrett."

"Not on your life. I don't get along with horses."

"So we walk. The triplets can carry—"

"Who's paying the wages, Morley?"

He did nothing but scowl.

"Right. The boss says we take boats as far as we can, *then* we do it the hard way. You have your boys pick up and pack up. We head out in fifteen minutes."

I went and hunted up Pop Tate and told him I'd be doing the job and would be leaving the city shortly. We dickered awhile about expense money. To end up with what I wanted I had to give him what he wanted, a pretty complete outline of my plans.

I could change them, of course.

I don't like letting people in on everything. It subverts my reputation for being unpredictable.

16

The river barge *Binkey's Sequin* reminded me of a shopkeeper's wife. She was middle-aged, middle class, a little run down, a little overweight, extremely stubborn and set in her ways, needing masterful coaxing and cajoling to get her to give her loving best, but also faithful and warm and unsinkably optimistic in her care for her children. Morley hated her at first sight. He prefers them sleek, lean, taut, and fast.

Master Arbanos, her skipper, was an oversize gnome of that ethnic minority the ignorant sometimes confuse with hobgoblins (though any idiot knows hobgoblins don't come out in the daytime because the sunlight would broil their eyeballs). After he got us settled in what, with a smile of self-mockery, he called the cabin, he pulled me aside and told me, "We won't be able to sail till morning. Hope that don't throw you off schedule."

"No." But being naturally nosy and suspicious, I wanted to know why.

"Cargo's late. Best part, that is. Twenty-five cask of the TunFaire Gold, that they don't trust nobody but me and my brother to get down the river unbruised."

TunFaire Gold is a premium wine with a reputation for traveling poorly.

"So here I sit," he complained, "with eight ton of potato, two ton of onion, three ton of pig-iron billet, and forty hogshead of navy salt pork turning to mold while I wait for them to baby that spoiled grape juice down from TagEnd. If I didn't get paid more for hauling that than the rest put together, I'd tell them

72

what to do with their TunFaire Gold poison! You bet I would."

Cargo manifests. How thoroughly exciting. "No problem for us. As long as we get there in a reasonable amount of time."

"Oh, won't be no problem with that. We'll get there almost the same time we would have."

"We will? Why?"

"We'll be going out with the tide, with an extra five knot of current running where the river is usually slowest. I just thought you might be in a hurry to move at this end, what with the way your friends are keeping out of sight down with the codfish smell. The way I hear tell, you landsider don't favor fish odor too much."

I had not mentioned the stench, being the naturally courteous guy that I am. But, "Now that you bring it up . . ."

"What?"

"Wait."

One of the Tate cousins or nephews was limping down the dock, checking ships with mad eyes. He was covered with dried blood. People stepped out of his way and stared after him.

He spotted me, staggered faster. I went to meet him.

"Mr. Garrett! They got Tinnie and Rose! They said if we don't give them Denny's papers—"

He collapsed. I caught him, lifted him up, and carried him aboard *Binkey's Sequin*. Master Arbanos gave me an appalled look. Before he started complaining, I tossed him a couple of marks. His personality shifted like a wolfman's under a full moon. You would have thought he was the boy's mother.

A draft of brandy bubbling in the gut got the kid into a state to tell his tale.

Rose and Tinnie, as was their custom, had gone out to do the afternoon marketing. Lester and the usual cousins and nephews and some kitchen help had accompanied them, again as was customary. When they were returning with the servants and two boys lugging vegetables and whatnot, disaster had struck, in the form of Vasco and a half-dozen thugs.

"They grabbed Rose and Tinnie before we could drop the groceries and get our weapons out. Uncle Lester was the only one who was able . . . They killed him, Mr. Garrett."

"You all do them any damage?" The kid wouldn't have been in such bad shape if they hadn't tried. I needed to know how much blood was in it to tell if the women had a chance.

"Some," he admitted. "I don't think we killed anybody. We had to back off first. That's when they said we could have them back if we gave them Denny's letters and notebooks and stuff."

Well, they had no real reason to commit murder. The blood was balanced. One of their lot for Uncle Lester. A trade could be made. The problem was, they would find out I was headed south if I had much to do with the exchange.

I grinned.

"Sounds bad to me," Morley said.

"Thought you were staying out of sight." I wondered how long he had been sitting on that sack of onions listening. Not that he had heard anything he shouldn't.

He shrugged.

"They tell you where to get in touch?" I asked the kid.

"Yes. The Iron—"

Old Man Tate himself materialized. I thought he never left the family compound. He stormed aboard, shaking all over. He was winded from his hike and so damned mad he couldn't do anything but sputter.

"Sit down, Pop," I said. "I'm working on it already."

He plopped onto another bag of onions, giving Morley a curt nod. Master Arbanos winced but kept his yap shut.

"Here's the lay," I said. "We've got to make the trade."

Tate sputtered but nodded, then wheezed, "If it was just Rose, I'd be tempted to tell them to go to hell."

"Right. Look, I put the papers and whatnot in a box and moved them out of your place so those clowns wouldn't get them when they broke in. I didn't figure them for this. Anyway, what we have to do now is set the exchange up in such a way that we get the women back in one piece. I think I can do that, but you'll have to trust me on it."

Tate started sputtering again.

Morley said, "He's the expert, Mr. Tate. Permit him to exercise his expertise." His tone was more diplomatic than what I usually manage.

"I'm listening." Tate glared at me.

"Master Arbanos. What time are we going to take off tomorrow?"

"Five minutes after the seventh hour."

"Right. Mr. Tate, you go over to the Iron . . ." I snapped my fingers at the kid.

"Iron Goblin," he said.

"The Iron Goblin. Tell whoever meets you there that he's to deliver the women here at five after the seventh hour tomorrow morning. Or no deal. I'll tell them where they can get the papers when the women look like they'll get back to their own people okay. In fact, if Master Arbanos will provide me pen and paper, I'll write the instructions."

Tate wanted to argue. He always wanted to argue. The old goat would disagree if you said the sky was blue. I let him simmer while I scratched a note. Master Arbanos was going to get rich selling me favors.

"Just pretend you're me," I told Tate when I finished. I folded the note and handed it to him. "Don't argue with them. Tell them that's it, take it or leave it."

"But—"

"They'll take it. They won't expect me to trust them. They would know I'd try to set up something so they can't mess us around. And they'll check around about me. They'll find out that I've done a couple of these things before and held up my end every time."

That was true. As far as it went. But this time a

snatch and switch was not the whole story. This time the snatch was part of something bigger.

I was starting to take things personally, too.

Tate got his spleen out, and yakked his fear into submission, then took my note and marched off. We got the kid cleaned up and bandaged and sent him home.

17

Vasco didn't want to play the game my way, though he brought the women when he came to argue. He came on time, too, which told me that he would do it my way if I didn't bend.

He left Rose and Tinnie fifty feet up the dock, guarded by a half-dozen men, and marched aboard. "Still in there pitching to get your throat cut, aren't you?" I asked.

His lips tightened but he refused to be baited. The sergeants teach you to control your temper, down in the Cantard. He looked around, did not see anything to disturb him.

He should have been disturbed. It had been all I could do to restrain Morley, who wanted to bushwack the bunch and leave them floating in the river.

"Before you start," I told Vasco, "you'd better realize that I've got no special need for those women. I don't have any for Denny's papers, either. Which is why I'll make the trade."

"Where are the papers, Garrett?"

"Where are the women?"

"Right there. You can't see . . . ?"

"I don't see them on the boat. You don't get squat till I think it's too late for you to screw me over."

"Why would I do that?"

"I don't know. You haven't shown a lot of sense so far."

"You won't needle me into doing something stupid, Garrett."

"I don't have to. You do fine without me. Get those

women over here." Master Arbanos was ready to cast off.

"What guarantee do I have that you're not cheating us?"

I ticked off points. "One: I always play these things straight. You know my reputation. Two: I don't need the papers for anything. Three: I know who you are, so I don't have to mess with you now. I can come for your head whenever I want it."

"Keep talking tough, Garrett. You'll get burned."

"Maybe you'll send Barbera after me?"

His mouth tightened even more. He jerked around, jumped to the wharf, gestured at his goons. They released the women. I waved them toward *Sequin*.

They came forward slowly. I guess they thought blood would fly any second.

Vasco stopped a few steps from the edge of the wharf. "So where are the papers, Garrett?"

I didn't have anything to say. He was still between me and the women. I just sort of looked around like a bored sightseer.

That's when I spotted the two guys from Morley's place, Big One and Ugly One. Not together, but both hanging around, relaxed, just part of the crowd eyeballing the goings-on.

I backed up a couple of steps like I was giving the gals room to jump aboard. I whispered down to Morley, who was crouched between onion sacks, "Take a peek at the guy sitting on the cotton bales."

"Give, Garrett," Vasco said.

I ignored him. The women had a few yards to go yet. Even Rose's sour face had begun to show some hope.

Master Arbanos began letting lines go.

Morley whispered, "I see him. What about him?"

"Who is he?"

"How the hell should I know? I never saw him before."

"I did. Once. The other night. Hanging around with the big guy over there leaning against those navy pork barrels." I started to tell him where and when, then decided it might be wise to save a little something for my old age.

"I don't know him, either," Morley said.

"Give, Garrett." Vasco had just about decided I was going to cheat him. He started after the women.

"Run!" I yelled at them. And to Vasco, "They're in a box in an abandoned house on the Way of the Harlequin, half a block west of Wizard's Reach."

"It's your ass if they aren't, Garrett."

"Anytime you think you can take a piece of it, Vasco. Anytime."

The boat began to drift away from the wharf. The women took my advice, sprinted and jumped. A delectable bundle of goodies plopped into my arms. Morley popped up and caught Rose, making suitable purrs at the advent of unexpected treasures. I tossed him a sneer.

Vasco trotted away, barking orders at his troops.

I couldn't restrain a chuckle.

"What's so funny?" Tinnie asked. She made no effort to peel herself from me. I thought about pushing her away—sometime next week.

"Just imagining what might happen when they try to collect those papers."

"You mean you lied to them?"

The wharf was fifteen feet away now. Ugly One got down off the cotton bales. He paid us no special attention. And I had trouble paying him any, either. Tinnie would not hold still.

"Oh, no. I told him the truth. I just didn't tell him all of it."

"Amateurs," Morley said, taking a break from Rose, who was doing to him what Tinnie was to me. "They had any professional smarts at all, they'd know that's the Dead Man's place. Slick, Garrett. Remind me not to get on your wrong side. You're so slick you'd slide uphill."

I glanced at the two men on the wharf and wondered.

"I told you I was going with you, Garrett," Rose crowed, as if she had planned the whole thing. She got over her frights fast.

"You might think," I told her. "You might think." I figured to have Master Arbanos put in a mile or two down and get shut of those females.

Damn! That Tinnie was merciless.

I decided I liked her.

About then old man Tate came charging out the dock, too late for anything but the bye-bye. "Master Arbanos, where are you going to put in so we can get rid of these women?" I figured I'd yell the news across to Tate.

"Leifmold."

Leifmold. All the way down to the coast.

He would not relent. He was deaf to offers of money on this. He had a reputation, a schedule, and a tide, and he would waste none of them for any puny bribe I could pay.

Rose grinned wickedly while I argued.

Tinnie's smile was more promising.

18

The trouble with that damned boat was that there was no privacy. You started a little hand-holding and ear blowing and there was Doris or Marsha or Dojango or some damned crewman exercising his eyes. It nearly drove Morley and me crazy. Rose seemed plenty willing to be friendly with him. Of course, he had the authentic golden touch.

I guess eating your vegetables is good for something.

Leifmold was not that long a journey. The first chance I got I pulled Morley aside and asked, "How are we going to ditch those two?"

"Bad choice of words, Garrett. Though I understand your frustration. Does our principal have reliable associates in Leifmold?"

"I don't know."

"Why not?"

"I never had any reason to ask."

"Too bad. Now we have to try to charm it out of those girls." He did not sound optimistic.

Rose laughed at us when we tried to get some word out of her. Tinnie just pretended she was deaf.

Morley and I went off to the stern and brooded together alone.

"Can't do it, Garrett," he grumbled after a while.

"Uhm," I grunted.

"No way."

"Uhm."

"Skirts in the Cantard. Worse than poison, what I hear. We go in there with women, we're dead. Guaranteed."

"I know. But we can't just run off on them, either."

He gave me a look. "If it wasn't poor business sense in this case, I'd say you were too romantic. Baggage is baggage. There isn't anything any one of them is sitting on that you can't get from another one."

There was a lot of traffic on the river, most of it taking advantage of the tide. And most of it faster than *Binkey's Sequin*. But there was one gaudy yachtlike vessel back upstream that seemed to have us on a leash. "I don't know how a guy with your attitude has your luck."

The yacht boasted a sail of red and yellow stripes. It had sleek lines. It smelled of wealth, which meant power. It could have passed us easily, but it just hung back.

"They want to be treated that way, Garrett. If you don't treat them like rats, they have to admit that they're responsible for their own behavior. And you know women. They never want to admit they get a kick out of messing around."

"How about trying this angle—if Master Arbanos is willing."

"I'm listening."

"We tie them up just before we make port. He hides them out while he's loading and unloading, then he takes them back to TunFaire. Just part of the cargo."

"Sounds good to me. When you talk to him, ask about that boat with the striped sail."

I had wondered if he'd noticed.

Master Arbanos held me up. The man was a buccaneer. But I was between a rock and a hard place, and he knew it. I paid. In the end it all came out of Tate's pocket, anyway.

I asked about the striped sail ship.

He looked at me like I was a moron. "Sorry, I forget you are not a riverman. That is *Typhoon*, personal vessel of Stormlord Thunderhead. Everyone on the river knows it. It runs to Leifmold and back all the time, showing the Stormlord's colors."

"Oh my, oh my, oh my," I murmured.

"The Stormlord never sails her himself. She is just

for show. Her master is a bitch cartha with the temper and moral of an alley cat. She has had trouble with everyone on the river. Some say will strike the striped sail and hoist the black one by night.''

"What does that mean?"

"That some think she turn river pirate **when** no one is looking."

"Is it just talk? Or is there something to it?" Bless me, but wouldn't it be my kind of luck to be aboard a barge pirates were stalking. The gods have a fellow especially assigned to complicate my life.

"Who knows? There are pirate. I have seen their leaving."

"And?" He wanted coaxing.

"They don't leave any witness. Which is why I never accept any cargo they find attractive."

Little wheels and gears clicked in my mind, like the works in a waterclock. A clock running a little slow, perhaps. What sort of cargo might attract a pirate working from a vessel belonging to one of the Stormlords? What was this whole business about?

Silver. Sweet silver. The fuel of the engines of sorcery.

One more complication?

Why the hell not? Every other angle had been covered, hadn't it?

I gave Master Arbanos a generous portion of the metal sugar. He assured me my will would be carried out where the women were concerned. They would be treated like royalty, and on *Sequin*'s return to TunFaire he would deliver them to old man Tate personally.

I could ask for nothing more.

Master Arbanos' crewfolk—all of them his relatives—moved the night before we were due to reach Leifmold. They caught the gals asleep.

Such caterwauling and cursing! I never. Rose I expected to be less than polite, but Tinnie I'd had pegged as at least half a lady. She turned out to be the louder of the two.

At least that went off without hitches.

*   *   *

The sea lay on our left. Leifmold climbed steep hills a mile to our right. We were waiting to pick up a pilot, whose expertise would be needed if *Binkey's Sequin* was to negotiate the traps laid for Venageti raiders. Morley was loafing in the bows. "Come here," he said, beckoning languorously. He was nibbling a raw potato stolen from the cargo. I gave it a disgusted look.

"Not bad if you sprinkle a little salt on," he said.

"And good for you, no doubt."

"Of course. Take a gander round the harbor there."

I did. And saw what he meant.

The striped-sail yacht was warping into a dock. She had passed us in the night and had pulled rank to get the first available pilot. "Needs keeping an eye on," I admitted.

"You read that guy Denny's papers. Did he mention Stormlord Thunderhead anywhere?"

"No. But a couple other wizards got memorialized. I'm willing to look for an indirect connection." When you consider the possibility of wizards being involved in anything, the smart thing to do is to assume the worst.

So chances were striped sail had nothing to do with us. But I would take the paranoid approach on the off chance.

The women raised all kinds of holler when we tied up, but nobody paid them any mind. Morley and Doris and Marsha and I went off looking for one of several coasters recommended to us by Master Arbanos. Morley left Dojango to watch the Stormlord's yacht. No one there ought to recognize him even if they were up to no good.

Our luck was in. We found a ship called *The Gilded Lady* planning to put out next morning. Her master was amenable to our buying passage. Morley started looking grey around the edges.

"You handled the river all right."

"No waves on the river, Garrett. Lots of waves along the coast, and the ship running parallel to them."

His eyes bugged. "Let's not talk about it. Let's find someplace to put up, then get out on the town. There's a place down here even better than mine—don't you ever tell anybody I admitted that—that you've really got to try."

"I'm not in a roots and nuts mood, Morley. Looking a long voyage in the eye, I need something with more body."

"Body? Don't you care what you're doing to your body? I promise, you'll like this place. Give you a little something different. All that red meat is going to kill you, anyway."

"We did red meat the other day, Morley. But since you bring up self-abuse, let's do some calculating. Who is more likely to die young? Me eating what I want or you messing around with other guys' women?"

"You're talking apples and oranges now, buddy."

"I'm talking dead is what I'm talking."

He did not have a rejoinder for fifteen seconds. Then he said only, "I'll die happy."

"So will I, Morley. And without hunks of nut stuck between my teeth."

"I give up," he said. "Go ahead. Commit slow suicide by poisoning yourself."

"That was my plan." A tavern sign caught my eye. It had been a dry trip down the river. "I'm going to tip a few."

Doris and Marsha recognized a beer joint when they saw one, too. They grunted back and forth. Morley started trading gibberish with them.

Oh, my. Did all the triplets have an alcohol problem?

I said, "As soon as we find a place for the night somebody better check on Dojango. At least so he knows where to find us."

Morley reached a compromise with Doris and Marsha. "They can have one bucket each. That's all."

"*Bucket?*"

"They're big boys, Garrett."

"So I noticed." We marched into the tavern. It was early yet, so there was no crowd. Still, a silence fell and grew so deep I knew we had walked in where we were not wanted.

I've never let that stop me. I tossed a coin on the bar. "A mug of brew for me and a bucket apiece for the big boys. And my buddy here will have whatever you can stomp out of a parsnip."

Cold-eyed stare. "We don't serve their kind."

"Well, now, they don't speak Karent very well. So when you look at them there, they're still smiling. But I don't think they'll keep on smiling if I have to translate that for them. You know how grolls are when they get mad."

He thought about arguing. He might have had there been forty or fifty more people to back his play. But Doris and Marsha had begun to get the drift. Their smiles vanished and their faces grew mottled.

"We want beer," I said. "Not your women."

He did not laugh. He headed for the tap. Not many people are fool enough to make a groll mad.

They do get mean.

"Not bad beer," I said, quaffing my third while Doris and Marsha nursed their milk pails. "And serving it up didn't break one bone, did it?"

The barman wasn't interested in bantering.

Most of his regulars had deserted him.

We followed their example.

About fifty sullen men had gathered outside. Their mood looked ugly. I told Morley, "I ought to pay closer attention to what neighborhood I'm in."

"I like the way you think, Garrett."

Half a brick thrown by somebody named Anonymous arced toward us. It had some arm behind it. Doris—or maybe it was Marsha—stabbed a paw out and snagged it. He looked it over for a second. Then he squeezed it and let the powder dribble between his fingers.

That impressed me, but not the mob.

So he snapped off the timber from which the tavern's sign hung. He stripped the sign off and flailed the timber around like a switch.

That got the message across. The mob began to evaporate.

Morley asked, "Could a mule do that?"

"No."

We were more circumspect in selecting a place to spend the night.

19

"So where the hell is he?" I demanded. There wasn't a shadow of Dojango.

Morley looked bleak. He had been looking bleak for a while. I thought maybe I should buy him a bunch of carrots or something. He muttered, "Guess we'll have to scout the alleys and taverns."

"I'm going to take a gander at that ship. Catch me on the pier when you find him."

Morley said something to the two remaining triplets. They grunted and moved out. I marched on down to where I could get a look at that striped-sail ship.

There wasn't much to see, a few men lugging things off, then lugging other things on. It wasn't hard to understand why Dojango bugged out. Watching is boring work. It takes a patient guy to lurk for a living.

A man came out on the rear deck, leaned on the rail, hawked, spat into the harbor.

"Interesting." He was Big One from Morley's place and the pier.

He began scanning the waterfront almost as if he had heard me. Then he shrugged and went into a cabin.

Curious.

Maybe Dojango would have stayed on the job if he had seen that guy before.

I lazed in the shade, wishing I had a keg to nurse and wondering what was taking Morley so long. Nothing else happened except that the stevedores finished loading and unloading.

I heard a soft scuff behind me. Maybe at last . . .

But when I looked I saw Big One. He was not in a friendly mood.

I dropped off the bale where I'd been loafing. Did this call for lethal instruments?

He walked right up and wacked the bale with a short club. No accusations. No questions. Nothing but business. I leaned out of the way and let him have one in the gut.

It did as much good as gut-punching a barrel of salt pork.

That club was meant to scramble my brains, I feared. I hauled out a knife.

I did not get to use it. The cavalry arrived in the guise of Doris or Marsha. The groll picked Big One up by one arm and held him out like a doll. A slow grin spread over his green face. Then he casually heaved him over the bales into the harbor.

Big One never made a sound.

They would have heard me cussing fifty miles away.

Doris—or Marsha, as the case may have been—beckoned me to follow. I did, grumbling. "I could have handled him." Probably about like I had handled Saucerhead, by pounding my body off his club till it broke.

This case was doing wonders for my self-esteem.

Dojango was not falling-down-drunk. He was climbing-the-walls-and-howling-at-the-moon-drunk. Marsha kept him under control while Doris explained what happened on the waterfront. Or Doris did while Marsha did. I passed my thoughts afterward.

"Bad business," Morley said. His sense of humor had deserted him.

Bad business indeed. But I had gone up against wizards before. You can handle them if your footwork is deft. They have more handles than your ordinary street thug. The big thing is, they're all as crooked as a hen's hind leg. They are in the middle of every stew of corruption. But they go for a squeaky-clean public image. It's smart to keep some tarnish in your trick bag and be ready to spread it around.

"We'll be out of here tomorrow. Our worries will be over."

"Our worries will be over about the time I learn to handicap the D'Gumi races."

"Meaning never?"

"Or maybe a little longer."

"I'm beginning to wonder if we ought not to reexamine your diet, Morley. Such unrelenting pessimism must have some deficiency at its base."

"The only deficiencies bothering me are of good luck, financial wherewithal, and female companionship."

"I thought you and Rose—"

"As you said, she wants something for nothing. She had a chance at a once-in-a-lifetime experience and she tried to sell herself to me! As if she had something special. As if a woman with her attitudes could ever develop whatever talent she did have. I'll never understand you people. What you do to your women . . ."

"What I do to them isn't any different than what you do to yours. Rose's problems are hers. I do get tired of hearing folks blame their faults on everybody else."

"Whoa, Garrett. Come on down off your stump."

"Sorry. I was just thinking how I was going to spend tomorrow."

"Say what?"

"Listening to Dojango groan and moan and heave his guts over the side while he blames his drinking problem on his mother or somebody."

Morley grinned.

20

Dojango gripped the rail and made an awful noise as he sacrificed to the gods of the sea. A soft whimper followed.

"What did I say?" I asked.

We were twenty feet from the quayside.

Morley was a little green himself. His trouble was all anticipation. The ship wasn't even noticeably rolling.

The ship's master approached. He had time for us now that the vessel was turning toward the channel. He said, "I spoke to the harbor master this morning. The war situation is quiet. We're clear all the way to Full Harbor if you want to stay with the ship that far."

"Of course we do."

Morley groaned. Dojango whimpered something about throwing himself overboard and ending it all. I grinned and set to dickering for the extra passage.

Halfway out of the channel the groll portion of the triplets began gabbling at Morley. When we went to see what they wanted, we found we were overhauling *Binkey's Sequin*. The Tate girls were out on deck. They spotted us as we slid past on the starboard side.

"I get the feeling they're upset about something," Morley said. He smiled and waved.

"Women have no sense of proportion," I said. I grinned and waved, too. "Wag a little tail at you and you're supposed to eat out of their hands." I looked at Tinnie and wondered if it might be worth it.

They blistered the air. I wondered if my personal sacrifices could be parlayed into a bonus from old man Tate.

We swooped past *Sequin* and dashed for the mouth

of the channel. Master Arbanos' vessel was a dark
lump in the distance as we began our turn to the
south.

"I'll be damned!"

It was a morning for meeting old friends. A river
scow entering the Leifmold channel carried Vasco and
his buddies. "That damned Dead Man," I muttered.
"He could have banged them around a little, at least."

They hadn't spotted us. I got everybody out of sight
so it would stay that way.

I had counted on the Dead Man to stall them longer
than he had. Now I worried. Had they done something I would regret?

"Keep an eye on these pirates," Morley grumped.
"They might murder us while we're laying in the scup-
pers puking our guts out." The ship had completed
her turn. She was rolling in the offshore swell.

Morley had no call to worry. The ship's crew treated
us perfectly. The journey was almost without event.
Once, the Stormlord's striped sail passed us, wallowing
and struggling through seas she was not designed to
face. She did not seem interested in us, and was not to
be seen in the harbor at our first port of call.

Once we saw a royal man-of-war farther out, and
another time a masterhead lookout yelled down that
he had a Venageti sail in sight. Nothing came of either
sighting. We entered Full Harbor eight days after de-
parting Leifmold. No striped sail was to be seen there,
either.

For once I felt a little optimistic.

21

"We're here," Morley growled the next morning. "What now?" He had stoked up on biscuits baked with lard and served with greasy gravy. It was the nearest he could get to a vegetarian breakfast.

"Now I try to pick up the woman's trail. Her family should still be here. They ought to know something."

It sounded too simple even to me. But sometimes things go your way. It would be sweet if I could find her at her dad's place, make my pitch, and head out with her yea or nay.

Full Harbor had changed and not changed. New buildings. New naval facilities. New streets laid out after the cleanup from the big Venageti attack three years ago. Same old whores and stews and pawnshops and overpriced inns and tailors preying on the loneliness of young sailors and Marines far from home and in the shadow of death. The gods know I wasted enough of my own time and pay in places like that. Reformers keep talking about shutting them down. They won't. The boys would have nothing left to fill their time.

I expected commentary from Morley Dotes. He disappointed me in a pleasant way. "You humans are a despair, that this is the best a soldier can expect."

Maybe it was his human side talking.

We are the only race that goes in for war habitually, in a big way. The others, especially the elves and dwarfs, have the occasional brawl, but seldom more often than once a generation, and then usually only a single battle, not much sorcery, winner take all.

Plenty of them get in on our doings as auxiliaries.

They can be useful but are unreliable. They have no concept of discipline.

"You're right. Let's find ourselves a base, then get to work."

We drew plenty of stares, being civilians, and them being what they were. I didn't like the attention. Mine is a business where I don't want to be remembered.

We found a place that would accept civs and breeds without devouring the income of ten years. It was about as sleazy as a place could get. I bribed the owner to keep alcohol away from the triplets, then Morley and I hit the streets.

Full Harbor, on the map, looks something like a lobster's head lying between its arms. The city proper, and its naval facilities, sits at the end of a fortified neck of land. The arms reach out and shield the bay from the worst storm-driven seas. The city's location makes it very defensible. The Venageti have managed to penetrate it only twice, each time losing the entire force committed. The farther you get from the water-front and naval facilities, the more "civilized" the city becomes. There are some low, wooded hills just inside the neck of the peninsula, right behind the Narrows Wall. They harbor the homes of the city's well-to-do.

No lords reside in the city. They refuse to risk themselves or their properties where the Venageti might show up with the unpredictable suddenness of a tropical storm.

They're funny that way—plenty willing to trek all over the Cantard risking themselves for glory and personal gain, but . . .

I don't understand them any more than I understand frogs. But I'm handicapped by my low birth.

Kayean's father had been one of the Syndics who dwelt in the hills, with a wife, four servants, and eight kids. Kayean was the oldest.

Memories returned, bringing a certain nostalgia, as I guided the rented carriage up and down pacific lanes.

"What're you looking all moony-eyed about?" Morley demanded. We had left the triplets at the inn, an action the wisdom of which I still doubted, though

Morley assured me he had not left a farthing between them.

"Remembering when. Young love. First love. Right here in these hills." I had not filled him in on every little detail. A bodyguard did not need to know all the sordid angles.

"I'm a bit of a nostalgic romantic myself, but I never figured you for one, Garrett."

"Me? The knight in rusty armor always clanking out to rescue undeserving maidens or to do battle with the dragons of some lunatic's imagination? I don't qualify?"

"You see? Romantic images. Though why should you mind working for nuts if they have money to spend? You can milk a man with an obsession like a spider milks a fly."

"I don't work that way."

"I know. You really *want* to rescue maidens and champion underdogs and lost causes—as long as you get enough grease to keep the joints in the armor from freezing up."

"I like a beer sometimes, too."

"You've got no ambition, Garrett. That's what's wrong with you."

"You could write a book about all the things you've found wrong with me, Morley."

"I'd rather write one about the things that are right. It'd be a lot less work. Just a short little fable. 'He's kind to his mother. Doesn't beat his wife. His kids never have to go in the snow barefoot.' "

"Sarky today, aren't we?"

"I'm off my feed. How much longer are we going to be looking for the ghosts of might-have-been?"

Not only sarky but a little too perceptive. I supposed I might as well confess. "I'm not being romantic. I'm lost."

"Lost? I thought you said you knew these parts like the back of your hand."

"I did. But things have changed. All the trees and bushes and stuff that were landmarks have grown or been cut down or—"

"Then we'll just have to ask somebody, won't we?

Yo!" he shouted at a gardener clipping a hedge. "What's the name of the guy we're looking for, Garrett?" The gardener stopped working and gave us the fisheye. He looked like a real friendly type. Poison you with his smile.

"Klaus Kronk." The first name was pronounced *claws* with a soft sibilant, but Morley took it for a nickname.

He climbed down and approached the gardener. "Tell me, my good fellow, where can we find the Syndic Claws Kronk?"

The good fellow gave him a puzzled look that turned into a sneer. "Let's see the color of your metal, darko."

Morley calmly picked him up and chucked him over his hedge, hopped over after him and tossed him back, thumped on him a little, twisted limbs and made him groan, then said, "Tell me, my good fellow, where can we find the Syndic Claws Kronk?" He wasn't even breathing hard.

The gardener decided that at least one of us was a psychopath. He stammered directions.

"Thank you," Morley said. "You have been most gracious and helpful. In token of my appreciation I hope you will accept this small gratuity." He dropped a couple of coins into the man's palm, closed his fingers over them, then rejoined me aboard our conveyance. "Take the first left and go all the way to the top of the hill."

I glanced back at the gardener, still seated beside the lane. A glint of mischief sparked in his swelling eyes.

"You think it's wise to make enemies out here, Morley?"

"We won't get any comebacks from him. He thinks I'm crazy."

"I can't imagine why anybody would think that about you, Morley."

We had only one turn left to make. A cemetery flanked both sides of the road. "You know where you

are now?" Morley asked. "A landmark like this ought
to be plenty memorable."

"More memorable than you know. I think our gardener friend got us. We'll see in a minute." I turned
between the red granite pillars that flanked the entrance to the Kronk family plot.

"He's dead?"

"We're about to find out."

He was. His was the last name incised in the stone
of the obelisk in the center of the plot. "Got it during
the last Venageti incursion, judging from the date," I
said. "Fits what I remember about him, too. He would
get out and howl for Karenta."

"What do we do now?"

"I guess we look for the rest of the family. He's the
only one who's established residence here."

He lifted one eyebrow.

"I can find my way from here. Kayean and I used to
walk up here at night to, uh . . ."

"In a graveyard?"

"Nothing like tombstones to remind you how little
time you have for the finer things in life."

"You humans are weird, Garrett. If you want an aph-
rodisiac, there's one that the sidhe tribes of the Benecel
river basin make from the roots of something like a
potato plant. It'll keep your soldier at attention for
hours. Not only that, but when you use it you're guaranteed there's no way you're going to become a papa."

Vegetarian sexual aids? Some people take good things
too far.

22

Starting from the cemetery I was able to find the Kronk place with only one miscue. From the lane the place next door looked more like the one I remembered than the correct one. We were partway up the flagstones when I spied the peacock cages under the magnolias.

"About turn and march," I said. "One house shy of our mark." I recalled how, if Kayean was not very careful sneaking in and out, those peafowl would raise six kinds of hell and there went the evening if it happened on the sneak-out side. Her old man knew what was going on but was never quick enough to catch her. She had been fast on her feet.

I explained that to Morley as we retreated to the lane.

"How the hell did a slob like you ever meet a quail living in a place like this?"

"I met her at a party for bachelor officers the admiral put on. All the most eligible young ladies of Full Harbor were there."

He gave me an overly dramatic look of disbelief.

I confessed, "I was there waiting tables."

"It must have been animal magnetism and the air of danger and forbidden fruit surrounding an affair with a member of the lower classes." He said it deadpan. I could not decide whether I should be irritated or not.

"Whatever it was, it was the greatest thing that had happened in my young life. Hasn't been much since to eclipse it, either."

"Like I said, a romantic." And there he let it lay.

*   *   *

"Lot of changes since I was here," I said. "The place has been completely done over."

"You sure it's the right one?"

"Yeah." All the memories assured me that it was. We had walked these grounds under the watchful chaperonage of a patient and loving mother who had seen the whole romance as a phase and would not have believed her eyes if she had walked in on us in the cemetery.

Morley took my word for it.

We were still fifty feet from the door when a man in livery stepped outside and came to meet us. "He don't look like he's glad we dropped by."

Morley grunted. "He don't look like your average houseboy, either."

He didn't. He looked like a Saucerhead Tharpe who was past his prime but still plenty dangerous. The way he fisheyed us said that, fancy clothes or not, we were not fooling him.

"Can I help you gents?"

I'd decided to go at it straight ahead, almost honest, and hope for the best. "I don't know. We're down from TunFaire looking for Klaus Kronk."

That seemed to take him from the blind side. He said, "And just when I thought I'd heard all the gags there was."

"We just a little bit ago found out he was dead."

"So what are you doing here instead of heading back where you came from if the guy you want is croaked?"

"The only reason I wanted to talk to him was to find out how I could get in touch with his oldest daughter. I know she's married, but I don't know who to. I thought maybe her mother or any others of the family who were still around might be able to point me in the right direction. Any of them here?"

He looked like it was getting too complicated for him. "You must be talking about the people who used to live here. They moved out a couple years ago."

The changes all seemed recent enough to support his statement. "You have any idea where she is?"

"Why the hell should I? I didn't even know her name till you told me."

"Thank you for your time and courtesy. We'll have to trace her some other way."

"What you want this machuska for, anyway?"

While I considered his question, Morley said, "Throw it in the pond and see which way the frogs jump."

"We represent the executors of an estate of which she is the principal legatee."

"I love it when you talk dirty lawyer," Morley said. He told our new buddy, "She inherited a bundle." In a ventriloquist's whisper, he told me, "Hit him with the number so we can see how big his eyes get."

"It looks like around a hundred thousand marks, less executors' fees."

His eyes did not get big. He didn't even bat one. Instead he muttered, "I thought I heard every gag there was," again.

So I repeated myself for him. "Thanks for your time and courtesy." I headed for the lane.

"Next stop?" Morley asked.

"We ask at the houses on either side. The people who lived there knew the family. They might give us something."

"If they're not gone, too. What did you think of that guy?"

"I'll try not to form an opinion till I've talked to a few more people."

We had a less belligerent but no more informative interview at the next house down the lane. The people there had only been in the place a year and all they knew about the Kronks was that Klaus was killed during the last Venageti invasion.

"You make anything of that?" I asked as we turned the rig around and headed for the peacock place.

"Of what?"

"He said Kronk was killed *during* the Venageti thing. Not *by* the Venageti."

"An imprecision due entirely to laziness, no doubt."

"Probably. But that's the kind of detail you keep an

ear out for. Sometimes they add up to a picture people don't know they're giving you, like brush strokes add up to a painting."

The peacocks raised thirteen kinds of hell when they discovered us. They crowed like they hadn't had anything to holler about for years.

"My god," I murmured. "She hasn't changed a bit."

"She was always old and ugly?" Morley asked, staring at the woman who observed our approach from a balcony on the side of the house.

"Hasn't even changed her clothes. Careful with her. She's some kind of half-hulder witch."

A little man in a green suit and red stocking cap raced across our path cackling something in a language I didn't understand. Morley grabbed a rock and started to throw it. I stopped him. "What're you doing?"

"They're vermin, Garrett. Maybe they run on their hind legs and make noises that sound like speech, but they're as much vermin as any rat." But he let the rock drop.

I have definite feelings about rats, even the kind that walk on their hind legs and talk and do socially useful things like dig graves. I understood Morley's mood if not his particular prejudice.

The Old Witch—I never heard her called anything else—grinned down at us. Hers was a classic gap-toothed grin. She looked like every witch from every witch story you've ever heard. There was no shaking my certainty that it was deliberate.

A mad cackle floated down. The peafowl answered as though to one of their own.

"Spooky," Morley said.

"That's her image. Her game. She's harmless."

"So you say."

"That was the word on her when I was here before. Crazy as a gnome on weed, but harmless."

"Nobody who harbors those little vipers is harmless. Or blameless. You let them skulk around your garden, they breed like rabbits, and first thing you know they've driven all the decent folk away with their malicious tricks."

We were up under the balcony now. I forbore mentioning his earlier response to a gardener's bigotry. It wouldn't have done any good. Folks always believe their own racism is the result of divine inspiration, incontestably valid.

My dislike for rat people is, of course, the exception to the rule of irrationality underlying such patterns of belief.

The Old Witch cackled again, and the peafowl took up the chorus once more. She called down, "He was murdered, you know."

"Who was?" I asked.

"The man you were looking for, Private Garrett. Syndic Klaus. They think no one knows. But they are wrong. They were seen. Weren't they, my little pretties?"

"How did you . . . ?"

"You think you and that girl could sneak through here night after night, running to that cemetery to slake your lusts, without the little people noticing? They tell me everything, they do. And I never forget a name or a face."

"Did I say they were vermin?" Morley demanded. "Lurking in the shadows of tombstones watching you. And probably laughing their little black hearts out because there is no sight more ridiculous than people coupling."

Maybe I reddened a little, but otherwise I ignored him. "Who killed him?" I asked. "And why?"

"We could name some names, couldn't we, my little pretties? But to what purpose? There is no point now."

"Could you at least tell me why he was killed?"

"He found out something that was not healthy for him to know." She cackled again. The peafowl cheered her on. It was a great joke. "Didn't he, my little pretties? Didn't he?"

"What might that have been?"

The laughter left her face and eyes. "You won't be hearing it from me. Maybe that machuska Kayean knows. Ask her when you find her. Or maybe she doesn't. I don't know. And I don't care."

That was the second time that day I'd heard Kayean called machuska,and only the second time I'd heard the word since I had gotten out of the Marines and the Cantard. It was a particularly spiteful bit of Venageti gutter slang labeling a human woman who has congress with members of other species. A word like our own kobold-knocker is a like nickname.

"Can you tell me where she is?"

"No. I don't know."

"Could you tell me where I might find some of her family?"

"I don't know. Maybe they all went to join her. Maybe they went somewhere to escape their shame." She cackled but she didn't put much heart into it. The peafowl didn't, either. Their feeble response was pure charity.

"Is there any way you can help me?"

"I can give you some advice."

I waited.

"Watch out who you play with among the headstones. Especially if you do find Kayean. She might show you one with her name on it."

"Time to get out of here," I told Morley. "In case it's catching."

He agreed. I thanked the Old Witch. We backed away in spite of her efforts to cling to our company.

"Was that worth it?" Morley asked.

"Absolutely."

A little fellow in green and red jumped into our path. He removed his cap and bowed, then rewarded Morley with a grandiloquent obscene gesture. He raced into the bushes giggling.

This time I didn't interfere with Morley's rock throwing. Lurk behind tombstones, would they?

The giggles ended with an abrupt "Yipe!"

"I hope I broke his skull," Morley growled. "What're we going to do now?"

"Go back to the inn and eat. Check on the triplets.

Guzzle some beer. Think. Spend the afternoon trying to turn something up in parish or civil records."

"Like what?"

"Like who she married if she was married here. She was a good Orthodox girl. She would have wanted the whole fancy, formal show. It might be easier to trace her through her husband if we knew his name."

"I don't want to be negative, Garrett, but I have a feeling the girl you knew and are looking for isn't the woman we're going to find."

I had the same sad feeling.

23

"Where the hell are they?" Morley roared at the innkeeper.

"How the hell should I know?" the man roared right back, obviously used to rough trade. "You said don't give them anything to drink. You didn't say nothing about nursemaiding them or keeping them off the streets. If you ask me, they looked like they was growed up enough to go out and play by themselves."

"He's right, Morley. Calm down." I didn't want him getting so stirred up he'd need to run ten miles to work it off. I had a feeling it would be smart if we stuck together as much as we could. Assuming the Old Witch knew what she was yakking about, somewhere there was a killer who might get unnerved by our poking around.

I repeated myself. "Calm down and think about it. You know them. What are they likely to be doing?"

"Anything," he grumbled. "That's why I'm not calm." But he took my advice and sprawled in a chair across the table. "I've got to find some decent food. Or something female. You see what's happening to me."

I didn't get a chance to put in my farthing's worth. Dojango came ambling in looking like a rooster on parade. He had his hands shoved into his pockets, his shoulders thrown back, and he was strutting.

"Calmly," I cautioned Morley.

Doris and Marsha each had a hide with the look of old, scuffed shoes, but they were grinning too. Strutting was too much for them. The ceiling was only twelve feet high.

Morley did very well. He asked, "What's up, Dojango?"

"We went out and got in a fight with about twenty sailors. Cleaned up the streets with them."

"Calmly," I told Morley, hanging on to his shoulder.

From the looks of Dojango, compared to his brothers, his part in the fight must have been mostly supervisory.

Morley suggested, "Maybe you'd better tell it from the beginning. Like start with what made you go out there in the first place."

"Oh. We were going down to watch the harbor in case anybody interesting came in. Like the guys on that striped-sail ship or the ones that snatched Garrett's girlfriends, or even the girls themselves."

Morley had the good grace to look abashed. "And?"

"We were headed back here when we ran into the sailors."

Doris—or maybe Marsha—rumbled something. Morley translated. "He says they called them bad names." He kept a straight face. "So. Besides making the streets safe from marauding, name-calling sailors, did you accomplish anything?"

"We saw the striped-sail ship come in. One guy—the one Marsha threw in the drink in Leifmold—got off. He hired a ricksha. We figured we would be too obvious if we tried to follow him, so we didn't try. But we did get close enough to hear him tell the ricksha man to take him to the civil city hall."

Full Harbor has two competing administrations, one civil, one military. Their feuding helps keep city life interesting.

"Good work," Morley grouched.

"Worth a beer?" Dojango asked.

Morley looked at me. I shrugged. They were his problem. He said, "All right."

"How about two?"

"What is this? A damned auction?"

Morley and I mounted the rig. He asked, "Where to now, peerless investigator?"

"I figured on hitting the civil city hall next, but Dojango changed my mind. I don't want to run into that guy again if I can help it."

"Your caution is commendable if a bit out of character. Keep an eye peeled for a decent place to eat."

"Get up," I told the horses. "Keep an eye out for a pasture where Morley can graze."

I don't understand it. We went into the church and there was nothing going on. Every day seems like a holy day of obligation for the Orthodox from what I've seen.

A priest in his twenties with a face that did not yet need shaving asked us, "How may I help you gentlemen?" He was unsettled. We weren't ten feet inside the door, but already we had betrayed ourselves as heathen. We had overlooked some genuflection or something.

Earlier I'd decided to deal straight with the church—without telling everything, of course. I told the priest I was trying to locate the former Kayean Kronk, of his parish, because she had a very large legacy pending in TunFaire. "I thought somebody who works here, or your records, might help me trace her. Can we talk to your boss?"

He winced before he said, "I'll tell him you're here and why. I'll ask if he'll see you."

Morley barely waited until the kid was out of earshot. "If you want to get along with these people, you should at least try to fake the cant."

"How do you do that when you don't have the foggiest what it is?"

"I thought you said you and the gal used to come here for services."

"I'm not a religious guy. I slept through them most of the time. The Venageti must not have made it this far during the invasion."

"Why do you say that?"

"Look at all the gold and silver. There aren't any Orthodox among the Venageti. They would have stripped the place and sent the plunder out on the first courier boat.''

The priest came hustling back. "Sair Lojda will give you five minutes to argue your case." As we followed him, he added, "The Sair is accustomed to dealing with unbelievers, but even from them he expects the honor and deference due his rank."

"I'll be sure not to slap him on the back and ask if he wants a beer," I said.

The Sair was the first to ask for my credentials. I made my pitch while he examined them. He did not give us the full five minutes allotted. He interrupted me. "You will have to see Father Rhyne. He was the Kronk family confessor and spiritual adviser. Mike, take these gentlemen to Father Rhyne."

"What are you grinning about?" I asked Morley as soon as we were out of the presence.

"When was the last time you had a priest take less than three hours even to tell you to have a nice day?"

"Oh."

"He was a dried-up little peckerwood, wasn't he?"

"Watch your tongue, Morley."

He was right. The Sair's face had reminded me of a half-spoiled peach that had dried in the desert for six months.

Father Rhyne was a bit remarkable, too. He was about five feet tall, almost as wide, bald as a buzzard's egg, but had enough hair from the ears down to reforest fifty desert craniums. He was naked to the waist and appeared to be doing exercises. I have never seen anyone with so much brush on his face and body.

"Couple of minutes more, men," he said. He went on, sweating puddles.

"All right. Throw me a towel, Mike. Trying to shed a few stone," he told us. "What can I do for you?"

I sang my song again, complete with all the choruses. I wondered if I would run out of bottles of beer on the wall before I picked up Kayean's trail.

He thought for a minute, then said, "Mike, would

you get the gentlemen some refreshments? Beer will do for me."

"Me too," I chirped.

"Ah. Another connoisseur. A gentleman after my own heart."

Morley grumbled something about brewing being an unconscionable waste of grains that could be stone-ground and baked into high-fiber breads that would give thousands the bulk they desperately needed in their diets.

Father Mike and Father Rhyne both looked at him like he was mad. I didn't contradict their suppositions. I told Father Mike, "See if you can't track down a rutabaga. If it doesn't put up too fierce a fight, squeeze it for a pint of blood and bring that to him."

"A glass of cold spring water will be sufficient," Morley said. Coldly. Sufficiently. I decided not to ride him so hard.

Once our guide stepped out, Father Rhyne confessed, "I wanted Mike out of the way for a while. He has a tendency to gossip. You don't want this spread around any more than need be. So you're looking for Kayean Kronk. Why here?"

"The Kronks were a religious family. This was their parish. I know she was married some time ago, but I don't even know her husband's name. It would have been in keeping with her character to have had a big parochial wedding. If she did, and it was here, then the groom's name would be on record."

"She was not married in the church. Not this parish or any other." There was something very odd and ominous about the way he said that.

"Is there any chance you could give me a useful lead or two, either toward her or a member of her family who might be willing to help?"

He eyed me a full half a minute. "You seem like an honest enough fellow, if not entirely forthright. But I expect our trades are a little alike in that respect. You satisfied the Sair, who has the eye of a buzzard when it comes to judging character. I'll help however I can as long as I don't have to violate the sanctity of the confessional."

"All right. How can you help me?"

"I don't know. I can't tell you where to find her."

"Is that privileged knowledge?"

"No. I don't know."

"What about the name of the guy she married?"

"I can't tell you that, either."

"Privilege? Or don't know?"

"Six of one, half dozen of the other."

"All right. I'll worry about getting a dozen out of that later. Can you tell me where I can get in touch with any of her family?"

"No." Before I could ask he raised a staying hand and said, "Ignorance, not privilege. The last I heard of any of the Kronks was about two years ago. Her brother Kayeth had been decorated and brevetted major of cavalry for his part in the victory at Latigo Wells."

Morley stirred just the slightest. Yes, another cavalryman. It might or might not mean something. Kayeth was younger than Kayean, which meant he was younger than Denny and me, which meant their periods of service might not have overlapped at all.

Idiot! They didn't need to overlap for them to have met if Denny was her lover after me.

"Do you recall what unit he was with?"

"No."

"No matter. That should be easy to find out. When was the last time you saw Kayean?"

He had to think about that. I figured he was having trouble remembering I was wrong. He was debating proprieties. He gave me an exact-to-the-minute time and date slightly more than six years ago, and added, "That is when she ceased to exist in the eyes of the church."

"Huh?"

Morley said, "He means she was excommunicated, Garrett."

Father Rhyne nodded.

"What for?"

"The reasons for excommunication are revealed only to the soul to be banished from grace."

"Wait a minute." I was confused. "Are we talking about the same woman?"

"Take it easy, Garrett," Morley said. "Excommunication don't necessarily mean she turned into some kind of religious desperado. They do you in because you won't let them extort your whole fortune. Or, if you're a woman, because you won't come across."

That was a deliberate provocation. Father Rhyne took it better than I expected. "I have heard that sort of thing happens up north. Not here. This is a church militant, here in this archdiocese. The priest who tried that would find himself staked like a vampire. The reasons for Kayean's excommunication were valid within the laws of the church."

I stepped in before Morley rendered his opinion of laws that judged him to be without a soul and therefore beyond the protection of its golden rules. "That's not really the sort of information that's likely to help me, Father. Unless the reasons for her excommunication have some bearing on where she is now."

Father Rhyne shook his head, but with just enough hesitance to show he was not sure.

"My job, and my only job, is to find the woman so I can tell her she has inherited a hundred thousand marks. Once I tell her, I'm supposed to ask if she wants it. If she does, I'm supposed to escort her to TunFaire because she has to claim it in person. If she doesn't want it, I have to get a legal deposition to that effect so that others down the list can benefit from the legacy. That's it. That's all."

"Nevertheless, you have a personal interest."

Glass Door Garrett, that is what they call me. See right through me. "The guy who died was a good friend of mine. I want to see what kind of woman would get him to leave her everything when he hadn't even seen her for seven years."

A twitch of a smile worked one corner of Rhyne's mouth. I stopped, confused. Morley said, "In the shadows behind the tombstones."

That did it. Of course. Rhyne had been Kayean's confessor. He'd never say a word, but he remembered sins confessed that included a Marine named Garrett.

"All right. We know where we stand. We know what my job is. I've asked the questions I think are pertinent—and a few that weren't and some that were probably impertinent—and I think you've answered me fairly. Can you think of anything you could volunteer that might be helpful?"

"Hang on a second, Garrett," Morley said. He drifted to the door as soundlessly as a cloud and jerked it open. Father Mike almost fell over.

I'd wondered what had been keeping him.

"Ah! That beer at last!" Father Rhyne had on a big, jovial host's grin, but his eyes were not smiling. "Just put the tray down and go about your duties, Mike. I'll talk to you later."

Father Mike went out looking like he hoped later would never come.

Rhyne chose to pretend that nothing untoward had happened. He poured beer from a monster of a pitcher into enormous earthenware mugs. Morley's water was in a blown-glass tankard of equal size. I'd barely taken my first sip before Father Rhyne parted from his mug and said, "Ahh!" He wiped his mouth with the fur on the back of his forearm, then belched like a young thunderhead. He poured himself a pint chaser.

Before he hoisted it, he said, "What information can I volunteer? I can tell you that you won't find her in Full Harbor. I can tell you to walk very carefully because I can infer, without absolute certitude, that there might be people who wouldn't want you to find her. I can tell you not to look for the image that lives in your memory because you will never find *her*."

I finished my brew. "Thank you. Good beer."

"We make it ourselves. Will there be anything more?"

"No . . . Well, something from off the wall. I've heard her father was murdered. Any comment?"

He got a very evasive look. "It's possible."

His expression told he would clamp his jaws on that cryptic statement. I returned my mug to the tray.

Morley followed my lead. He had downed enough water to show he appreciated the stuff in quantities too small to rock a boat. We headed for the door. I said, "Thanks for everything."

"Sure. If you do find her, tell her we haven't stopped loving her, even if we can't forgive her. That might help."

Our gazes locked. And I knew that fat little hairball did not mean "we" at all. I also knew the whole thing was as chaste and courtly as any perfect knight's affection for his lady in an old *roman*. "I'll do that, Father."

"Another one," Morley said when we got outside. "I've got to meet this woman." There was not an ounce of sarcasm in his tone.

24

"Are we making any headway?" Morley asked as we climbed aboard the rented rig.

"Oh, yes. We've eliminated some legwork, like making the rounds of every Orthodox parish in Full Harbor. We've added a visit to the army office at the military city hall to see if they will help us locate Major Kayeth Kronk."

I did not look forward to that. They'd probably assume we were Venageti spies.

"What now?"

"We can try that. We can try the civil city hall, too, though I don't think we'd get much there. Or we could go back to the inn and I could lay around staring at the ceiling and wondering what a sensible young woman can do to get herself excommunicated."

"That doesn't sound productive. And butting heads with the army, even to get them to tell us to get out and leave them alone, is likely to be an all-day job."

"The civil city hall it is, then."

We were headed up the steps when a voice roared, "Hey! You two."

We stopped, turned. Near the rig stood a city employee, the type who carries weapons and is supposed to protect citizens from their neighbors' villainies, but who spends most of his time force-feeding his purse and sparing the reputations of the wealthy and powerful. "This yours?"

"Yes."

"You can't leave it here. We don't want no horse apples tracked all over the hall."

Despite his friendly way of putting it, his position had merit. I marched down the steps. "Have you a suggestion what I can do with it?"

He did not know who we were. We had come in a fancy rig. We were well dressed. Morley looked a bit like a bodyguard. I wore a look of cherubic innocence. A suspicion slithered through his slow wit. I had handed him that straight line so he would stick his foot in his mouth. Then I would choke him on it.

"We usually ask visitors to leave their conveyances in the courtyard behind the hall, sir. I could move it back there for you, if you like."

"That's very thoughtful of you. I'd appreciate that very much." I dug out a tip about one and a half times the going rate for such a task. Enough to impress, not enough to arouse resentment or suspicion.

"Thank you, sir."

We watched him drive into a narrow passageway between one end of the hall and the city jail.

"Slick, Garrett."

"What?"

"You should have been a con man. You sold him using nothing but intonation, bearing, and gesture. Slick."

"It was an experiment. If he'd had two ounces of brain to rub together, it wouldn't have worked."

"If he had two ounces of brain he'd be making an honest living."

I think Morley's attitude toward so-called civil servants is as cynical as mine.

The next public employee we encountered—on a more than which-way-do-we-go? basis—had two ounces of brains. Just barely.

I was digging through what passed for vital statistics in Full Harbor and finding that four of the Kronk children were not listed at all. Morley, in pursuit of an inspiration of his own, dug through the property plats and brought one over. He sat on the floor reading it.

Two-Ounces appeared out of nowhere and bellowed, "What the hell do you think you're doing?"

"Research," I replied in my reasonable voice.

"Get the hell out of here!"

"Why?" Reasonable again, of course.

That got him for a moment. Both ounces went stumbling after something with more authority than a bottom-rung city flunky's "because I said so."

Morley dealt himself a hand. "These are public records legally open to public inspection."

That left Two-Ounces armed only with bluster because he didn't know for sure. "I'm going to call some guards and have you wise guys thrown out on your asses."

"That won't be necessary." Morley closed the plat book. "No need for a scene. The matter can wait till after you've explained to the judge tomorrow morning."

"Judge? What judge?"

"The judge who's going to ask you why a couple of honest investigators like ourselves, sent down from TunFaire, can't look at documents any vagrant off the streets of Full Harbor has a right to see." He went off to return his plat book.

Two-Ounces stared at me while I neatened up after myself. I think he saw nothing but potential disaster. There is no man so insecure as a bottom-level functionary in a sinecure he has held for a long time. He's done nothing for so long that nothing is all he can do. The prospect of unemployment is a mortal terror.

"Ready?" Morley asked, returning.

"When you are."

"Let's go. See you in the morning, friend."

The man turned slowly to watch us go, his face still drained. But the poison had begun to creep into his eyes. It was the hatred and power greed that make vicious liars out of people who tell you they're public servants.

25

"How'd I do?" Morley asked as we pushed out the front door. He was grinning

"Not bad. Maybe one slice too much ham."

He wanted to debate but I cut him short. "You learn anything?"

"Not unless you care that the house was sold by Madame Kronk, a decent interval after the date on that memorial obelisk, to a character with the unlikely name of Zeck Zack, for what seems like a reasonable market price. You ever heard of him?"

"No."

"You find out anything?"

"Only that the civil city administration keeps pretty loose track of who's dying and being born."

"Oh. So with those Kronks being prominent, imagine what they've got on ordinary, real folks."

I shrugged. "You leave no stone unturned till you find a trail. Where's that clown who took the carriage?"

"Probably at the nearest swill pit guzzling your tip."

"Then we'll just get it ourselves. We're big boys. We can handle it." We turned into the alley between the hall and the jail. It was clean for a city alley—probably because of where it was—but gloomy because of the hour.

Morley said, "We could probably find a judge we could bribe to back us with that guy."

"I don't think old man Tate would buy it when it showed up on my expense sheet."

A large somebody stepped out of the wall a dozen feet ahead. His appearance was vague in that light.

Morley said, "Behind you," let out a screech, and flung himself through the air.

I whirled, ducking. Just in time. A club whipped the air where my head had been. I gave the guy a kick in the root of his fantasies, then clipped him on the cheek as he bent to pray. Behind him was a guy who was more surprised than me. I jumped and grabbed his arm, tried giving him a knee. He tried to pull a knife while he stared over my shoulder, a big wad of fear in his eyes.

I figured Morley was about finished behind me.

My man tried to knee me and I tried to knee him again and sometime during our dance he decided he really ought to get the hell out of there. He twisted away and started hiking.

I was satisfied. I turned to check behind me.

Morley's man was out. Morley himself was bent double, holding up a wall, puking his guts out. His man must have gotten in a good one.

My first was down, thrashing and twitching and making disgusting handsaw noises. The light was too poor to be sure, but I thought his color looked bad.

"What did you do to him?" Morley croaked.

"Kicked him."

"Maybe he swallowed his tongue." Morley went down on one knee. He moved gingerly.

The guy finished up with one wild convulsion, then he was done. Literally.

Morley trailed fingertips over the corpse's cheek. One of my rings had cut him. The cut had a nasty color.

I looked at my hand.

So did Morley.

The poison chamber on one of the rings had been torn open by the force of the blow.

"We'll have to get rid of him," Morley said.

"Fast. Before somebody stumbles in here."

"I'll get the rig. You drag them to the side so they don't get run over." He ran away as fast as he could.

I wondered if I would see him again. It might be in his interest to find a back way out and just keep on going.

He returned but it seemed like he'd been gone for about twenty hours. He tied off the traces and clambered into the back of the rig. "Hoist him up here."

I hoisted. Morley pulled. When the cadaver was in, Morley set it up with its back against the driver's seat.

"People will see him."

"You just worry about driving. I'll handle this. I've done it before."

I had done my share of driving that day. Horses and I can enjoy an armed truce while they are in harness. But this was too grand an opportunity for that devil tribe to revert to the war rules. "You'd better handle the traces."

"I'll be busy back here. Get moving before somebody comes or the other one wakes up."

I climbed up and took the traces.

"We're just a bunch of guys out on the town. Don't hurry. But get us out of this section fast."

"Make up your mind!" I snapped. But I knew what he meant.

At first Morley sat back with his arm around his buddy slurring some song so thickly that Garrett could only understand about every third word. Later he started cussing the corpse out, telling him what a fool damned no-good he was for getting blasted before the sun even went down. "You ought to be ashamed of yourself, what am I going to tell your old lady, how're we supposed to have any fun dragging you around? You ought to be ashamed."

Later still, once we were in an area where a bunch of drunks in a carriage were as unusual as eggs under a hen, Morley stopped rambling and asked, "Who were those guys, Garrett? Any idea?"

"No."

"Think it was a robbery?"

"You know better. The place, the timing, the behavior of that clerk, the disappearance of the guard from out front, all say it wasn't."

"Off the striped-sail ship? One of them went to the hall."

"I doubt it. Only a local could set up something

like that so fast. We've obviously stepped on a toe somewhere."

"Why?"

"My guess is it was a warning whipping, a Saucerhead job. Pound us around awhile, then tell us to take the next boat home. But we blew up in their hands."

"That's what I figure. Then the real questions are who sent them and why do we make him nervous?"

"Him?"

"I don't think we need to count the Old Witch. Do you?"

"No. Nor the church people, probably. I guess we'll have to find out who Zeck Zack is."

"Too bad we can't ask this guy here."

"You checked him?"

"Dry as a bone. It's time we started thinking about how to break up the party."

"We can't dump him in the drink here. After dark Marines watch the shores like hawks in case Venageti agents try to sneak in. They never catch anybody, but that doesn't stop them." I did my share of watching in my time. I was very young and very serious about it.

My successors would be just as young and just as serious.

Morley said, "Find the busiest, sleaziest cathouse you can. We go in drunk with him between us. We find a dark corner in the waiting room, squat, order drinks for three, tell the madam not to bother our buddy because he's dead drunk, take our turns at the trade, then get out. They won't bother him till the crowd thins out because they'll want to roll him. By then they'll have forgotten us and he'll be their problem."

"Suppose we run into somebody who knows him?"

"There are risks in everything. If we dump him here in an alley, whoever sent him will know what happened. My way he'll have to wonder. That was blockshaush in the ring, wasn't it?" He used the elvish name for the poison. On our side of the line we call it black sauce.

"Yes."

"Good. By the time his boss finds him it'll be too

late for even a master wizard to tell he was poisoned."
He sounded very thoughtful. I knew what he was
thinking. He was wondering what other uncharacteristic
surprises I had in store. He was thinking I was tight
with the Dead Man, and that was probably why I was
carrying poison. He was wondering just how much and
what kind of advice the Dead Man had given me.

I figured a little worry would do him good. It might
take his mind off his stomach for a while.

We ditched our friend Morley's way. I expected
tribes of his buddies to swarm, but it came off smooth.
The guy's boss would never really know what had
happened,

Who *was* his boss? Why did he want to discourage
me from doing my job?

26

I packed a lunch, knowing it would be a long day of runaround at the military city hall. Because they would not let Morley in, I told him to go find out what he could about Zeck Zack. The triplets I sent to watch incoming harbor traffic again.

"But be careful," I told Dojango. "They might decide to take you in to ask if you're Venageti spies."

"Actually, that possibility occurred to us yesterday," Dojango told me. "We've lived on the fringes of the law long enough to know when we're pushing our luck."

Maybe so. Maybe so.

I hefted my picnic basket and went to work.

First there was a clerk, then a senior clerk, then various sergeants followed by a couple of lieutenants who gave me to a captain who admitted he did not think I would have much luck before he dropped me in the lap of a major. One and all checked my bona fides before sending me on. Sometimes twice.

I kept a smile on my mug, stayed polite, and kept my tongue on a tight rein. I could play the game.

I figured I would earn every mark I would gouge from Tate for that day. Besides, it was all part of the plan.

Outlast the bastards.

The major was halfway human, and he even looked like he might have a sense of humor. He apologized for the shuffle and I offered to share my lunch.

"You packed a lunch?"

"Sure. I've dealt with the army before. If it was something complicated, I would have brought a blanket and an overnight bag. You get in the craw of the system and stay there, disturbing routine, somebody is going to go out on a limb, take a chance, tell you what you want to know or make a decision to throw you out, just to get you out from under foot. I get paid exorbitantly for letting people give me the runaround, so I don't mind."

For a moment I thought I had misjudged him. He was not pleased. Knee-jerk response. Give him credit. He gave it a think before he came back. "You're a cynic, aren't you?"

"Occupational hazard. The people I meet leave my faith in human nature mostly negative."

"Right. Let's try again, with the understanding that I'll be the man who ends your quest with an answer or by having you booted out. You want?"

"Some way of getting in touch with Major Kayeth Kronk, cavalryman, the only one of the woman's family of whom I have been able to catch wind. I want to ask if he knows where I can get in touch with his sister. The simple, obvious thing for the army to do is tell me he's out at Fort Whatever. I'd go interview him. But it won't work that way. The army will act on the perfectly reasonable assumption that the entire Venageti War Council has been holding its collective breath for years, waiting to discover the major's whereabouts. So any communications will have to be managed the hard way."

"You are a cynic."

"I'm also right. Not so?"

"Probably. What's your hard way?"

"I write him a long letter explaining the situation and asking him to meet me here or, if that's impossible, to respond to a list of questions. The weakness of the method is that I end up having to trust the army both to deliver the letter and to get the reply back to me. My cynical side tells me that that's too much to expect."

He looked at me from a face of stone. He knew I was setting him up for something and was trying to figure out how I was boxing him in. "That's probably the best you'll get. If that. It isn't the army's problem. But we do help with family matters where we can."

"Any help I get will be appreciated. Even if it isn't much help."

He had not figured any angles yet, which might mean that he did not know how a headquarters really worked. "I'll check with my boss. You check with me tomorrow morning. Just to be safe, bring your letter with you, unsealed but ready to go."

That took care of the aboveboard.

I figured I'd been around long enough—and had explained my problem to enough people—for the word to have spread throughout the headquarters. So I thanked the major, shook his hand, and said I would be heading back to my inn. Did he want to keep the rest of the lunch?

No.

I dawdled through hallways. I loitered in corners. Finally, he found me. *He* being the first staffer to convince himself that I was not a Venageti agent, and therefore safe, and therefore maybe he could pick up a small gratuity by telling me where I could find the man I wanted.

That had been the whole point of taking the runaround.

"Fort Caprice?" I asked back. He nodded. I crossed his palm with silver. We both got out of there.

I went off disappointed. Major Kronk did not, at least now, belong to the same outfit that Denny and his buddies had.

Dojango and his brothers got back to the inn before I did. When I arrived they were eating like they meant to use up my expense money before the end of the week.

Dojango reported, "Nothing to report, actually. Nothing came in today. But we did bribe a piermaster to let us go down there mornings and wait for the rest of our family to arrive. Quite a coup, I thought, actually."

"Quite a coup," I agreed. I forbore asking where they had gotten the wherewithal to grease a piermaster. Nothing about those boys was going to surprise me anymore.

And I have yet to report half their tricks.

* * *

Morley wandered in an hour after I did. "Any luck, Garrett?"

"I found out where her brother is stationed. You?"

"Some."

"Zeck Zack?"

"An interesting character. Nothing secretive about him, supposedly. Everybody knows him. Nothing obvious to connect him with your Kronk people. He's a centaur, an auxiliary veteran who was given citizenship for his service. He's some sort of middleman between the centaur tribes and the merchants of Full Harbor. The darkest rumor about him is that he indulges in a little night trading. He likes to play with human women. The bigger and fatter, the better."

"Can't hang a guy for that," I said, demonstrating my vast tolerance.

"Lucky me."

As proven by the prevalence of accidents like Morley and his buddies, cross-race contact is a sport too popular for us to go lynching the players.

Morley went on, "He does own the house, but he's never there because he's never in the city."

"But there's more."

"Oh?"

"You have a gleam in your eye."

"Probably because I finally found a decent place to eat and got a wholesome meal inside me."

"No. It's more an 'I know something you don't' kind of gleam."

"You've got me." But he sat on it till I threatened to take him for a boat ride.

"All right. Yesterday somebody decided we were too snoopy and deserved a thumping. Had those guys on to us before we started. We bumped a sore tooth somewhere. Unless our friends from the striped-sail ship were behind it."

"Or Vasco is in town without us knowing it," I added.

"That too. But I thought I'd start with the folks we'd talked to. The down-lane neighbor and Old Witch:

no chance. The guy at Zeck Zack's: surly as hell, no
help, maybe, but I couldn't be sure. I bribed the
vermin to keep an eye on the place. So?"

"Come on! You went to the church?"

"I asked around before I dropped in. You remember what you said about the gold and silver?"

"Yes."

"That church was inside Venageti lines for thirteen
days. Afterward, the Sair was praised for talking the
Venageti into sparing the church. Then he and his
flock talked the army into releasing a hundred twenty
prisoners of war as a counter gesture. Everyone thinks
he's a great man, full of compassion for the enemies of
his church."

I already knew, but he wanted me to ask. So I did.
"But you know different, eh? What do you know,
Morley?"

"A third of those soldiers he sent home, all supposedly common infantry, were Venageti officers who
could have been ransomed or put to the question.
They surrendered at the church after exchanging uni-
forms with dead soldiers. At the order of the chief
Venageti undercover agent in Full Harbor."

"The Sair?"

"You got it."

"You go on like you were there."

"I talked to somebody who was."

I raised an eyebrow. I do that very well. It's one of
my outstanding talents.

"I took Father Mike for a walk. After I assured him
that I have no interest in politics, and would not use
what he told me against him, he told me about it. He's
the old boy's helper."

"Are all the priests in on it?"

"Just the two. The old boy sent the others to safety
when the Venageti began closing in. I guess you can
figure why."

"Fewer witnesses. So the old boy sicced the dogs on
us because he thought we might dig something up on
him."

"No."

"Wait a minute. . ."

"Father Mike was very positive."

"Who, then, if you eliminate everybody?"

"Always room for another player in the game. I didn't get to talk to the hairy priest. Nor to anybody the others mentioned us to, and everybody admitted they did, though they couldn't remember to who—except that crazy witch. And at her place we had the vermin listening in. There's no telling who *they* reported to."

"Yeah." This needed some thought. "You've still got the gleam in your eye. You must have gotten around like a bolt of lightning."

"Us breeds can move when we need to. Hybrid vigor."

"So?"

"Your friend Kronk died at that church the day it was liberated. Father Mike was vague about details. Kronk was one of the dozen partisans the Venageti took prisoner. Father Mike didn't think he knew about him and the Sair, but he could have. He doesn't think Kronk was killed while the Venageti were still in control. The body wasn't found till six hours after the army moved in. But two others died at the same time. I have the names of the surviving prisoners if you decide to go howling off down that path."

"That's not what I'm here to do. But give me the names and we'll keep them in mind. In case we keep stumbling over some of them. I see the gleam has gone out. Does that mean the well is dry?"

"Yes. What now?"

"Now I write a long letter to Major Kronk for another major's benefit, while all this information simmers."

"Marinates, you mean. I'm sure you'll soak your brain in a few gallons of beer."

I did not feel up to repartee. Too much to digest. "Tomorrow morning I see my major. Then we do a few more interviews. If we don't strike something hot, the day after we're off into the Cantard."

"Maybe we can bribe a priest to pray for a break," Morley said. "I'm here, but I'm not thrilled about going out there."

"And I am?"

27

There were breaks. They were mixed to say the least.

I went to see my major right after I breakfasted, three eggs gently fried in the grease of a half pound of bacon slowly cooked to a crisp, a mountain of griddle cakes on the side, heavily buttered and buried in strawberry jam. Morley was despondent. He began holding a wake for my health.

He went out when I did, on the trail of roots and berries, barks and grasses, that would hold still long enough for him to prey upon them.

The triplets headed for the waterfront to wait for their relatives. I sincerely hoped they had none anywhere. I figured my luck was running so hot a platoon would descend on me like orphans left on the church steps.

I didn't have to wait long or put up with much before I was told I could see the major. My outlook began to improve.

The major took my message after a rudimentary greeting, checked it for messages to the Venageti War Council, said, "This looks acceptable. It will go out in the next courier pouch headed the right direction."

"Not going to test for invisible ink?"

He gave me one of those good hard stares they practice in front of the mirror when they're shavetails. I let it slide off. "You're cocky today, aren't you?"

"It's a personality defect. I spent five years on the inside of the service. It's hard to take it seriously when it doesn't have a noose around your neck."

"Do you really care if your letter gets delivered?"

I didn't tell him I never expected it to get beyond

the nearest trash receptacle. He gave me a reassuring pat on the shoulder and said, "Don't bother us anymore. We'll let you know when there's an answer." I couldn't tell him I'd brought it in only for form's sake.

But he could figure that out for himself.

"I see that you don't care about this letter. Someone on the staff obviously took pity and told you. For a suitably warm expression of gratitude."

I remained silent.

"I see," he said. "I thought so. You needn't be surprised. Not only can a few of us think, there're some—mostly majors and colonels—who can figure out how to lace their own boots in the morning. But I won't ask you about it if you'll answer a few questions about something else."

"Why?"

"Say I'm looking for a fresh viewpoint on something."

"Shoot."

"I'll start with a list of names. When you hear one you know, tell me what you know about him or her."

"That's all?"

"For now."

"Go ahead."

I scored three and a half out of maybe thirty. One was Zeck Zack. One was a Venageti commander my outfit had fought in the islands who later participated in the attack upon Full Harbor. The third was a dwarfish sharpie who had been executed for misappropriation, fraud, and profiteering, which basically meant he had gotten caught stealing from the army without paying kickbacks to the right officers. The half was a name I knew I had heard somewhere sometime but could not remember where or when or in connection with what. As far as I knew Zeck Zack was the only character there who was still alive.

I lied about recognizing one more name, that of a man who had been imprisoned with Klaus Kronk the day he had died.

"Is that all?" I could see no connection among the names on the list. Maybe there was none, really. Or maybe it would have been obvious to someone who knew who the hell all those people were.

"Just about. You seem to be what you pretend. You've been doing a lot of poking around. Have you stumbled across anything that might interest a man in my position?" He assumed I knew what his position was. I did, now.

"No," I lied. I had figured to do my patriotic duty by reporting the Sair. Sometime after arriving I had made an unconscious decision to pass.

"Would you consider doing a little work for Karenta while you're doing the job you have already? Wouldn't cost you much time and shouldn't take you out of your way."

"No."

He looked like he wanted to argue.

"I did my so-called patriotic chore," I declared. "Five years of my life making sure their gang of thieves didn't get one up on our gang of thieves. There is no way I'm getting onto that treadmill again."

A thought occurred to me. That happens occasionally. He saw it spark.

"Yes?"

"I might work a trade." I had the priest to sell. "If you tell me where to find Kayean Kronk."

"I can't."

"Oh?"

"I never heard of her till you came in yesterday. She's no one who's ever interested this office."

"I guess that's that, then. Thanks for your time and courtesy." I headed for the door.

"Garrett. Drop by when you get back from Fort . . ." He glared at me like I'd almost tricked him into revealing the Emperor's secret name. "Drop by when you get back. We may have a story or two to swap."

"All right."

I got out before he decided to look at me a little closer.

It was too nice a morning just to head for the inn to pick up Morley so we could visit the civil city hall again. It seemed a day made for lying around sniffing a clean seabreeze. I headed for the waterfront.

The triplets probably needed help watching for their relatives, anyway. They would be so hard to spot.

I found them doing exactly what I planned to do, sprawled in the sun atop a mountain of army grain sacks awaiting transport to the forts in the Cantard. I'd never have spotted them from the harbor side. I clambered up with a cold keg under my arm. I sent it around once before I asked, "How's it going, Dojango? Any sign of the family?"

The keg was half weight by the time it got back to me. I took a good long guzzle before I passed it on.

"Actually, Garrett, your timing is perfect. Come here." He drew on the keg before he moved.

They had shifted a few sacks so they formed a parapet of sorts. They could watch from concealment yet could claim the shifted sacks made pillows for the grolls if anybody asked.

"Some of your cousins, I think."

"Actually."

A ragged old coaster lay about thirty feet in the lee of the only pier space available. Lee was the very operative word. The ship was taking the breeze on her beam. About fifty guys were pulling on hawsers, trying to haul her in.

She was not coming.

In fact, she was winning the tug-of-war.

"Why don't I go trade this empty in on a full keg?" Dojango asked.

"Yeah. Why don't you?" I gave him some money.

A guy could work up a powerful thirst watching that much grunting and cursing and sweating and yelling for help.

The ship was interesting because Vasco, Quinn, and some other old friends were stomping around her deck in a storm of frustration.

I thought about canceling Fort Caprice and just watching them instead, on the chance they would lead me to Kayean. I looked at that from a couple of angles, then rejected it. They had not come to Full

Harbor to see Kayean. They had come to keep me
from seeing her.

I studied the striped-sail for a while. It seemed
deserted except for the short and wide thing, who was
napping in the shade cast by the low sterncastle.
Dojango arrived with the keg. We soon had another
dead soldier. Dojango ventured the suggestion that we
send for reinforcements again.

"I sadly fear we have to go to work. Do your
cousins know your brothers?"

"Not by sight, actually. But they must know you're
traveling with grolls."

"They aren't the only grolls in the world." I stripped
down while I explained what I wanted to do.

"I think it's insane, actually. But it might be fun to
watch." His part would be to observe and guard the
valuables.

"Tell the boys."

Below, a gust caught the coaster. She heeled. Men
yelled. Four or five went into the water.

"They know what to do."

"Let's go." I tumbled down the front of the pile.
Doris and Marsha tumbled after me, grinning their
great goofy groll grins. They trotted to the ends of a
couple of hawsers and started heaving. I grabbed another. I wish I could say my strength made the
difference.

That coaster fought like a granddaddy trout, but in
she came.

Vasco and Quinn must have gotten my stage directions. They spotted me as the dock hands started
swarming around Doris and Marsha, trying to slap
their backs. Somebody yelled. I faked big eyes as men
came leaping onto the wharf.

I lit out.

I did not see Dojango atop the sack pile as I raced
past. That meant nothing had changed at the striped-
sail ship. I whipped that way with a herd of boots
pounding behind me.

Hard right turn onto the yacht's gangway.

Short, Wide, and Hideous opened his eyes and hit

his feet. I made the deck before he could head me off.
Then he spotted the pack behind me.

He stopped.

I did not. I pulled straight ahead and dove over the
far rail. I groaned on the way down.

The water was so slimy I'd be lucky if I didn't
bounce.

We joined up again back at the inn. After I ordered
a keg to celebrate, Dojango told me what he had seen.

Vasco, Quinn, and four others had chased me. That
I did not need to be told. They had started up the
gangway when they had spotted Short, Wide, and
Hideous. They had stopped dead. Then they had scattered like roaches surprised by a sudden light.

"They didn't even go back to their boat for their
stuff," Dojango said. He laughed and drew himself
another beer.

"What about the guy on the yacht? What did he
do?"

"He ran inside."

"And?"

"And nothing, actually. Nothing happened at all."

"Something will," I prophesied.

We killed the keg while we waited for Morley.

28

Morley was a long time showing. When he did, I knew he had not been running *from* anything—unless it was himself. He wasn't scared of anything else.

"A little trot to settle your meal?" I asked.

"Started out that way. I came back here, you weren't in yet, so I thought I'd get in five or ten miles while I had time. I've gotten out of training since we left TunFaire."

He seemed a little pallid for Morley Dotes. "Something happen? You get yourself into trouble?"

"Not exactly. Let me catch my breath. Tell me what you did."

I did. He seemed mildly amused by my gambit on the waterfront.

"Your turn," I said.

"First a conclusion, then two sets of facts which may support it. My conclusion is, you're in over your head, Garrett. We keep cutting the trails of people with big clout. And they're starting to notice."

"And the facts?"

"My run took me out near the Narrows. I decided to see if my tribute to the vermin had earned me anything but scorn. Wonder of wonders, they had something. Zeck Zack is back in town. He arrived early this morning. The comings and goings started an hour later. I gave them a bonus and told them to keep an eye on him."

"One set of facts, Morley. How about the set that has you spooked?"

He did not argue, which was proof enough that he was nervous.

"I decided to drop in on Father Rhyne. I figured I'd go in the back way so I wouldn't inconvenience anybody, what with a rowdy service going on in the main hall."

He was stalling getting to the point, which meant it was something that did not please him.

"He came up dead, Garrett. Sitting at his writing table, dead as a man can get, still not cold."

"Killed?"

"I don't know. I didn't see any wounds, but that leaves plenty of room."

Plenty of room for sorcery or poison.

"He didn't seem like the kind of guy who drops dead coincidentally after people come around asking questions that only he can answer. Especially when you consider the fact that his boss and Father Mike have turned ghost."

He meant they had vanished. "When?"

"Sometime after breakfast. The prune was at first services. Father Mike was at breakfast. When I mentioned to somebody that Father Rhyne didn't look too healthy neither of them could be found. Nobody saw them leave."

"Maybe they decided they couldn't trust you not to be a tattletale."

"Maybe. Father Rhyne did try to leave a message, however he died. I don't know who he meant it for, but since you're looking for a married woman, I grabbed it."

He gave me a wad of paper. I smoothed it out on the table. There were just two words on it, printed big in a very shaky hand.

BLOOD WEDDING

"Blood wedding? What does that mean?"

"I don't know, Garrett. I do know this. Rhyne was number four. They're dropping like flies around us."

He was right. Four deaths. Three of them on the manslaughter level: the burglar in Denny's apartment, Uncle Lester, and the thug from the alley beside the civil city hall. And now one unexplained. "It does seem that way."

"Any change in plans?"

"No. Let's go see the boys at city hall."

Inspired by a silver memory-jostle, the guard outside frankly admitted that he had been paid to disappear for an hour. He gave us an excellent description of an ordinary guy who could have been right there on the street with us. I suspected he was the guy who had gotten away in the alley.

The clerk was not pleased to see us. In fact, he tried to take a sudden, unauthorized leave of absence. Morley was on him like a wolf on a rabbit. We took the committee into the records room to confer.

He claimed almost as much ignorance as the guard. But he said they had come to see him again awhile after we busted up the ambush to ask about us. The clerk said they talked it over and decided we were not the people they had expected, confederates of a man who had been there earlier. They had jumped the wrong people.

So who the hell were we?

The words *investigators from TunFaire* had done nothing to cheer them up.

We turned him loose, then, and headed for the inn.

"He wasn't coming across with everything," I said.

"He's on somebody's pad. He's more scared of them than he ever could be of us."

29

We roomed in what could hardly be classified as a room. It was a converted stable attached to the inn. It was not elegant, which was why we spent a lot of time in the common room. We took it because it was the only place the grolls could quarter comfortably.

That night we retreated there earlier than usual, none of us being in the mood for the jostle of the evening trade, when all the neighbors came to guzzle and swap lies. Besides, I wanted to get an early start in the morning.

I still had to turn the carriage in and pick up mounts.

The rest of our outfitting we had managed to get in whenever we were not off chasing chimeras.

It looked like a quiet evening. Not even Dojango felt much like talking. He had a hangover and Morley wouldn't let him near any hair of the dog.

Breeds just don't handle their alcohol well.

A subtle change in the roar from the common room caught my ear, though I couldn't pin down exactly what it was. Morley caught it, too. He cocked an ear, frowned. "Dojango, see what's happening."

Dojango went out. He was back in about four blinks. "Six guys rousting the innkeeper. They want you and Garrett, actually. They look plenty bad, too, Morley."

Morley grunted. Then he grumbled and growled and snarled and barked in grollish. Doris and Marsha sat down on either side of the door, several feet away. Dojango came over and got behind Morley. Morley told me, "Let's get as far from the door as we can. Give them plenty of room to come in if they come."

The grolls' skins began changing color. They faded into the landscape.

"I didn't know they could do that."

"They don't brag about it. Ready, Dojango?"

"I need a drink, actually. I need one bad, actually."

"You'll be all right."

Ka-boom! The door exploded inward and a couple of Saucerhead Tharpe types came mincing after it. Their fearless leader followed. A rear guard of three more muscle wads came in after him. The storm troops spread out so the boss could eyeball us from between them.

He stopped.

He didn't like what he saw.

We were waiting for him.

Morley said a few words. Doris and Marsha growled back. Our guests looked around. One of them said, "Oh, shit."

Morley smiled at the head invader and asked, "Shall we go ahead with it, then?"

"Uh . . . we just dropped in to deliver a message."

"How thoughtful," I said. "What was it, so long you each had to memorize a whole word? And don't you guys find all that wood and iron a little encumbering?"

"The streets aren't safe at night."

"I'll bet they aren't. It isn't that safe inside some places, either."

"Don't overdo it," Morley told me.

"What's the message?"

"I doubt there's much point my delivering it, considering the circumstances."

"But I insist. Here I am visiting a strange city, where I didn't think I knew anyone, and someone is sending me greetings. It's exciting, and I'm curious. Dojango, go get a keg and some mugs so we can entertain properly."

Dojango gave our visitors a wide berth leaving. They did nothing after he left. I guess the shift in odds wasn't encouraging.

I rescued a small philter packet from my duffel. "What was that message again?"

The voice seemed small for the man when he said,"Get out of Full Harbor. If I have cause to get in touch with you again, you're dead."

"That's not what I'd call neighborly. And he doesn't bother to say who he is or why he's concerned for my health. Or even if I've done something to offend."

He began to simmer despite the situation. Morley was right. A slice too much.

Dojango came with the keg and mugs.

"Tap it. Friend, I'd like to talk to a man so interested in me he'd send you around. Just to find out why, if nothing else. Who sent you?"

He set his jaw. I'd expected that. I opened the packet I'd gotten and tapped bits of its contents into the heads of the beers Dojango drew. "This is a harmless spice guaranteed to put an elephant out for ten hours and a man for twenty-four." I gestured.

Dojango got hold of his nerve and took a mug to a man near one of the grolls. The thug refused to take it. Morley barked something. Marsha—or Doris—snagged man and mug and put the contents of one inside the other with less trouble than a mother getting milk down a toddler. Then he stripped the thug to the altogether and tossed him out our only window.

If the man had any sense at all, he would get himself hidden fast, before the drug took hold. Folks in Full Harbor have very strong feelings about public nudity. Caught, he could end up spending the rest of his life in the Cantard mines.

The rest of the muscle decided it was time to go. The other groll held the door until his brother came to help. After things settled down, I asked, "Who sent you?"

"You're a dead man."

"A thought which will comfort and warm you during those long nights in the mines." I gave Dojango another mug. This time the other groll took a turn feeding baby. "I keep going till I get that name. You're last. If I have to do you, you get a short dose. Just enough to make you forget who and where you are,

but not enough to put you down so you don't go
wandering into trouble."

"For heaven's sake, Switz," one of the thugs said as
I handed Dojango another mug. "We aren't getting
paid enough for this. He's got us by the balls."

"Shut up."

Another said, "You ain't going to see me in no
mines."

"Shut up. It can be fixed."

"Bull. You know damned well he wouldn't bother.
He'd say we deserved it. He don't have that kind of
pull, anyway."

"Shut up."

One of the grolls snagged the loudest complainer.

"Wait a goddamned minute!" he yelled at me. "It
was Zeck Zack that sent us."

I was startled. I made use of my reaction. "Who the
hell is Zeck Zack?"

Fearless leader groaned.

Morley gestured. The grolls put our man down but
did not turn him loose. I said, "We won't be sending
the rest of you after all. But I'm still going to need you
sleeping. Set yourselves down someplace comfortable.
We'll serve up the brew."

The leader said,"You're dead meat, Trask."

"I bet I'll last longer than you," the other thug replied.

While they bickered I got everything settled. I got
the three to drink their beer. We settled back for a
listen to our songbird.

"One thing," he said. "The first guy you threw out.
He's my brother. You get him back in here or I don't
say nothing."

"Morley?"

Morley sent Dojango and Doris.

Trask was able to tell us almost nothing we didn't
already know. He had no idea why Zeck Zack wanted
us thumped and run out of town. He had not seen the
centaur. Only Switz saw or heard from Zeck Zack. He
didn't know if the centaur was in town or not. Probably not, because he almost never was.

I asked a lot of questions and got almost nothing

more. Zeck Zack shielded his infantry from trouble-some knowledge about himself.

"You kept your part of the bargain, with one pro-viso that benefited your brother." The brother was back inside and redressed, sloppily. "So I'll keep mine, with a proviso that will benefit me. Dojango is going to tie you up just tightly enough so it will take you a couple of hours to get loose. When you do, take your brother and get lost."

Dojango did the honors. He had been sneaking some off the keg and was getting braver by the minute.

"Not bad for improvisation," Morley said.

"Yeah. Thought so myself."

"What now?"

"We strip the other three and dump them where they're sure to get got, then we go see a centaur named Zeck Zack."

Morley didn't like it, but he went along. He was making top money and staying out of the hands of his creditors, and what more could a guy want? Cabbages and cattail hearts?

30

Morley led the way down the old path from the cemetery to the house. I knew the trail but he had the night eyes. Each fifty paces he stopped and asked the darkness, "Hornbuckle?"

He didn't get an answer until we neared the waking radius of the peafowl.

I was amazed by the grolls. For all their height and mass, they moved through the woods with more stealth than a human.

"Sit," Morley said when tittering answered him at last.

We sat.

Diminutive forms pranced around and among us. Morley gave each a piece of sugar candy, the most certain bribe there is. They wanted more. He promised it. If . . . They scattered to do our scouting for us.

I'll bet Morley hated himself. He certainly looked disgusted as he tucked the rest of the candy inside his shirt.

I asked, "Can we trust them?"

"Not much. But they want the rest of the candy. I don't plan to run out till we're on our way again."

After that we stayed quiet, waiting. I got itchy between the shoulder blades, that feeling you get when someone is watching. Or you think someone is.

That scalawag Hornbuckle flipped Morley a mock salute.

"How many?"

"Four. Two humans. Very nervous. One centaur. Worried and grumpy. One *other*. They're awaiting a report from someone and that someone is late. Sugar?"

"Not yet. Are there wardspells? Alarms? Booby traps? Dangerous guard animals?"

"None."

"Any reason for us to fear?"

"They are wicked creatures. All."

"Silence the peafowl so we can pass."

"Sugar?"

"All the sugar I have when we come out."

"You might not get out."

"Why not?"

Titter. "They are wicked creatures. Very wicked. Especially one."

"All right." Morley took out his candy. "One piece for you. A half piece for each of your friends. The rest if we come out. Tell me the best way to get to them."

Their boy Switz did it to us, so we did it to them.

Kaboom! One groll after another went through the huge double doors of the ballroom. Then Morley. Then me. Then Dojango to guard our rear.

It was thoughtful of them to have waited in the only room where the grolls would have space to maneuver. The ceilings were eighteen feet high.

They scattered like squeaking mice when the cat pounces.

Doris and Marsha each snagged a man. Morley streaked between them, pursuing a shadowy something that crashed through a window at the far end of the ballroom.

Where the hell was the centaur?

There he was, a one-critter cavalry charge. I managed a leg whip that tangled some fetlocks or forelocks or whatever they're called. It was a sin, what his hooves did to the carpets and flooring.

Impetus flung me against something made of mahogany or teak, very hard and very immovable. I practiced exhaling a bushel more air than any human being normally inhales. Somebody was hollering.

"Help, Morley! I got him, Morley! Help!"

I staggered to my feet.

Dojango had him all right.

Zeck Zack was about average for his tribe, about the size of a small pony. He was not built to carry a hundred thirty pounds of Dojango on his back. His problem was complicated by Dojango having his arms and legs wrapped around his skinny chest. He couldn't breathe. He staggered around, banging into things, then went down on his knees.

I got a choke rope on him, pried Dojango loose, then looked around.

The grolls had their men subdued. Morley was coming back from the window empty-handed and looking puzzled.

I caught my breath, straightened my clothing, and led Zeck Zack into a better light, where Morley patted him down for hardware and other lethal surprises. The centaur remained glassy-eyed.

"What happened?" I asked Morley.

"I don't know. I got there three seconds after it went through the glass. And there was nothing. Not a sign of it."

"What was it?"

"I can't even tell you that. I never got a good look."

The grolls brought the two men over and plunked them down on the floor. They were in a playful mood after events at the inn. They had plucked these birds, too.

"Did you see me, Morley?" Dojango bubbled. "Did you see me? I mean, actually, I took the damned thing down. Did you see me, Morley?"

"Yes. I saw. Shut up, Dojango."

Morley seemed troubled.

He kept looking toward the broken window.

"Well, you've got him, Garrett. Are you going to do something with him?"

"Yeah. All right." I looked at Zeck Zack. "I have a problem, Mr. Zeck." Centaurs stick their family names up front, figuring their antecedents are more important. "People keep trying to whip me and I can't figure out why."

Zeck Zack had nothing to say. He'd heard me, though.

"All right. I'm going to tell you a story. Then you can tell me one. If I like yours we can part as friends."

Still no reaction. I had a feeling Zeck Zack was tough, and had been through the narrow passage before. He was cool enough. He would do what had to be done.

"Once upon a time up north a guy died. He left everything to a gal he knew when he was in the army. His father hired me to come find her and see if she wanted the legacy. A simple job. A kind I do all the time. Only this time I get people ambushing me and sending thugs to work me over, and nobody anywhere giving me a straight answer. So you might say I'm a little fussed."

I gave him a chance to comment. He did not. I hadn't thought he would.

"People are trying to push me. So now I'm pushing back. I'm asking questions. I want answers. What's with this woman Kayean that's worth knocking heads?"

He had nothing to say.

"What's in this to die for? Are you ready to die for it?"

I got a reaction that time. Just a flicker around the eyes. He didn't think I looked the killer type. But he didn't know me so couldn't be sure.

"He's starting to listen, Garrett," Morley said. "But we ought to convene this somewhere else. The one that got away could bring reinforcements."

"I have faith in sugar as an alarm potential. You know anything about centaurs? I've never dealt with one."

"A little. They're vain, avaricious, mean in most senses of the word, miserly. Overall, not much to recommend. Did I mention that most of them are thieves and liars?"

"Where are their pressure points?"

"Did I mention cowardly? You're on the right track with that rope. Strangle him slowly. He'll come across."

"I don't want to do it the hard way. Nobody's been

hurt yet. I'd rather talk, work something out where we could get off each other's backs, and get on with finding the woman. I'm tired of this job. Too many people are interested in us and I don't know why."

Zeck Zack sort of nibbled at the bait. He spoke for the first time, piping. I almost laughed at his voice. "Can you prove you're what you say you are? If you were nothing more, there would be no difficulty between us."

A wedge!

Morley told Dojango, "Tie up those guys so Doris and Marsha can have their hands free." One of the two was the greeter who had thought we were hilarious gagsters. He looked the worse for wear.

The grolls helped form a circle around Zeck Zack once they were free of their baby-sitting chores. I handed over every piece of documentation I had. He examined it all minutely. Meanwhile, Morley got antsy.

Zeck Zack said, "This is all silly enough to be true. I'll give you the benefit of the doubt. For the moment."

Morley said, "Garrett, we're running out of time. Choke him."

"That would do you no good," Zeck Zack said. "I might tell you many interesting things but I would tell you nothing of value. My position is exposed. Therefore, I am allowed to know nothing of importance. However, I do know one thing of value to you. If you are what you say you are."

I waited.

"I know someone who knows someone who could bring you face-to-face with the woman."

"Yeah?"

"Did I mention treacherous?" Morley asked.

"One more test, of sorts," Zeck Zack said. "I will recite a list of names, phrases, places. You tell me if you know or have heard of them. I have an ear for the truth."

I've lied successfully to men who thought that. Many times. "Go ahead."

I scored a mere one half on this one. The same half I scored on the army list. Zeck Zack was amazed by what he heard with his ear for the truth. "You could just be what you say." He gave me a squint-eyed look. "Yes. It might even make sense . . . I think I know what is happening. It should be put to the test."

He did some thinking. The rest of us did some waiting, Morley with very poor grace.

Zeck Zack asked,"Where can I leave you a message?"

I used my best raised eyebrow.

"Not trusting me, you will, of course, remove from your present lodgings. I will not possess sufficient manpower to locate you again quickly. I am going to attempt to arrange for you to see the woman and complete your mission. If I am successful, I must be able to get that word to you."

I had a strong feeling he meant to do just what he said, though not out of any inclination to make my life easier. He had motives I couldn't fathom. Everyone but me seemed to have shadowed motives.

"The innkeeper where we're staying now. We'll leave him feeling kindly toward us." I removed the choke rope. "I'm going to play a hunch, a long shot, and take a chance on you, centaur. Maybe because I'm getting desperate. If you've been bullshitting me to get your behind out of a bind, or if you're planning on taking another crack at me, you have a problem."

"Indeed I do. As I said, I am exposed. And vulnerable, as you have demonstrated tonight."

I thought I would leave everything on that very unsatisfactory note.

Morley, who had been eager to evacuate some time ago, now jumped all over me for wasting half a night.

"Come on, Morley. It's time to go."

31

We sat on a patch of grass not far from the witch's house, surrounded by little folk stoned on sugar. Only a couple were sober enough to titter occasionally.

Morley had turned from argumentative to reflective. "You know what made it interesting, Garrett? That list. Sixteen items. But six of them were the same thing: a name, translated into six different languages. Curious. Especially because it isn't a name either of us recognizes in any of its forms."

"What was that?"

He rattled off a jawbreaker. "I'd give you the Karentine, but it wouldn't make any sense."

"Try it anyway. Karentine is all I speak."

"There're two possible translations. Dawn of Night's Mercy. Or Dawn of Night's Madness."

"That doesn't make sense."

"I told you it wouldn't."

"What language uses the same word for *mercy* and *madness?*"

"Dark elfin."

"Oh," I glanced toward the centaur's house. Not a thing had happened since our departure. I looked at the witch's place. A light burned in an upper-story window. It hadn't been burning when we'd come down the path. "Why don't you guys head on up to the cemetery? I'll catch up in a few minutes. There's something I want to check out."

I expected Morley to give me an argument. He didn't. He just grunted, got to his feet, got the triplets moving, and vanished into the night.

Somebody small with a man-sized grin had passed

out leaning against me. I tilted him over gently, patted his shoulder when he mumbled something, rose, and headed for the house. I prowled around looking into windows.

"I'm up here, Private Garrett."

"Good. I was hoping to see you. But I was a little leery of waking you." I couldn't see her.

She laughed. Her laughter was mostly merriment, but it also carried a trace of mockery. She didn't believe me. But she knew I didn't expect her to.

"How can I help you, Private Garrett?"

"You could start by not calling me Private Garrett. I'm out of the Marines. I'd just as soon forget them. Then you can tell me if you know anything about somebody named Dawn of Night's Mercy or Dawn of Night's Madness."

She was silent so long I feared she had deserted me. Then she threw down the dark elvish *gobblewhat* Morley had used, applying a distinctly interrogative inflection.

"That's right."

"*Gobblewhat* is not a person, Mr. Garrett. It is a prophecy, and an unpleasant one from your point of view. The name *Gobblewhat* is dark elfin, but the prophecy is not. It is an echo, a rumor, an aspiration, out of a deeper night."

Being what she was, she naturally stoked the drama on her declamation, then clammed up, leaving her answer obscure.

I tried asking questions. That was a waste of time. She was done talking about *gobblewhat*. She closed the subject by saying, "That was spur of the moment. What did you really want?"

There was no point playing games. "Are you still in business? I'd like to buy a few of your special tools."

She ripped off a first-class witch's cackle. It was hilarious. I grinned. The peafowl even got into the act, though their mirth was confused and sleepy. "Go around to the front door," she told me. "You'll find it unlocked."

*   *   *

When I rejoined Morley and the triplets, I carried five tiny, folded pieces of paper. I had hidden each carefully. Each bore a potent and potentially useful spell. I was still repeating the witch's instructions to myself. Basically, all I had to remember was to unfold the papers at the appropriate moment, though a couple required a whispered word at the right time.

Morley said, "So. You survived the trail. I was about to go looking for you. What now?"

"We go back and get what sleep we can. Then early tomorrow we hit the road for Fort Caprice."

"I thought you were going to let the centaur do the finding for you."

"Contrary to the false notion formed earlier, I don't trust him to do anything. If he comes through, fine. Meantime, I go on looking. He expects us to hide from him. I can't think of a better place than out in the Cantard. Two birds, one stone."

Morley was as thrilled as I might have expected. "I had to ask, didn't I?"

32

Fort Caprice was a bust.

It was four days out of Full Harbor, pushing hard all the way, shielded every step by more luck than any five fools deserved. Not only did we not encounter one of our own Karentine patrols, but we didn't fall in with Venageti rangers or representatives of any of the nonhuman races of the Cantard, most of which are at least marginally involved in the war. Their loyalties shift like a chameleon's color, according to where they think the most profit lies.

Fort Caprice was not in the heart of the caldron, though. The richest silver country lay a hundred miles farther south.

Major Kayeth Kronk proved to be brevet-Colonel Kronk now, at the tender age of twenty-six. I did not remind him that we had met before, though I'm sure he remembered me before we reached the end of our short interview. I told him I was looking for his sister Kayean, and told him why. And he told me that he didn't have a sister Kayean.

And that was all he would say about it. When I kept after him he got stubborn. Then he got mad and had a couple of soldiers show me the street.

We poked around among the hangers-on Fort Caprice had acquired—like fleas, ticks, and worms to a hound—and found out nothing more interesting than which men were watering their wine and which women would send you away with something you hadn't had when you arrived. So we made the four-day journey back to Full Harbor, with fool's luck cleansing the way ahead of us again.

It was a lovely time to visit the Cantard.

I hoped the centaur would come through so I wouldn't have to do it again.

That would be tempting fate a bit too far.

We were out of Full Harbor nine days, all told.

33

The major from the military city hall was waiting at the gate through the Narrows Wall. There was nothing magical about it once I realized that without sorcery, a trip to Fort Caprice takes a predictable amount of time. He cut me out of my herd.

"Any luck?" he asked.

"Zip. Zero. Zilch. What can I do for you?"

"I have another list of names."

"And getting my reaction is important enough for you to lay in wait for me out here?"

"Maybe."

"Fire away."

He did.

I knew five of the twelve names this time. Father Mike. Father Rhyne. Sair Lojda. Martello Quinn and Aben Kurts, of Denny's old crowd. I admitted knowing the latter two only as friends of a friend, saying I thought they were in shipping. Then I asked, "What ties this together? What's up?"

"All these people, and three more for whom we have no names, have died or disappeared during the last eleven days. I'm certain you would recognize more if you saw them. Imelo Clark was a guard at the civil city hall. Egan Rust was a clerk there. You interviewed them. I was not sure you had any connection with Kurts and Quinn, but since you did, then I assume there's also one with Laught and the three unknowns, all of whom seem to have come off a yacht from TunFaire."

"What the hell are you trying to say?"

"Don't get your hackles up, Garrett. You're safe.

153

You were out of town during the excitement. In fact, the only time I place you or yours near anyone at a critical time is Father Rhyne. I'm satisfied your associate found him dead."

I didn't say anything. My thoughts were pounding off in twenty directions. What the hell was going on?

"It seems apparent that, in most of these cases, someone is cleaning up after you. It's a wonder you haven't been turned invisible yourself."

Thoughtlessly, I admitted, "It's been tried a couple times."

He wanted details. He demanded details. I gave him some without mentioning centaurs or dead men or much else that would do him any real good. He thought it was crafty of us, setting the one group up for a career in the mines.

He observed, "I have a feeling that there are a lot of things you wouldn't tell me no matter how nicely I ask. Like where the others from TunFaire fit in."

"I wouldn't be even a little shy about telling you that if I knew. What's the story on them, anyway?"

Kurts and Quinn had died the evening we left Full Harbor. They had been found in an alley on the far south side. At first it had looked like they had fallen foul of robbers. Laught—identified because his name and that of the yacht were stitched on the inside of his jumper—died later that night in the graveyard where Kayean and I had played when we were kids. At almost the same time a tremendous explosion and fire had consumed the yacht. No one knew how many had died in that. The unburned remains of the yacht had sunk. It was a miracle the whole waterfront hadn't gone up.

"That's pretty rough stuff," I said. "The stakes must be big. I don't want to sound dumb or impertinent, but what's your interest? Seems to me it's a civil problem, gaudy as it is."

"Full Harbor's reason for existing is military. Anything gaudy could effect the city's military situation. Garrett, I'm convinced you know things I want to know. But I'm not going to press you. When you feel like baring your soul, drop in. And I'll trade you the name of the man she married. Meantime, I'll just use you as a stalking horse."

"Yeah." I waved bye-bye, but my heart was not in it. I was pondering that equine-derived chestnut.

Morley and the triplets joined me. "Who was that?" Morley asked. I told him. He asked,"He have anything interesting to say?"

I told him all that, too.

"Gang warfare and vampires," he mused. "What a city."

"Vampires?"

"Several people claim they were attacked this week. It's all the talk. You know how those stories get going. People will see vampires in every shadow for a month."

34

We slept at the same inn. We couldn't be safer elsewhere, and the quarters were the best available for grolls.

The innkeeper had five messages for me. They were from Zeck Zack, had come at a rate of one daily, and had become increasingly strident. I got the impression he wanted to see me.

"Tomorrow is soon enough," I told Morley. "Tonight I'm going to lay around and ruminate and drink beer to get the Cantard dust out of my throat. I'm not much closer to the woman but I'm starting to see the outlines of the other stuff. Except for Vasco and his crowd, I don't think it has anything to do with silver. I think three or four conspiracies with completely alien or only marginally overlapping goals have collided here, maybe with the woman being the link. I don't think I'm the only one going around wondering, Who the hell are those guys? What do they want?"

I let it go there. Morley could chew on it if he wanted. I snuggled up with my beer and tried to let my mind go blank.

Some might say I did not have to work very hard.

Zeck Zack turned up next day. He got righteous with me.

"Do I work for you?" I asked.

He looked around. A lot of unfriendly faces were turned his way. Centaurs are not popular, which is probably why Zeck Zack spent so little time at his city house. He desisted, though he kept simmering. He handed me a sealed letter. "Your instructions are in there. You are to come alone."

156

"Have you been smoking weed?"

"What?"

"I don't go anywhere alone. People have been dying around this town. Four of them right out around your place."

"You will go alone or they will not let you see her."

"Then I'll find her my own way."

Morley walked in then, coming back from grazing. He slapped Zeck Zack across the rump, a familiarity and indignity that almost sent him into paroxysms. Morley said, "There was another vampire thing last night, Garrett. Sounded like the real article."

"Remind me to wear my high-collar shirt when I go barhopping tonight." His pursed lips told me he had something more on his mind but wouldn't say what until I got rid of the centaur.

I told Zeck Zack, "You see? It's dangerous to wander the streets alone."

"I will put it to them. They are going to be very irritated with both of us. They have gone to a great deal of trouble to make the woman available. But, perhaps, for that reason they will accede to your petition."

I did my eyebrow trick. My petition? "Right. Check it out. You know where to find me."

He extended a hand. "The instructions? They will have to be changed."

I gave them back. He left, giving me a couple of dark looks.

"He wanted me to come to the meet all by myself, on the lonesome," I told Morley. "Just me face-to-face with 'them,' whoever 'they' are."

"Whoever, they have him peeing down his leg. And he has a reputation for being a tough bastard."

"I noticed he had a case of nerves. What's up?"

"The place is being watched. Somebody followed me out and back. I didn't give it a good scout because I didn't want them to know they'd been made, but I spotted two more. I figured that's iceberg."

"Damn! The works. A whole crew. And now they know I'm dealing with Zeck Zack."

"Spilled milk. Who do you figure for it?"

"That army bastard. I don't know why. Vasco or the striped-sail crowd wouldn't have the resources. The centaur doesn't need to know every breath we take. He hopes he has us on the hook."

"Maybe the major needs a closer look."

"Maybe. Though I don't even know his name. And I'd rather not. I'd just as soon get on with the job I'm getting paid to do."

Morley nodded. "It's getting thick. I find myself looking forward to the trip home—in my more insane, impatient moments."

I slouched in my seat. "I guess we spend the day on in-and-out, getting a scout on how many and how good they are. We can make like we're getting ready for another trip out of town. We can eat the food on the way home if the meet goes down and I get what I need."

"We'll have to work a way for all of us to shake them, too."

"Yeah. This thing couldn't get any more complicated if you hired three wizards to knot it up."

35

I was wrong, of course. It could get more complicated. And it did.

Morley, the triplets, and I spent the day running the bird dogs, and scoped out both daytime and nighttime routines for shaking them, though it looked like there would be at least twenty of them on us around the clock. It isn't hard to shake watchers when you know they're around, especially in a city as crazy as Full Harbor.

Morley had gone out for supper. I was having mine with Dojango in the common room. His brothers were in our quarters, where they felt more comfortable.

Dojango wasn't a bad sort to pass the time with, if you made allowances. He knew more crude stories than anyone I'd ever met, though he didn't deliver them very well. Actually.

Further complication waltzed through the door.

"Saucerhead Tharpe!" I groaned.

"And Spiney Prevallet," Dojango said of the guy who was the last of the four to enter. "Doris! Marsha!" He could put a snap in his voice when he wanted. It carried over the common-room noise.

The two in the middle need no introduction. My old flames, Tinnie and Rose. Tinnie stomped past Saucerhead, who was giving the grolls the once-over and not liking what he saw. I said, "I see the Venageti didn't get you. And I thought their sailors had an unfailing eye for the finest."

She halted in a widespread stance within slapping range, but her fists settled on her hips. "You're a brass-balled son-of-a-bitch, Garrett. You know that?"

"Yeah. I've heard that talk, too. And it's true, so
don't think you can flatter me. Have a nice trip? How
long you been in town?" I kept one eye on Rose who
looked as vicious as an entire pack of wolves circling
in for the kill. Saucerhead and Spiney, with better
sense and no emotional investment, put their hands in
their pockets and kept them there. "Had supper yet?
Sit down. My treat. It isn't the Unicorn Gambit, but
the food sticks to your ribs."

"You . . . ! You . . . !" Tinnie stammered. "Don't
you sit there and act like you didn't do anything.
Don't treat me like one of your flapping old army
buddies, you bastard." The fire was fading from her
eyes. She had become conscious of the silence surrounding us, of all the staring eyes and knowing smirks.

"You're not being very ladylike," I noted. "Sit down,
my one true love. Let me ply you with food and
spirits."

"Bought with Uncle Willard's money?"

"Of course. It's a legitimate business expense."

A smile flirted with her lips despite her determina-
tion to be angry. She plopped into the chair Morley
usually inhabited.

"Dojango, would you scare up enough seats for the
rest of our guests?"

He looked at me like I was crazy, but he did it.

"You're lucky you got here when you did. An hour
from now this place will be standing room only. Hello,
Saucerhead. I paid your fee against your account at
Morley's place. All right?"

"Yeah. Sure. That's what I wanted. How you doing,
Garrett?" He was embarrassed to be seen in the company of two real live women. What was it going to do
to his reputation?

"Not so good. I've fallen right into the middle of the
damnedest thing I ever saw."

Civilized behavior begets civilized behavior. Rose
decided to play the game and was the perfect lady as
Dojango held her chair. "Rose," I said. "You're looking lovelier than ever,"

"It must be the sea air. And a change of diet."

I looked at Tinnie. "Not roots and berries, I hope."
Tinnie winked.

I faced Spiney Prevallet. "Mr. Prevallet. I've heard
of you but don't think we've ever met."

"Garrett. No, we haven't. I've heard of you, too."
And that was all he had to say for the evening. It was
enough to set my teeth on edge. His voice was neutral
but as cold as the bottom side of a coffin.

If Morley and Saucerhead are the best at what they
do, Spiney Prevallet is crowding them. And he's said
to be less squeamish and less choosy about the jobs he
takes.

The landlord himself came to take orders. Men like
him have a sixth sense. He wanted to size up the
trouble before it happened. I smiled at him a lot.

"You've had trouble?" Rose asked. She sounded
hopeful.

"A little. More, you'd say I've been trouble. Everybody I talk to turns up dead."

That got their attention. I gave them an edited and
censored account of my adventures. Somehow, I forgot to mention Zeck Zack.

I was still talking and wondering how to get rid of
them, in case the centaur showed, when Morley walked
in.

He never batted an eye. He walked up behind Rose,
who had her back to the door, and trailed his fingertips lightly up the side of her neck. "A miracle. I
would have sworn the pirates would have—"

Tinnie cut in. "Garrett already used that line. Only
with him it was Venageti sailors."

"Then add plagiarism to his list of sins." Morley
placed a small box on the table before me. "That
four-legged wonder of a cook sent you this kelp salad.
Since you've already eaten, maybe you should save it
for a snack."

I peeked despite his warning. Kelp salad, all right.
"He gave it to you?"

"To bring over. He knew we had company and
didn't want to intrude."

"I don't have much use for kelp, but since he went to all the trouble . . ."

Morley kept stroking Rose's neck and shoulders. He nodded once to Tinnie, ignored Spiney and Saucerhead completely. If, as I suspected, the kelp concealed Zeck Zack's instructions for making the meet, we had a problem. I expect that had Morley's undivided attention.

"Did you bribe Master Arbanos somehow?" I asked Tinnie.

"That little water rat? He did exactly what you told him to. He handed us over to Uncle Willard personally."

"I'm sorry I missed that."

"You're going to get your chance to take part in a reenactment."

"How did you manage—"

Rose said, "Our good Uncle Lester bestowed a small legacy on each of us."

"I see." Women with their own money do tend to get independent, don't they?

That box of salad sat there staring at me, begging to be opened, and I hadn't one idea how to get rid of them.

"Why are you here, Tinnie? Rose I understand. A hundred thousand marks makes for a big greed." Morley was over talking to the grolls, now. I hoped his mind was more fertile than mine.

"I have a grudge to settle with a certain bastard who had me tied up and shipped like a sack of turnips."

"After he had the brass-balled gall to get you out of the hands of kidnappers. What can you do with a churl like that?" I countered.

She had the grace to redden.

Morley came over and begged Dojango for his seat, which was next to Rose. With bad grace Dojango gave way and joined his brothers.

I saw it then, and Morley knew when I knew. He gave me the ghost of a smile and went to work charming Rose.

Dojango ducked through the door to our quarters.

Five minutes later I developed an irresistible need for the loo. I grabbed my box and promised to be right back. I trickled fingers through Tinnie's hair. She slapped my hand but it was only a pat.

Dojango was waiting. "Out the window. Night course. Morley says you'd better read your instructions and dump them down the loo first."

I had that much sense. I didn't figure he needed reminding, though. "Who's next?"

"Morley. He comes to see why you're taking so long. He's worried. Then Doris goes, then me. Marsha stalls and distracts them by keeping them from getting through the door."

"Sounds good. If it works."

36

I ambled up the lane toward the Orthodox cemetery, where we were to meet at the Kronk family plot. Convenient, that. Zeck Zack or his messenger was supposed to take us to the meet from another plot just two hundred yards away, come midnight.

I reached the place where the first man to arrive was supposed to lie in the weeds for anybody following the rest. "Morley? I'm clean."

Dojango came out of the darkness, not Morley. "What took so long?"

"I had more tails than an uighur. All pros. Took awhile to shake them. Where's Morley?"

"Pushing sugar."

"Doris and Marsha?"

"At the plot. They just got here, too. They almost forgot. They were having fun trotting around town watching the humans huff and puff trying to keep up."

"The ladies?"

"You and Morley better forget those two and take up kicking beehives."

"Mad, huh?"

"Furious, actually."

Morley came back from his pandering. "Just in time, Garrett. Let's go check something out." He marched off through the graveyard.

His destination proved to be a decrepit mausoleum. He examined its door. I couldn't see what he saw. He grunted. "Hunh. Maybe they knew what they were talking about. Marsha. Open it up."

The groll obliged. There was no sound of seals

breaking. There was almost no sound at all. Curious in a door that should have been unmoved for generations.

Then the stench rolled out.

I considered a crack about ducking the stampeding buzzards, but desisted. Death is no joke.

"We need a light, Morley," Dojango said.

"I figured we would. I borrowed a lucifer stone from my bitty buddy Hornbuckle." He removed it from its protective sack. It was a young one, burning bright.

I didn't want to go inside, but I did. I stayed only as long as I could hold my breath, which was long enough to get an education. It was pretty bad, but I did recognize what was left of Father Mike, the Sair, and the clerk from the civil city hall. I had no idea who the others were.

Marsha closed it up. We walked to the Kronk plot in silence. Finally, Morley said, "Somebody's garbage dump."

"Who put them there?"

"Soldiers. I quote Hornbuckle: 'Soldiers without livery.' "

"I see." I saw a great deal. It had nothing to do with finding Kayean, but a lot to do with a nameless major.

Morley said, "On no evidence at all I'll bet you fifty marks your major was part of the outfit that liberated the church the day your girlfriend's father died."

"No bet. Not even at ten to one."

A man in the major's position wouldn't quietly dispose of the top Venageti agent in his territory. Not when he could bring him in and harvest all sorts of rewards. Not unless that agent could name some very interesting names, like maybe that of an agent even better placed than he.

"Investigators from TunFaire, you had to say. He thinks we're the King's men and we're looking for him. What other reason for the interest in people named Kronk?"

"Or the Emperor's men." I shook my head. "My poor sweet, silly Kayean. She had to make the worst choices in fathers and husbands."

Morley frowned. "Husbands? You don't even know who he is."

"I don't have to to know he's somebody Zeck Zack and his bosses want to keep us away from. It can't be her. There's no evidence that she's anything but a woman carrying on a profitable correspondence with an old flame.".

Morley grunted. "What about your major?"

"You know me. I'd rather negotiate, like with the centaur. Or I just let them ride and hope for the best, like with Vasco and his bunch. I've only killed two men since I got out of the Marines, and one of them was by accident. But I think somebody is going to have to chop the head off this snake before it crushes us all."

We scouted the terrain thoroughly. There was no sign the centaur planned anything cagey, but that wasn't especially reassuring.

Zeck Zack came for us himself, which said something about his relationship to the shadow folk behind him. "You're early," he accused.

"So are you."

"I told them I needed time to scout you for treachery. In truth, I wanted time to talk."

"You trust us, then?"

"As much as one dares, given the circumstances. Your claims received independent corroboration from persons who had no wish to further your mission."

"Who?"

"I believe they called themselves Quinn and Kurts."

So. I had to reorganize my notions about who had done what to whom that bloody night.

"Mr. Garrett, I've gone to a great deal of trouble on your behalf. For myself as well, I admit, for it could mean my neck if the knowledge of the movement of certain letters reached the wrong persons. But still, on your behalf I have saved your lives by convincing them that the surest way to handle you is to let you get your affidavit. You might also note the removal of two deadly enemies, which improves your odds."

"You want something."

"Sir?"

"Besides me not mentioning any letters—a subject I wouldn't mind chatting about, just to satisfy my curiosity—there must be something else. Call it a hunch."

"Yes. I might as well be direct. There is so little time."

"So?"

"In my youth I was guilty of, shall we say, a mortal indiscretion. A certain gentleman acquired proofs sufficient to place me in extreme jeopardy should they come to the attention of either my employers or the Karentine military. He used the threat to compel me to perform tasks that only worsen my chances of living to old age. The whereabouts of the evidence is known only to him. He does not allow me to get anywhere near him. You, however, could walk right up to him."

"I get the picture." I had no intention of skragging anybody for him, but I played the game out. I wanted him to stay my buddy. "Who?"

He wanted to get cagey.

"Come on. I don't agree to anything till I hear a name."

He had made up his mind to tell me if I pressed. He did. "A priest named Sair Lojda. At the Orthodox church at—"

"I know him." Morley and I exchanged glances. So the centaur didn't know that the Sair had gone invisible. Far be it from me to respect a dead villain so much I failed to profit from him. "You've got a deal, buddy. He's dead meat right now. If I see the woman, get what I want, and leave in one piece, I'll show you the body before the sun comes up."

"Pact?"

"Pact and sworn."

"Good. Let's go. They'll be getting impatient."

37

Zeck Zack led us down the trail to his house. The peacocks raised twelve kinds of hell. "I'm going to roast the lot someday," the centaur said. "Every damn night they wake me up with that whooping."

He took us in through the tradesman's entrance Kayean used to sneak out. Then it was through servants' corridors to the front antechamber.

"Dark as hell in here," Morley complained. "What have you got against light, centaur?"

If it was bad for him and the triplets, it was worse for Zeck Zack and me. We had no night eyes at all.

There was a ghost of light in the antechamber. It leaked in from the ballroom. It was just enough to betray the form of a man awaiting us.

The centaur said, "At this point you must shed all your weapons. Indeed, everything you're carrying that is made of metal. Past this point you may go armed only with the weapons given you by nature."

I started shucking. I could smell the end of the chase. I would give Zeck Zack the benefit of the doubt.

"Damn, it's cold in here," Dojango muttered.

He was right. And here I'd thought my teeth were chattering because I had to go in there armed only with the weapons given me by nature. I announced, "I'm ready."

Zeck Zack said, "Step up and let the man double-check, Mr. Garrett." He made no apologies.

I stepped forward. A pasty face the color of grubs appeared before me for a moment. Eyes of no color stared into mine. They were filled with an old hopelessness.

He patted me down smoothly and efficiently. Professionally. He did only one thing unprofessional.

He slipped something into my pocket.

It was done slickly. He touched me just heavily enough to make sure I noticed. Then he went to frisk Morley.

One lone candle illuminated the ballroom. It sat, with a quill and inkwell, on an otherwise barren table at the chamber's geographical center. The table was four feet wide and eight feet long, long side toward me. Two chairs faced one another across it. I went and stood behind the one on my side, dropped my credentials and all the legal stuff on the table. Shivering, I shoved my hands into my pockets and waited.

I hadn't imagined anything. I palmed a folded piece of paper.

I checked the disposition of my troops. Morley was to my left, my weak side, two steps out and one back. Dojango was the same to my right. The grolls were behind me. Morley's nose twitched and pointed three times. Three beings shared the room with us, all in front.

One came floating out of the darkness.

She was beautiful. And something else. Ethereal, a poet might have said. Spooky is good enough for me.

She moved so lightly she seemed to float. Her gown whispered around her. Gauzy and voluminous, it was as white as any white ever was. Her skin was so colorless it almost matched her apparel. Her hair was the blond called platinum. Her eyes were ice blue and without expression, except they narrowed as she neared the light, as though it was too bright. Her lips were a thin wound vaguely purpled by the cold. She wore no makeup.

"You're Kayean Kronk?" I asked when she halted behind her chair.

She inclined her head in a barely perceptible nod.

"Let's sit, then. Let's get it over with."

She pulled her chair back and drifted into it.

I glanced at Morley and Dojango as I settled. They

were staring into the darkness, as rigid and fierce as trained wolves on point. I didn't know Dojango had it in him.

I looked across the table. She waited, her hands folded.

I gave her the whole thing, Denny dying, leaving his bundle, her having to come to TunFaire with me if she wanted to claim the legacy, or having to execute a sworn and sealed affidavit that would renounce and abjure, in perpetuity, all claims upon the estate of Denny Tate.

While I tried to talk what Morley called dirty-lawyer talk I shuffled and referred to my papers and used that to cover unfolding the thing that had been deposited in my pocket. It was a note of course.

It said:

> *Come take her out. Soon. Please. While there is still a chance for her redemption*

I shivered and tried to convince myself that it was the cold.

I read on, and under the guise of jotting notes jotted a note:

> *Open the enclosure only in her presence. Do so elsewhere and all hope dies.*

I folded in one of the charms I had obtained from the Old Witch. Hands-at-the-door had not removed those, if he had detected them at all. I got the paper into a pocket and concentrated on concentrating on that spooky woman.

I tried to sound incredulous. "Are you honestly rejecting one hundred thousand marks? Less fees, of course. In *silver*?"

A ghost of a hint of revulsion feather-touched her eyes as she nodded. It was the only emotion she betrayed during the interview.

"Very well. I won't pretend to understand, but I'll draw up the affidavit." I began scratching slowly on a piece of paper. "One of my associates will witness my signature. One of your companions will have to witness yours."

Again she nodded.

I completed the thing, signed. "Morley. I need your chop."

He came and gave me it. He was still as taut as a drawn bowstring.

I pushed the paper, ink, and pen across. "Is that satisfactory?"

She considered the paper just long enough, then nodded, collected everything, floated up, and drifted away into the darkness.

I put my papers and such together, rose, waited behind my chair. Soon enough the apparition drifted back. She placed the signed affidavit on the table, just beside the candle. Thus there was no possibility of physical contact, as there might be if she offered it to me directly. I gathered it up and tucked it away.

"I thank you for your time and courtesy, madame. I will trouble you no more." I headed for the anteroom.

I noted that neither Morley, Dojango, nor the grolls turned around to retreat. There are times when not having night eyes can be a blessing.

Slipping my counternote to my correspondent was easy. Zeck Zack was so anxious to get us out of his house, and so eager to get himself out, too, that he was blind. In half a minute he was fussing unmercifully, trying to get us moving down the dark halls before we had recovered half of our hardware.

38

The peafowl carried on like wild dogs had them surrounded and help would come only if they yelled loud
enough to rattle the clouds. I sympathized. Lately I
felt the same way. But if I yelled, *they* would know
where I was and start closing in.

As we approached the witch's house, the air quiv-
ered. A cackle fluttered down like gaunt, soggy snow-
flakes. Out of everywhere and nowhere, she asked,
"Did you enjoy your taste of the prophecy, Mr. Garrett?" More soggy cackle.

Morley and the boys might not have heard. Zeck
Zack glanced at the house, puzzled. I just put my head
down and marched, not wanting to think about it.

The centaur was determined to stick with us. I expected him to press on the matter of Sair Lojda, and
he didn't disappoint me. He started in halfway to the
graveyard. I told him, "Wait," and refused to listen.

Morley picked the spot to squat, the one we had
used before keeping our date with Zeck Zack. Morley
sat down. So did I. Morley said, "We need to talk."

"Yeah."

Zeck Zack grumbled, "This is where you tell me
how sorry you are, can't keep your half of the bargain?"

"No," Morley said. "We can deliver on that fast
enough to make your head spin. The problem is, *you*
didn't deliver."

I looked at Morley. He explained, "You gave her
the paper upside down. She didn't turn it. She couldn't
read. It's reasonable to assume that your Kayean could."

"She could. You're right. That wasn't her. Didn't

begin to resemble her. They just plain didn't know I knew her."

Zeck Zack looked upset. I didn't bother to ask. I did say, "One question, old horse. When you bought that house, was it your idea, theirs, or the priest's?"

"The priest's."

"One cycle of coincidence unmasked. Did he find what he was afraid might be hidden there?"

"No."

"Did you? I'm sure you looked."

He was regaining his balance. He grinned. "I took that place apart. I needed some back leverage."

"I can take that as a no?"

"Right."

"Garrett," Morley said, "is that paper going to satisfy you? It'll get you your ten percent."

"That's not what I said I'd do. I haven't found her yet."

He grunted. I couldn't be sure in that light, but thought he seemed relieved and pleased. "Then we have plans to make, things to do, and our butts to cover." He rose. "Your pal there jacked us around, but maybe he didn't have any choice. I say we deliver our half. Maybe he'll suffer a fit of gratitude. Come on."

There was an edge to his voice I didn't like.

I'm not sure Zeck Zack followed Morley. Maybe he just didn't want to go back down to that house. Or maybe he thought he would get to watch the priest die.

Morley hiked straight to the mausoleum we'd visited earlier. "Open it up, Marsha."

Marsha obliged.

Zeck Zack noted the little giveaway details that said the tomb was in use. "You already did it? Before . . . you dumped him here?"

Morley gave him the lucifer stone. "See for yourself. Pardon us if we don't join you. We've been in there once already tonight. We don't have your iron stomach."

Their gazes locked. Right then Zeck Zack would

have murdered him cheerfully. The odds didn't favor
him. He spun, raised the stone, stamped inside.

Morley said something in grollish.

Marsha slammed the door.

"Morley!"

"A little night trading, I told you the first time I
reported on him. Like a little innocent smuggling, I
thought. What do you want to bet he procures for
them?"

I had known Morley a long time, though not well.
I'd seen him angry, but never out of control. And
never eaten up with hatred.

"You know what we walked into down there, don't
you, Garrett?"

"I know." And Father Rhyne's last message and
Kayean's excommunication made sense. Of a sort. So
did the attacks and rumors of attacks.

Morley calmed down. "Something had to be done.
He could have trotted straight down there and told
them we weren't taken in. He'll be all right for a
while. We already know he has a strong stomach. We
can turn him loose later, if you want. Anyway, a few
days in there might incline him to tell us how to find
her."

"I'll know how to reach her soon enough." Though
Morley gave me the fisheye, I didn't elucidate.

"You sure you know what you're doing? There wasn't
anything in your deal about digging her out of a nest
of the night people."

"I know." I knew only too well. And I am cursed
with an imagination capable of conjuring up the worst
possibilities.

"If we blow it and get taken, me and the triplets are
just dead. We don't have enough human blood to be
any use to them. But you. . ."

"I said I know, Morley. Back off. We have the
major to worry about. He knows we were in touch
with the centaur. I expect he knows the priest was
blackmailing Zeck Zack. With the priest gone that
leverage is gone. So are we. Meaning we might have
learned something that made us run for cover. He's

going to tear this town apart. He's going to have guys sitting on every way out. We can't stay here. When the sun comes up the sextons will start planting the day's crop of stiffs. They'll wonder what we're doing hanging around. We can't go back to the inn. Everybody will be watching that."

"Don't get yourself in an uproar. We've got the woods to hide in. We've got ourselves a night trader who knows ways to get people and things in and out of town. I say let's worry about our friends of the nest and let your major worry about himself."

Morley had a point of sorts, though he didn't realize it. The more the major scurried around looking for us, the more likely he was to draw the attention of superiors who might want to know what was going on. And few if any of the men he commanded would be Venageti operatives. Their suspicions dared not be aroused.

He had to juggle carefully.

39

I wakened to an itchy nose, tittering, and the *harumph-harumph* of grollish laughter. I opened my eyes. Something brown and fuzzy waved in my face. Behind it was one of the little folk, seated in the crotch of a bush. I controlled my temper and got my forequarters upright, leaning against a tree. I was stiff and sore from sleeping on the ground.

No doubt Morley would argue that it was good for me.

"Where the hell are Morley and Dojango?"

The only answer I got was some big grollish grins and titters from the undergrowth.

"All right. Be that way."

"Sugar?" A tiny voice piped.

"If I'd had any, you would have swiped it while I was sleeping."

"With those great beasties watching over you?" the one in the bush asked.

I didn't feel like arguing. Morning is always too early for anything but self-pity, and even that's usually too much trouble. "Is there anyone in or around the centaur's house?" You have to strive for precision with those folk. "Human or otherwise?"

"Sugar?"

"No sugar."

"Bye, now."

So. No pay, no play. Little mercenaries. I considered going down and burglarizing the centaur's kitchen. But I wasn't hungry enough to bet that Zeck Zack's masters had done the rational thing and gotten the hell out the minute my affidavit and I departed. Besides, I didn't feel like getting up and doing anything.

I sat there trying to reconcile the Kayean who dwelt among the nightmares with the Kayean I had known. I shuffled through what I remembered from her letters to Denny. Nothing there but the occasional hint that she was not happy. Never a word about her where-abouts or circumstances. She hadn't been proud of herself.

No sense worrying about it. That would give me nothing but a headache and the heebie-jeebies. She could explain when I got to her.

Morley showed up around noon, staggering under a load of junk. "What's all that?" I demanded. "You planning an invasion? Where's Dojango? What the hell have you been up to?"

"Taking bids on your butt from Vasco, Rose, and your major. It was hot going till they got up to a quarter mark. Here." He dumped half his load beside me. I noted a sack that looked like it might contain comestibles. I hit it first.

"What is all this stuff?"

"Raw materials. For the arsenal we'll need if we're going into a nest after your lady. They'd smell metal hardware ten miles off. You any good at flaking stone arrow points?"

"I don't know. I've never tried."

He looked exasperated. "Didn't they teach you any-thing practical in that Marine Corps of yours?"

"Three thousand ways to kill Venageti. I'm a tool user, not a toolmaker."

"I guess the load falls on Doris and Marsha again." He gobbled grollish, and gave the big guys a bunch of stuff. Two minutes later, snarling and rumbling, they were chipping out arrowheads with a touch as delicate as a mouse's. They were good, and they were fast.

Morley said, "They're put out. They say it's dwarf's work. They want to know why they can't just make themselves some ten-foot clubs and go in and break skulls. Grolls are slow sometimes."

I could whittle a bit so I set to making myself a sword from an ironwood lath. It's a good hard wood that will almost take an edge, but won't hold one the way steel will. So I gave myself only one. The back-stroke side I channeled and set with waste from the arrowhead flaking. That gave me a vicious tool.

Time rolled by. I shed my troubles in my concentration on my craftsmanship.

"Have mercy, Garrett!" Morley snapped. "Do you really have to put in the blood gutters?"

I looked at the thing in my hand. I sure was doing it up purple. I tried it for balance. "Close. Needs a little more work. A little more polish to lessen the drag during the cut."

"And you call me bloodthirsty."

"I'd rather carry a saber."

"Come off it. One time we're going to use this stuff. Finish it up. I cut some bolts, there. Fletch them and sharpen them. I'll harden and poison the tips when I'm done here." He was removing metal parts from crossbows and replacing them. The reworked weapons wouldn't hold up, but, like he said, it was just the one raid.

"Old Man Tate is going to pee blue vinegar over the expenses. Why poison? It won't do you any good." I dragged bolts, glue, feathers, and thread together and started in.

"Because not everybody we meet is going to be immune."

True. The bloodslaves would fight ferociously to defend their chances of someday joining the order of masters.

"You know anything about the nests in the Cantard, Garrett?"

"Who knows anything about any of them anywhere?"

"True. They wouldn't survive. But?"

"There are rumors. Because of the military situation, they don't have to be as circumspect in the Cantard. Plenty of easy prey, too. Nobody misses a soldier here or there. The nests are supposed to be bigger than usual because of that. When I was sta-

tioned down here, there were supposed to be six nests.
That got reduced when some Karentine agents snatched
a Venageti warlord's daughter and let it out that she
had been carried off to a nest. The warlord forgot
everything else, went off to the rescue, found the nest
and cleansed it, and got himself killed for his trouble.
While his army was busy hunting night people, one of
ours was sneaking up behind them. And that's all I
know. Except to guess that they're happy to see so
much silver leaving this part of the world."

"They would know everything about silver, wouldn't
they?"

"They would know everything about what everyone
was doing, that's for sure. Which explains how Kayean
was able to make Denny rich."

Silver is as poisonous to the night people as cobra
venom is to humans. It kills them fast and makes it
stick. Not much else does. Other metals bother them
to a lesser degree.

"Speaking of sneaks," Morley said.

Dojango appeared, burdened with poles and bow-
staves and whatnot. He was tipsy. He said, "It's set for
tomorrow night."

"How much did you have?" Morley demanded.

"Don't worry, cousin. I came here clean. Actually.
They'll have the horses and gear waiting at an abandoned mill they said is three miles up something called
North Creek. They said they'd only wait one night.
They said they would take the animals and stuff out
tomorrow morning and bring them back the next day
if we don't show. They seemed a little nervous about
being out in the countryside, actually."

"Guess we'll have to resurrect our centaur. Sit down
and start turning those dowels into arrows. Garrett.
You know this North Creek?"

"Yes." I was tempted to ask who he thought was in
charge, but kept my mouth shut. Morley had taken
care of things that needed doing.

Dojango started making arrows. "Some interesting
news started going around just before I came back up.
About the time we were taking a peek into that tomb

last night, Glory Mooncalled, *unsupported*, actually, attacked Indigo Springs."

"Indigo Springs?" I asked. "That's a hundred miles farther south than the army's ever gone. And he tried it without wizards?"

Dojango smirked. "He not only tried it, he pulled it off, actually. Caught them sleeping. Killed Warlord Shomatzo-Zha and his whole staff in the first assault, then wiped out half their army. The rest ran off into the desert barefoot, wearing nothing but their nightshirts."

"Good hunting for the night people," Morley grumbled.

"And unicorns, centaur slavers, wild dogs, hippogriffs, and any other kind of critter that wants a piece of them, " Dojango added. "This is going to mean problems, Morley. If we have to spend much time out there."

"How come?"

"If it's true, it's an unprecedented disaster for Venageti arms. When Glory Mooncalled changed sides, he swore vengeance on five warlords. For years he's been waltzing them around the Cantard, making fools of them. Now he's struck deep into traditionally safe territory and stomped one of the five the way I'd stomp a bug."

"So?"

"So the Venageti are going to start flailing around like a boxer with blood in his eyes, hoping they hit something. Karentine forces will begin to move, trying to take advantage. Every nonhuman tribe in the Cantard will be out trying to profit from the confusion. In a week it'll be so hairy it'll be worth your life to squat to poop if you don't have somebody to stand guard."

"Then we'd better move fast, hadn't we?" Morley asked.

A sentiment with which I agreed wholeheartedly. But my sneak to the bloodslave guarding the things in Zeck Zack's ballroom had paid no dividends yet and I doubted that my revelation would come for days—if at all.

40

Zeck Zack was as cooperative as a centaur could be after his sojourn with the dead. He didn't balk until having led us from the city via an underwall smugglers tunnel, he discovered that he had been enlisted in our enterprise for the duration.

Morley was in a puckish mood.

"But sir, surely you see all your caterwauling is without foundation. If you will reflect seriously you cannot help but confess the rectitude of our position. If we were to release you, as you so unreasonably insist, you would dash back through the tunnel and instantly set about wreaking evil upon us, imagining us to be the authors of your ill fortune rather than assuming that onus yourself, as is the fact."

I had arrayed my army in squad diamond, with a groll out front, another behind, Dojango on the right and Morley on the left. Night-blind, I marched at the heart of the formation, ready to rush to any quarter suddenly threatened. Zeck Zack stumbled along between Morley and me.

It wasn't long before the centaur surrendered to the inevitable. He betrayed a hitherto sequestered facet of character and began arguing with Morley in the same florid language and overblown, overly polite formulations.

The men who had brought our horses and gear were thrilled to see us. Our advent meant they couldn't just take everything back and sell it again. Nor, they decided after eyeballing the grolls, could they murder us and do the same.

We parted ways immediately upon delivery. They

were of the school that maintains wandering around at night could get you killed. We kept moving on the hypothesis that the wise man puts ground between himself and people who want to kill him.

Not a lot of ground. Those horses had heard of me and just to make trouble they insisted that the sensible thing to do was stay put.

Nobody was out to kill *them*. Nobody behind them, anyway.

Their attitude didn't improve when the sun rose and they found themselves headed into the Cantard.

Morley accused me of anthropomorphizing and exaggerating the natural reluctance of dumb beasts to go into unfamiliar territory.

It just goes to show they had him fooled. They're crafty in their malice, unicorns under the skin.

Having had no revelation, I set a course due west. Thither lay the most barren territory in the Karentine end of the Cantard, the desert of colorful buttes and mesas people in TunFaire picture when they think of the Cantard. I decided to head there because it seemed a logical place for the night people to have established a nest. It was so inhospitable as to be repugnant to most races. There were no discovered resources to bring exploiters with their guardians. Ample prey existed close by—especially when there were Zeck Zacks to do the rounding up.

Our second day out Morley began to suspect that I was not sure of my course. He went to work on the centaur.

"There's no point to it, Morley," I said. "They wouldn't be stupid enough to trust him."

Doris grumbled something from behind us. I could now tell the grolls apart. I had made them wear different hats.

"What?" I asked.

"He says there's a dog following us."

"Uh-oh."

"Trouble?"

"Probably. We'll have to ambush it to find out. Watch for a place where the wind is toward us."

Three possibilities suggested themselves. The dog could be a domestic stray seeking human company. Damned unlikely. It could be an outcast from a wild pack. That meant rabies. Or, most unpleasant and most likely, it could be an outrunner scouting for game.

Marsha found a likely bunch of boulders on the lower slope of the butte we were rounding. He headed up a steep, twisting alley between, into shadows and clicky echoes. Morley, Dojango, and I dismounted and followed, rehearsing the balky animals in the vulgates of several languages.

"What did I tell you about horses, Morley?"

Doris hunkered between rocks and started blending in.

"Keep going, Morley. They're sight as well as scent hunters. It'll need to see movement."

Morley grumbled. Marsha grumbled back, surly, but continued climbing. A bit later there was one brief squeal of doggie outrage from below, canceled by a meaty smack.

The horses were not reluctant going downhill. Lazy monsters.

Doris had squashed the mongrel good. He stood over it grinning as though he had conquered an entire army troop.

"Yech!" I said "Looks like a rat run over by a wagon. Lucky he missed its head." I squatted, examined ears. "Well, damn!"

"What?" Morley asked.

"It was an outrunner. A trained outrunner. See the holes through the ears? Punched there by unicorn teeth. There's a hunting party somewhere within a few miles of us. They'll track the dog when he doesn't turn up. That means we have to leave enough nasty surprises to discourage them, because we aren't going to outrun them if they take our scent."

"How many?"

"One adult male and all the females of his harem that aren't too pregnant or cluttered up with young. Maybe some adolescent females that haven't run away yet. Anywhere from six to a dozen. If they do catch up, concentrate on the dominant female. The male won't get involved. He leaves the hunting and heavy stuff to the womenfolk. He saves himself for giving orders, mounting females, killing his male offspring if they stray from their mothers, and trying to kidnap the most attractive females from other harems."

"Sounds like a sensible arrangement."

"Somehow, I figured you'd feel that way."

"Wouldn't killing the boss break up the harem?"

"The way I hear, if that happened they'd just keep coming till they were dead or we all were."

"That is true," Zeck Zack said. "A most despicable beast, the unicorn. Nature's most bankrupt experiment. But one day my folk will complete their extermination. . . ." He shut up, having recalled that the rest of us held a different view of the identity of nature's most bankrupt experiment.

We hurried on. After a while Zeck Zack resumed talking so he could explain some of the nastier devices his folk used to booby-trap their backtrails. Some were quite gruesomely ingenious.

He had contributed nothing but carping before. His sudden helpfulness suggested the proximity of unicorns scared the tailfeathers off him.

41

After pausing at a brackish stream to water and gather firewood, we scrambled up several hundred feet of scree around the knees of a monster monolith of a butte and made camp in a pocket that couldn't be approached in silence by a mouse. The view was excellent. None of us, with our varied eyes, or even with the spyglass, could see anything moving in the twilight.

We settled down to a small, sheltered fire. Being in the mood myself, we broached one of the baby kegs and passed it around. It held only enough for a good draft each for me, Zeck Zack, Dojango, and sips for the grolls. "Yech!" was my assessment. "Drinking that was the second mistake I've made in this life."

"I won't be so forward as to ask what the other might have been," Morley said, "suspecting it might have been being born." He smirked. "I presume beer jostled on the back of a pack animal in the hot sun loses something."

"You might say. What possessed you, Dojango?"

"A slick-talking salesman."

We sat around the fire after eating, mostly watching it die down, occasionally assaying a story or a joke, but largely tossing out notions about how we might deal with the unicorns if it came to that. I didn't contribute much. I'd begun to fret about my revelation.

Something must have gone wrong. There had been time for them to reach the nest, I felt. Had the bloodslave betrayed himself? Had he been found out?

Without him prospects were poor. We could wander the Cantard looking until we were old men.

At some point I would have to admit defeat and

head north with my false affidavit. I supposed we'd
give up when our stores were depleted to just enough
for the overland journey to Taelreef, the friendly port
nearest us after Full Harbor. Going back into the
shadow of the major's claw seemed plain foolhardy
from there in the desert.

One of the grolls was telling Morley a story. Morley
kept snickering. I ignored them and began drowsing.

"Hey. Garrett. You got to hear this story Doris just
told me. It'll tear you up."

I scowled and opened my eyes. The fire had died to
sullen red coals casting little useful light. Even so, I
could see that Morley's words didn't fit his expression.
"Another one of those long-winded shaggy-dog fables
about how the fox tricked the bear out of berries, then
ate them and got the runs and diarrheaed himself to
death?" That had been the most accessible of the
grollish stories so far, and even it had lacked a clear
point or moral.

"No. You'll get this one right away. And even if
you don't, laugh a lot so you don't hurt his feelings."

"If we must, we must."

"We must." He moved over beside me. In a low
voice, he said, "It starts out like this. We're being
watched by two of the night people. Laugh."

I managed, without looking around. Sometimes I do
all right.

Doris called something to Marsha, who responded
with hearty grollish laughter. It sounded like they had
bet on my response and Marsha had won.

"Doris and Marsha are going to jump them. Maybe
they can handle them, maybe they can't. Don't look
around. When I'm done telling the story, we're going
to get up and walk toward Doris. Chuckle and nod."

"I think I can manage without the stage directions."
I chuckled and nodded.

"When Doris moves, you follow him and do whatever needs doing. I'll go with Marsha."

"Dojango?" I slapped my knee and guffawed.

"He watches the centaur."

Zeck Zack had backed himself into a tight place

where nothing could come at him from behind. His legs were folded under him; his chin rested upon his folded arms; he appeared to be sound asleep.

"Ready?" Morley asked.

I put on my hero face that said I was a fearless old vampire killer from way back. "Lead on, my man. I'm right behind you."

"Big laugh."

I hee-hawed like it was the one about the bride who didn't know the bird had to be cleaned before it went into the roaster. Morley pasted a grin on and rose. I did so too, and tried shaking some of the stiffness out of my legs. We walked toward Doris.

Doris and Marsha moved with astonishing swiftness. I had run only two steps when I glimpsed a dark flutter among the rocks. Doris hit it. A great thrashing and flailing started. Another broke out behind me. I didn't look back.

When I got there, Doris had the vampire in a fierce bear hug, facing away from him. Sinews popped and crackled. Strong as he was, the groll was having trouble keeping the hold. Blood leaked from talon slashes on his hide. The blood smell maddened the vampire further. His fangs ripped the air an inch from the groll's arm.

Let that devil sink one and Doris was done for. It would inject a soporific venom capable of felling a mastodon.

I stood with a knife in one hand and silver half mark in the other, wondering what to do. Whenever a foot flailed out at me, I tried to cut the tendon above the heel.

Suddenly there was a flicker of light. Dojango was feeding the fire.

Doris pushed the vampire's ankles between his knees. I flung forward, trying to drive my blade into one of the devil's knees, to hobble it. It twisted half an inch. My point hit bone and cut downward through flesh harder than summer sausage.

A wound to the bone, a foot long, and when I was done about three drops of liquid leaked out. The

vampire loosed one flat, shrill keen of pain and rage.
Its eyes burned down at me, trying to catch mine with
their deadly hypnotic gaze.

I slammed the half mark into the wound before it
could start healing.

It was done so quickly, deftly, and instinctively that
even now it amazes me.

The vampire froze for many seconds. Then dead lips
peeled back and loosed a howl that terrified the stones
and must have been audible twenty miles away; immortality betrayed. I clamped both hands on the wound
to keep the coin in place. The night beast bent back
like a man in the last throes of tetanus, hissed, gur-
gled, shook so violently we barely held on.

The flesh beneath my hands began to soften. Around
the coin it turned to jelly. It oozed between my fingers.

Doris threw the thing down. The fire painted his
great green face in light and shadow patches of hatred.
The vampire lay among the rocks, still hissing, clawing
at its leg. It was a very strong one. The poison should
have finished it sooner. But they're all strong, or they
couldn't be what they are.

Doris snagged a boulder twice as long as me and
smashed the thing's head.

For several seconds I watched flesh turn to jelly and
slide off bones. Then, as though the vampire's end was
a signal, my revelation came.

I knew a direction.

When daylight came . . .

If daylight came. Morley and Marsha were embat-
tled still. Doris was on his way to help. He collected
his ten-foot club as he went. I shook all over and went
to help myself.

Somehow, as we approached, the second vampire
broke loose. It hit the ground, then hurled itself through
the air in one of those hundred-foot bounds that have
led the ignorant to believe they can fly.

The leap brought it straight toward me.

I don't think it was intentional. I think it jumped
blind, with the fire in its eyes. But he saw me as he

came. His mouth opened, his fangs gleamed, his eyes flared, his claws reached. . . .

"He" or "it"? It had been male when it was alive. It could still sire its own kind. But did it deserve . . . ?

Doris's club met him with a solid *whump!* The vampire arced right back the way he had come and fell at Marsha's feet. Marsha bounced a boulder off him before he could move—if he could have moved.

I didn't go on. I headed for the fire and another of those skunky kegs and hopefully some unsober reflection.

Dojango was shaking worse than I was, but he was on the job, feeding the fire with one hand, keeping a crossbow aimed at Zeck Zack with the other. He didn't look up to see who or what was coming toward him.

Another twenty-mile shriek shredded the fabric of the night.

42

"I make it twelve," I said. "One lame. If I stare through this glass anymore, my eye is going to fall out."

Morley took the spyglass, studied the unicorns playing around the water course and pretending they didn't know we were nearby.

Morley handed the glass to Dojango. He told Zeck Zack, "One of your traps worked."

The centaur wasn't talking to us this morning.

I retreated to higher ground, a better view, and contemplation of last night's revelation, which remained with me.

It amounted to a direction, a line on which Kayean and I were points. The trouble was, the line ran through me, so I had no certain idea which of the two ways pointed toward Kayean and which ran away.

The Old Witch hadn't mentioned that problem.

I favored going southeast. That would put the nest nearer Full Harbor and the roads toward the war zone. It also put a large, promising mesa astride the line.

"Hey," I called down. "Somebody bring me the glass."

Morley came grumbling up. "Who was your butt boy yesterday?"

"A genie. But somebody threw his beer keg on the fire last night." I trained the glass on the mesa, asked, "What took you so long with that thing last night?"

"I was trying to get it to talk. It was a new one, barely up from being a bloodslave. Not born to the

blood. I thought it might crack. Hey! The stallion and
two of the mares are taking off."

So they were. They headed up our back trail at a
grand gallop. The other unicorns moved out of sight
behind the scruffy trees lining the watercourse. I swung
the glass. "Did you learn anything we can use?"

"Nothing you'd find interesting. What is it?"

"Somebody coming right up our back trail. Too far
to tell for sure, but it looks like a big party."

He took the glass. "Fortune, thou toothless, grinning bitch. Here we are treed by unicorns and there—I'd
give you odds—comes your major friend."

"No bet till they're close enough to show faces."

"You want a sure thing, don't you?"

"I've never had a gambling debt hanging over my
head."

He scowled and returned the glass.

The male unicorn was back. He and the trained
dogs lurked behind the living screen bordering the
creek, waiting for us to make a break. The females
had moved to a tributary dry wash a mile away.

Answering a question, I told Morley, "They'll jump
out and try to panic the horses, which isn't hard unless
the horses are well trained. If they succeed, they'll
pick off a few, eat the horses where they fall, and
carry the riders back to those who missed out on the
hunt. If the horsemen regroup and come back at them,
they'll just scatter and wait. People aren't going to
bother carrying off dead horses."

"They ought to be close enough to see something."

I raised the glass. The riders were close enough to
pick individuals from the dust but not close enough to
distinguish features. "I'd guess fifteen horsemen and
two wagons. See what you think."

He watched awhile, grunted. "They ride like soldiers. Looks like we trade bad trouble for worse. At
least *they* seem to know where they're going."

"I know where I'm going, too. That mesa."

"Back the way we traveled for an entire day? When
were you struck by this marvelous revelation?"

I ignored him. He didn't need to know.

The riders passed the female unicorns' hiding place. "Going to hit them from behind." I took the glass back. "Well. What do you know. Did you check that lead wagon?"

"No."

"Can you think of two women who might be roaming the Cantard with Saucerhead Tharpe?"

"What? Give me that damned thing." He looked. "That stupid bitch. Hell. Your pal Vasco and his boys are there, too. Regular reunion of the Garrett Appreciation Society. Looks like they're prisoners. I count ten soldiers and one officer."

My turn at the glass showed me he was right. "That's my Major No-Name. This puts me in a moral bind."

"Yeah?"

"I can't let those women get hurt."

"The hell. They asked for it. What would they do if they were up here and you were down there?"

I didn't get to answer that one. The unicorns burst out of the dry wash. At first it seemed their strategy was perfect. The soldiers' horses darted every direction. Then suddenly they were all facing the rush. The soldiers held leveled lances.

The groups crashed together. The unicorns broke first, running for the wash. One soldier and two horses were down. The unicorns had lost no one, but they had collected the majority of wounds.

An arrow smacked into the shoulder of the slowest. She stumbled, went down on her knees. Before she could rise, soldiers with lances overtook her. Major No-Name called something taunting. He sent five men to plink arrows into the wash. Angered, the unicorns came roaring out. In another brief mix-up, another soldier, another unicorn, and two more horses died. No-Name held his ground and mocked the attackers. The soldiers who lost their mounts took replacements from their prisoners.

"He do have a hate for unicorns, I think," Morley said.

"Here comes the boss female after orders."

"I'm going back down. Give me the high sign if he tells her to take the dogs with her."

"Will do."

The major was expecting a fight. He made a make-shift fort of his wagons and baggage off his pack animals, put all the extra animals inside the barricade, armed his prisoners, and had them wait on the wagons. I wondered what he told them.

The male unicorn was either stupid or had lost a favorite. They do become mercurial when that happens.

I signaled Morley. I thought I knew what he had in mind. I didn't like it but I could see no alternative.

So. The dogs went howling toward the major's group. The unicorns charged behind. A fine, merry dust-up got started.

The male unicorn didn't want to watch. Morley proved that by racing from the foot of the scree to the watercourse unchallenged.

Zeck Zack was after him before he was halfway across. There is nothing on four legs faster—in the short run—than a motivated centaur.

The unicorn heard hoofbeats. He popped up to see what was happening.

It was too late. Zeck Zack was all over him, and showed us he had handled a unicorn one-on-one in younger days. It didn't last long.

All the while I was bounding down the slope. It was move-out time.

43

Everything and everyone was ready when I got down. I scrambled aboard my horse. For once we agreed on absolutely everything. We were a team with a single mind. That mind said, "Make tracks."

I got out ahead of the crowd so I could lead by example. I steered around the base of the butte so we were headed east again, until we reached a point where I could see the battleground. That journey took an hour and a half.

We halted. I raised the spyglass. Nothing moved except the vultures. From that lower angle of vision it was hard to tell how great the disaster had been. I could distinguish one wagon on its side. A vulture perched on a wheel.

"Somebody ought to take a closer look," I said, staring at Zeck Zack.

He nodded. Without comment he borrowed a couple of javelins and trotted off. The morning had wrought marvelous changes in him. "He might be back in the army," I told Morley. Dotes just grunted. I added, "Don't forget, somebody thought enough of him to get him Karentine citizenship."

"It isn't what you were, it's what you are, Garrett. And that creature is the worst kind of night trader. The kind that sells your kind to *them*."

Yeah.

Zeck Zack circled the mess a few times, closing in, then he raised a javelin and beckoned, knowing I had the glass on him.

"Let's go."

It was grisly. The dogs were all dead. So were most

of the unicorns and a dozen horses. But there was not a human cadaver to be seen.

"They went on," the centaur said.

I told Morley, "For a Venageti he sure sticks tight to Karentine field doctrine. Challenge unicorns when you can. Carry away your dead. Poison the flesh of the animals you leave behind." Every dead animal had been cut dozens of times. Each cut was stained a royal blue where crystalline poison had been rubbed into the wound.

No one was going to profit from dead army animals.

I counted eight slain unicorns. They had kept at it until the dominant female had been killed. The survivors would be in bad shape.

Unicorns in that part of the Cantard would seek easier prey for a while.

I raised the glass and searched the base of the butte. There they were, looking back at us.

"See them?" Morley asked.

"Yeah. Burying their dead. Can't make out anybody special except Saucerhead."

Zeck Zack took a cue from that and galloped off toward the butte shadow where the major was returning the earth's children to her.

"Trying to ingratiate himself," Morley said. "So you'll be a little loose on the rein when the time comes."

"When do you figure he'll run?"

"When we start into the nest. We won't dare waste time chasing him. And with us keeping them busy, his chance of making it would be good. This is his country and he can still pick them up and put them down when he wants."

I watched Dojango for a minute. He was collecting souvenirs. He had cut the dew claws off a unicorn, had knocked out some of its razor teeth, and was trying to figure how to take its horn. That would bring fifty marks bounty in Full Harbor and more as a curio in TunFaire.

"What are you going to do about it?" Morley asked.

"Let him run. I won't have any more use for him."

Zeck Zack came prancing back. He reported that four soldiers and the major had survived, and four other men as well. I knew about Saucerhead. One of the others sounded like Vasco. The remaining two could have been anybody.

"Survived don't mean unscathed, either," the centaur said. "They got cut up pretty good."

"What about the women?"

"Not much scathing there. A little frayed around the edges, as anyone would be after that."

Morley muttered, "Bet we can thank that dope Saucerhead for that."

Zeck Zack went right on. "One of them kept screaming at me to tell you she going to crack your eggs, fry them, and feed them to the unicorns. When the boss soldier tried to shut her up, she bit him and gave him a knee in *his* eggs."

"My lovely little Rose. What a wonderful wife she'll make some poor sod. Well. Let's go." I urged my mount to face east. Our unity had begun to unravel.

"She does bounce back, doesn't she?" Morley said in a tone that sounded suspiciously like admiration. "You just going to ride off?"

"Yes. The major isn't going to make prisoners of anybody again. That's going to turn into a three-way marriage of convenience that'll be as rowdy as those marriages get. But they'll take care of each other. Do you think you could get Doris and Marsha to pull a wagon? We might have a use for it."

The one wagon was not damaged, just overturned and lacking a team.

"It's army. We wouldn't want to get caught with it."

"We won't."

He spoke to the grolls. They responded in what sounded like impolite terms. He told me, "They want to collect unicorn horns. Those could be more use than any wagon. Stick one of *them* in the heart with a horn and it's all over, sure as silver. And they can't smell horns coming."

"Deal, then. Wagon for horns. Those people back

there are going to be burying and bickering for a long time."

The grolls took the deal. *Crash!* Down went the wagon onto its wheels. The grolls scampered from unicorn to unicorn, perhaps dreaming of buying a brewery.

A pair of adolescent females, outraged by the trophy taking and not too badly injured, charged out of the wash. It was disconcerting, watching the absent-minded way the grolls clubbed them to death.

44

We didn't try for the nest mesa that day. I wanted to go in early, when they had settled for the day, not late when they were about to awaken. Once they were soundly asleep, while the sun was high, it was almost impossible to wake them. Even the elder bloodslaves would have trouble responding.

So legend went.

We got out of sight of our pursuers, then went to work hiding our trail and laying false scents. Zeck Zack worked hard making himself useful. He knew all the tricks. He even had the grolls hand-carry the wagon two miles off to leave false wheel marks.

We set up for the night atop the corpse of a small butte not more than two miles from the face of the nest mesa. My head throbbed with the nearness of Kayean. From that vantage I could see most of the scrap facing the mesa and our back-trail.

"No fire tonight," Zeck Zack said as I crouched behind the spy glass trying to tell what kind of luck the major was having. "Also scatter a little and stay near the stones that got the hottest during the day. That is how they find their prey from a distance. Through their warmth. It would be wise, too, to keep too much metal from accumulating in one place."

"You wouldn't give them a holler, would you? To score a few points?"

"I've never been known for an inclination toward suicide. I am known to be quick-tempered, rash, foolish, sometimes even stupid. But not suicidal. I enjoy the good things in life too much." Wearing a distant look, he echoed himself, "Too much."

"You might remember that the major wants you as much as he wants me. Your blackmailing priest was a buddy of his and you know it," I added.

"He has to get out of the Cantard before he can cause me any grief. He has to get through tonight. Last night he was too strong for them. Tonight he won't be. Especially if they haven't fed for a while. And they have not. The two who came to Full Harbor could not restrain themselves, though their attacks put them at great risk."

"Why would they spot him more quickly than us?"

"Eleven humans are easier to find than one."

"Oh." The day was getting on toward failing. Those who were tracking us were having no luck and seemed now to be more interested in settling for the night.

"There." The centaur pointed. A darkness was rising from the mesa face.

I shifted the glass. "Bats. A billion bats." And coming up from a point right on the line through my head, my mystical connection with Kayean.

Morley came in from scouting around. For a city boy he caught on fast. I repeated the centaur's advice. He gave Zeck Zack the fish eye, then nodded curtly. "Makes sense. Don't sleep too soundly tonight, Garrett."

Right. With us here on the lip of it, I'd be lucky to get the old forty winks. You never admit it to the guys you're with, but you get scared. Damned scared. And this time there might be a bigger stake than just death. I could be dead and have to keep walking.

If you ask me, the difference between a hero and a coward is that a hero finds some damnfool way to con himself into going ahead instead of doing the sensible thing.

They never did give me much credit for sense.

I did sleep, because a hand shaking my shoulder woke me up. Morley.

I heard it before he told me. A hell of a row over by the foot of the mesa. Gods, how I had wanted to run over and warn them when they had chosen to camp less than a mile from the gate to the nest. But, like

Zeck Zack, I am not renowned for my suicidal tendencies.

As Morley said, the women were at little risk, and they were the only ones we had to give a damn about. Still, I had a soft spot for Saucerhead Tharpe. Saucerhead was implausibly romantic. He deserved preservation as the last of a knightly breed.

I got up where I could see just as the last of two campfires yonder died. Not two minutes after that the screaming and banging stopped. And about two minutes after that somebody finally said something. Dojango: "Guess we don't have to worry about the army anymore."

No. I guess not.

Nobody got any more sleep. I stared at the stars and wondered about the size of certain mouths, and about how much Rose, Vasco, and the major had yakked it up among themselves. Between them they had enough to work out what I meant to do. Did they have guts enough to stay buttoned up on the chance I might get them out?

"Going to have to be careful work over there tomorrow," Morley said sometime in the wee hours. He didn't have to ask if I was awake. He knew. Just as I knew that he and the others were awake and hanging onto something silver.

45

We started the crossing two hours later than I'd originally planned. That gave the sun two more hours to get up and glare at the gate to the nest. Two more hours for the night people to sink more deeply into slumber. Two more hours for us to prepare and two more hours for us to get crazier with fear. Every instinct screamed, "Get out of there!"

Morley spent that time rechecking every damned thing we would carry: flares, fire bombs, spears, crossbows, swords, knives, unicorn horns—the list was endless. I watched the gate through the spyglass, looked for secondary outlets, and helped the triplets polish off the last few kegs of beer. Zeck Zack mapped a convoluted route across that would be out of sight of spying eyes. The grolls, once the beer was gone, amused themselves by bringing enough water to do the horses for a couple of days. Dojango rigged up hitches they could pull if we didn't come back. Not much was said. The few lame jokes that were told got roll-on-the-ground laughs. Anything to ease the tension.

Morley distributed the lethal instruments and flares and rehearsed everyone on using them. We packed it all up, filled canteens, drank too much water, and finally the sun was high enough to suit me. "Let's go."

Morley muttered, "Wish I knew if they knew we were coming. Then we might not have to leave all the metal hardware. Especially the silver."

He was talking to no one but himself. My own contribution to nonconversation was, "I haven't been so loaded down with junk since we landed on Malgar

201

Island." I'd been scared witless that day, too. Now those Venageti looked like friendly puppies.

The centaur's route took us to the wasted camp. He knew we wanted to know.

We had an idea, of course. We'd watched the vultures circle for hours.

We heard them squabbling first. Then we heard the flies. Out on the Cantard those sidefliers of death get so thick they sound like swarms of bees.

Then we pushed between boulders and saw it.

I guess it was no more gruesome than any other massacre. But the bodies were so badly torn by attackers, vultures, wild dogs, and whatnot, that we had to count heads to find out that only four of the major's party had been left for the carrion eaters. Two pasty-skinned, black-clad bloodslaves had been left too, but they remained untouched. Even the flies and ants shunned them.

Nobody said anything. None of the dead could be identified; there was nothing to say. We went on, fear perhaps tempered by the rage that makes men hunt down the maneater, be it wolf, rogue tiger, or one of *them*.

Nearer the gate we spread out, Morley and I flanking the hole and doing a cautious scout for surprises. Nothing seemed untoward. We assembled closer to the cave. Bat reek rolled over us. There was no sign of vampires, but I had a bit of red hair twisted around my finger. It had come off a thorn bush nearby.

Morley and I went in first, each with a sword and unicorn horn. Dojango followed with flares and fire bombs. The grolls backed him with spears and crossbows. Zeck Zack was rear guard because we expected him to turn ghost on us anyway. He wouldn't have to stumble over anybody when he decided to leave.

We would change up on weapons and tactics if we reached the nest proper.

I gave a signal. We all closed our eyes, excepting the centaur. He counted a hundred silently, snake-hissed. Eyes barely cracked, we mouse-footed into the mouth of hell.

We advanced a few steps, stopped, listened. Morley

and I knelt to let the triplets have more freedom to support us. We continued in that fashion. The deeper we sank into the darkness, the more frequently we paused.

By right of better eyes Dojango should have been in my place. But Morley feared his nerves weren't up to it. I agreed. Dojango had buckled down and tightened up a lot, but he wasn't ready for the front line.

Gods, the stench in that hole!

The first hundred feet weren't too bad. The floor was level and clean. The ceiling was high. There was daylight at our backs. And there was no sign that anyone was waiting for us.

Then the floor dropped and turned right. The ceiling lowered until the grolls had to duck-walk. The darkness tightened and filled with the rustle and flutter of bats disturbed. Within a few yards we were saturated with the filth that was the source of the stench. The air grew chill.

Zeck Zack hissed.

We stopped. I was amazed that he could move so quietly on hooved feet. I'd assumed he was hell-bent for wherever already.

The hiss was the only sound. The centaur handed something forward. It gleamed through Dojango's fingers as he passed it.

It was the lucifer stone Morley had given the centaur before shutting him in that tomb.

An iron chill dragged its claws up my back. By the stone's light I saw Morley entertaining the same question: was the centaur announcing payback time? Burying us here would solve several of his problems.

I watched Morley struggle with the urge to kill Zeck Zack. He put it down. Barely. He gave me the stone because I had poorer eyes. I folded it into my right hand, under my fingers, against the grip of my wooden sword. I could lift a finger or two and leak light when I needed it.

Onward. Already the sun, freedom, and fresh air seemed a thousand years and miles behind us. Progress slowed as we examined every cranny for ambushers.

It looked like a dried-out corpse. Mouth open. Eye

sockets empty. Hair gray and wild. One buzzard claw came reaching out of a crack at me. I fell away, throwing a wild backhand stroke with the stone-set edge of my sword. Bone parted like dry sticks.

The thing that had pushed those old bones leaped out.

A groll's spear drove through it. Dull eyes stared into mine as it pitched forward onto the unicorn horn I raised to meet it. Cold, stale, awful breath washed my face. Again I saw that look I had seen on that butte about a century ago: immortality betrayed.

It tried to sink fangs into my throat. They weren't yet well developed. Its disease was not far advanced.

I was terrified anyway.

A Dojango toe connected with its head.

I grabbed the lucifer stone and got up. Neither old bones nor the bloodslave did. But brothers of the latter had come for the party, too.

They had no weapons but tooth. claw, ferocity, and a conviction of invincibility. None of that did them any good.

Morley and I held them. Dojango retreated behind his brothers and lit a flare. The night people made little squeaks and pawed at their eyes. A moment later it was over.

There were only four of them, plus somebody who had been dead for years. It had seemed like a battalion.

Morley and I inspected each other for wounds. He had one shallow gash but waved off attention. He wasn't human enough to have to worry.

The enemy had been met. He had been overcome in the opening encounter. Our nerve solidified. Our fear came under control. Dojango was proud of himself. He had proven he could think despite his terror.

We regained our breath and went on. Without the centaur Zeck Zack. There was no telling when he had deserted. Probably during the excitement, when he was sure no one would notice him going.

Behind us, the flare burned out. The bats began to settle down. The air grew colder.

46

The second bunch were more difficult than the first, though they were no more successful. They were bloodslaves farther along the scarlet path, harder to kill, but as vulnerable to blinding and more sensitive to the power of the unicorn horn. They did make us work up a sweat.

The third bunch was bad.

They let us know we were near the nest. They were bloodslaves who had slipped past all the perils of snares and pitfalls and were so far advanced in the disease that they were on the verge of joining the masters. Which meant they were almost as fast and strong and deadly as the two we had destroyed on the butte. After we skewered one with a horn it was almost impossible to touch the other three, even with them flare-blind. In the darkness where they dwelt, they had little use for sight. They ignored their pain and used their ears.

One got past me and Morley. The grolls pinned him with their spears, then finished him with unicorn horns. Dojango's fear-fevered arm gave us the other two. He hit them with fire bombs. We finished them while they thrashed in the flames and screamed.

"And that's it for the element of surprise," Morley said. "If ever there was one."

"Yeah."

They were the first words spoken since our entry underground, save a soft grollish curse from Doris on breaking a unicorn horn pinning a bloodslave.

The fires died. We readied ourselves. "Not far now," I guessed. Morley grunted. "The odds have got to be better," I said. Morley grunted again. Some conversationalist. He looked odd in the glow of lucifer stone. Was he going to flake out?

He got himself organized inside, stepped forward, whacking the flat of his sword with his horn and listening to the echo. After about fifty steps there was no echo.

I let light leak between my fingers.

No cave wall. No ceiling. "Dojango. Give Doris a flare."

The groll knew what to do. They threw for height and distance.

We were on the platform overlooking a floor about forty feet below. Man-made stairs ran down a widening sweep. Below, nearly a hundred . . . *creatures* . . . faced us and started screaming, pawing at their eyes. The dozen or so in white made me think of maggots on a dead dog.

Marsha snapped a spear down the stairs. It hit a youngster who had been rushing up when the flare ignited. He tumbled.

"How do you figure chewing it now that you've bitten it off?" Morley asked. He shivered in the cold.

"Sure won't do any good to change our minds. We have to keep pushing, keep them panicked."

He growled at the grolls. I looked out along the line that began in my head, and saw a half-dozen women in white, some leading children born to the blood. I couldn't pick her out.

Morley seemed to be looking for someone, too.

"There they are." Dojango indicated cages to one side. A score of prisoners stared at us, most of them forlornly.

The flare was almost out, but the grolls had shed and opened their packs and were pasting the crowd with fire bombs. Dojango was assembling a powerful lamp. Morley and I snatched bows and scattered arrows wherever it looked like the panic was fading.

I told Morley, "Like the pregnant lady told her guy, it's time we took steps." I started down the stair, again armed with sword and unicorn horn, straining against the weight of my pack of lethal confections. Morley elected the same weapons and snuggled his pack a little tighter. Dojango chose to bear horn and cross-bow. His pack was empty, so he left it. The grolls shrugged their packs back on but didn't arm them-selves with anything but their clubs, which they had dragged in through all the difficulties of the entry cave, tied to their belts and trailing like fat, stiff tails.

"Prisoners first?" Morley asked.

"I wouldn't. Even if they could be trusted they'd get in the way. Straight ahead. Where the women are going. That will be where the masters hole up."

We reached the cavern floor. The grolls went ahead, swinging their clubs. Muttering to himself, Morley minced around an ankle-deep pool of filth. He flicked a toe at a night creature. Some were trying to fight back now.

Tinnie and Rose added shrieks to the uproar. In a free second I saluted them with my sword. They didn't appreciate the gesture.

Morley kicked a human thighbone out of his path. "You ever wondered what bloodslaves feed on while the disease is running its course?"

"No. And I don't want you to tell me."

We climbed toward the gap through which the fe-males had fled. It was a hole maybe four feet tall and three wide. It was clogged with bloodslaves trying to reach the protection of their masters.

The grolls hammered them with all the passion of miners who'd hit a gravel reef.

"And you wanted to bring mules," Morley crowed.

Dojango's crossbow thunked, creaked, thunked again as he sniped at a hero with designs on the lamp we had left at the entrance.

The night people began to press in. Not good. Armed or not, there is only so much that can be done against such numbers.

I still had a few tricks folded up my sleeves and tucked into my boots, but I wanted to hoard those as long as I could.

The grolls opened the hole.

Morley spoke to them. They threw once-human trash
aside and wriggled through. I followed with the lucifer
stone. Morley came last.

Nothing tried coming through after us.

"Well. We made it to the heart of the nest. Just like
the heroes in the old stories. Only that was the hard
part for them. The hard part is just beginning for us."

The brides of blood had ranged themselves before
the stone biers of their lovers, who had not awakened.
There were fifteen of them. In only four had the disease
run its full course. One of those I had faced across a
table in Full Harbor, in a house where I had loved
another in whom the disease was only a few years
along and still reversible. Beside her stood a man
whose face betrayed him as he who had passed me a
note. She shuddered when she met my gaze, slipped
her hand into his.

Well. Did you ever want to cry?

From the hole behind us Dojango said, "They've got
the lamp. And the fires are out. Don't look like they're
up for breaking in here, though."

"Figure we got troubles enough already. She here,
Garrett?"

"Yeah."

"Cut her out of the herd and let's get on with it."

I beckoned Kayean.

She came, eyes downcast, towing the man. The
other brides, and the eight or so bloodslaves with them,
hissed and shuffled.

The tip of Morley's unicorn horn intercepted Kayean's
man and rested on his throat. "Where is he, Clement?"

"Kill him here, Dotes. Don't take him back."

"If I don't take him back, they'll kill me. Where is
he?"

Which was all very interesting.

What the hell was going on?

"Back there." The bloodslaves pointed past the
brides. "Hiding with the children. You won't get him
out without waking the masters." He stared at me,
eyes filled with appeal. "Take her out. Before they
wake up."

An excellent suggestion, and one I would have loved to have put into effect. Except that, though unspoken, we had come in knowing that if we went out again we would be leaving *them* dead behind us.

It had less to do with emotion than necessity. If we left them alive, they would be after us as soon as the sun went down. There would be no outrunning them. And they dared not let us go. They would have the Karentine army all over them as soon as we reported the location of the nest.

"We need to talk, Morley."

"Later. Come out of there, Valentine."

Something stirred, hissed, back among the biers. The hissing formed words, but just barely. "Come get me."

I said, "Folks, things are going to get nasty in a minute. Some are going to die the real death. You don't want it to be you. I'm taking volunteers to sneak out to the big cavern. We pull this off, you can migrate to another nest." And if we didn't we would be their midnight snack.

After a few seconds one of the newer females started toward us, eyes downcast. Most male bloodslaves become what they are by choice. Few women do. They are selected and collected for the masters by night traders like Zeck Zack.

One of the old females objected. She tried to stop the deserter.

Dojango's bolt hit her square in the forehead, driving four inches into her brain,

She fell and flopped around. The bolt wasn't enough to kill her, but plenty to scramble her mind.

I let the volunteer through. "Anybody else?"

The old females looked at the fallen one, listened to the creak of the crossbow rewinding, hissed back and forth, and decided to leave us to the mercy of their masters. One by one, the crowd departed. The little ones too.

They have no loyalty to one another at all.

47

"Kill that thing," Morley snapped. He repeated himself in grollish.

Marsha thumped the flopping woman till she stopped.

"Valentine. Come out."

Hissing again. I raised the lucifer stone overhead so I could look at this creature who so interested Morley Dotes.

Then a lot came together.

I knew that face. Valentine Permanos.

Six years back the kingpin's chief lieutenant, one Valentine Permanos, and his brother Clement had vanished with half the kingpin's fortune. There had been rumors about them running to Full Harbor. Morley would have to come across with more numbers to make it all add up, but I saw enough of the edges to relax with my allies.

"Let's do it, Garrett," Dotes said, getting a two-handed grip on his unicorn horn.

Valentine Permanos began shaking one of the still forms

His face was a horror. They say the swiftness of the disease's progress depends a great deal on the will of its victim. This one was much farther gone than his brother. He *wanted* to become one of *them*.

I recalled old rumors that he had been dying a slow death when he scooted on the kingpin.

Morley drove his horn straight into the heart of the first vampire he reached. So did I. The body shuddered. Its eyes opened for a moment and filled with that look of betrayal, then glazed over.

Morley did another one. So did I. He got a third. I

lined one up. Morley cursed. "Dojango. Throw me another horn."

"That's a hundred marks, Morley. What's wrong with the one you got, actually?"

"It's stuck in his goddamn ribs! Now throw me another horn."

I moved to my fourth victim. My shakes were going away. Six more after this one. Over the hump. We would be headed out in a few minutes.

I drove the horn down.

With no warning, the one Valentine was shaking flung itself toward me.

I twisted away. Dojango's hasty bolt ripped its face open. Morley whacked it with his horn. The ceiling was so low the grolls had to stay on their knees. Still, Doris managed to bounce his club off the vampire's chest.

The monster leaped back from whence it had come, eyes burning, amazed, hissing something we weren't meant to understand. I noted the huge ruby pendant it wore, than grabbed Morley's shoulder and kept him from pursuing it. "Get back here! Now!" I backed up. "That's the bloodmaster himself. Touch me. Everybody touch me."

"What the hell?"

"Do it!"

Hands clasped onto me. "Close your eyes." I palmed a sweaty slip from my sleeve, ripped it open. I counted to ten, expecting claws and fangs to rip me with each beat.

I opened my eyes.

They were all up now. They had their hands to their temples and their maws open in soundless screams. They swayed back and forth with the madness.

"Two minutes!" I yelled. "Less than two minutes to finish it! Let's go!"

I admit I did less than charge headlong. I didn't completely trust the Old Witch's magic. And the bloodmaster looked like he was less than incapacitated.

It was gruesome work, work in which I take no pride even though it was *them* we slaughtered and threw behind us so the grolls could hammer their

heads to pulp. We didn't get through it easily, either,
for even in their two minutes of madness, they knew
they were being attacked. I picked up a dozen shallow
claw gashes that would require careful attention later.
Morley nearly got his throat ripped out because, out
of some weird nobility, he tried to leave the bloodmaster
for me.

Groll clubs hammered that old monster's skull, and
not a second too soon. Dojango was yelling about
goings-on in the big cavern, where the crowd had
decided to get involved after all. Morley was busy
trying to get his prisoner sewed up. I yelled at the
grolls to turn around, then threw Kayean and her guy
out of the way so they wouldn't get stomped. Doris
chucked Dojango back, started stabbing with his club,
driving the bloodslaves back.

I heard a sharp whine, turned.

Morley was pulling a unicorn's horn out of Clement's chest.

I snarled, "That wasn't necessary." I glanced at
Kayean, wondering if she was going to go now. She
sank down beside Clement and held his hand again. I
faced the hole, shucked my pack, and pitched a few fire
bombs past the grolls. That drove the bloodslaves back.

"Let's go!" I ordered. I glanced back. Morley was
on his way, dragging his prisoner. Kayean was rising
reluctantly, her face as cool as the death she'd nearly
become. But Dojango . . .

"Damn you, Dojango, what the hell are you doing?"

"Hey, Garrett. You know what a genuine bloodmaster's bloodstone is worth? Look at this sucker. It
must be three or four thousand years old."

Three or four thousand years. For that long the
monster had preyed upon humanity. I hoped they had
a special place for him where they stoked the fires
especially hot.

I dove through the hole behind the grolls and scattered the rest of my fire bombs and arced a couple of
flares into the crowd. The screaming picked up again.
I dropped to one knee, wooden sword ready, while
the grolls flailed around with unprecedented fury.

A hand dropped onto my shoulder. I glanced up into sad, gentle, possibly forgiving eyes.

Morley plopped pack and prisoner on the other side of me and started flinging his bombs. I heard Dojango's crossbow thunk. Morley asked, "What the hell did you do in there, Garrett?"

"Later."

"I know sorcery when I smell it. What else do you have up your sleeve?"

"Let's free the prisoners and start hiking." The denizens of the pit had faded back, but they were gathering before the steps of the tunnel to the world. They had not given up. If they stopped us, their way of life would remain secure. They could wait until one of their born-to-the-blood children was old enough and tough enough to make himself bloodmaster.

An arrow arced down out of the gloom and thunked into Marsha's shoulder. Someone had gotten to the gear we had left at the entrance to the cavern. What was merely a nuisance to a hide-thick groll could be lethal to the rest of us.

"Move it!" I snarled. "Your meat up top, Dojango."

Rose and Tinnie howled like an alley full of cat fights. We pushed over to the cages. Most of the captives were as colorless as their captors. The night people didn't drain them quickly, like a spider. Most were too far gone to realize what was happening. I was surprised they were even alive. As somebody had said, the Cantard had been too quiet for the hunting to be good. "Hello, Saucerhead." I ignored the women's cage. "Are you going to be as stubborn as usual? I don't want to leave you here."

Give it to Saucerhead. Not much brains but plenty of spunk. He worked up a grin. "No problem, Garrett. I'm unemployed. I got fired on account of I couldn't keep us from getting into this fix."

He had enough wounds to show he'd damned well tried. He was blue with the cold, the artic chill I'd hardly noticed in my frenzy to get in and get out.

"You're free to take a job, then. Consider yourself on retainer."

"You got it, Garrett."

"How about you, Vasco? Still think you can get rich by stopping me? Look here. This is Denny's girl. How much longer you figure she would have been good? A year? Maybe. If you were lucky. All your buddies died for nothing."

"Don't preach at me, Garrett. Don't push. Just get me out of here. I'll bury my own dead." His teeth chattered.

"How about you, Spiney?"

"I never had any quarrel with you, Garrett. I got none now."

"Good enough." There were two Karentine soldiers in with them. They were the worse for wear, too. I didn't think it worth my time to ask if they would give me any grief.

Meantime, Morley chatted up the ladies. They were in a separate cage. Rose was ready to deliver the moon if we would just get her out. *Me* was the word I heard, not *us*. Lovable, thoughtful, family-oriented Rose. Tinnie behaved with as much decorum as the circumstances allowed. I decided to give her a closer look if we ever got out of there.

"Think we ought to turn them loose?" Morley asked.

"Up to you. They might slow us down."

It takes longer to tell than it took to happen. Even so, Dojango decided he'd had enough. "You guys quit jacking around or my brothers and I walk without you." He had the bloodstone and several unicorn horns, and though he was feeling wealthy, he was also worried about living to enjoy his gains.

His crossbow thunked. An instant later an arrow hissed overhead.

"He's got a point, Morley."

Morley spoke to the grolls. They opened all the cages with a few well-placed club strokes. Over Dojango's protests, Morley and I passed out unicorn horns. The grolls tossed our last few flares onto the steps and we headed for freedom.

48

Freedom was a coy bitch.

Our first charge looked like it would carry through. But they swarmed, threw everything at us, utterly determined to keep the secret of the nest. And I mean threw everything: filth, bones, rocks, themselves. And some were almost as tough as their masters. We lost every one of the older prisoners who had tagged along. They were unarmed and as slow as men in a syrup bath.

One of the soldiers fell. Vasco took a wound but managed to keep his feet. I collected another assortment of scratches. Saucerhead went down and had trouble getting up. When Doris grabbed him and started carrying him, the monsters swarmed all over him. I thought he was a goner for sure. When I saw he was still alive, I had to overcome self-disgust for momentarily wishing he'd died so we wouldn't have to drag him out.

Then the night people fell back and were silent. I wondered why, noting there were only about thirty of them left willing to fight. Then I noticed that the last two flares were about to die.

In moments they would have us in their element: darkness.

Time, then, for another one from up my sleeve. One I had expected to have to use earlier than this. "Everybody get in close, here. Leave something sharp-pointed out, face uphill, and close your eyes."

There were those who wanted to ask questions and those who wanted to argue. I lied, "Those who don't do what I say are going to end up blind."

Morley snapped orders in grollish. The triplets did what I wanted. That damned Doris was up and lugging Saucerhead again.

The last flare died.

Rustle and scrape as the night people began moving.

This one was actually in my boot, not up my sleeve. I said, "Close your eyes!" and ripped the paper open.

A blast of sulfurous air overrode the stench of the cavern. Light slammed through my eyelids. Night people shrieked. I counted to ten slowly. "Eyes open. Let's move." The enveloping light had waned to a tolerable glare. The Old Witch had said it was good for several hours. The light was much like that of the sun. The night people found it excruciating. If they didn't get out of it quickly, it would destroy what served them as sanity.

We went up the steps. I ripped rags off a fallen bloodslave, threw them over Kayean to shield her from the light. She was already in pain. Morley and Dojango wanted to stop and play with the bows we had left.

"Get out while you can!" I snarled. "Our luck has been too damned fantastic already. Let's not push it."

Marsha grabbed Dojango and started dragging. Everybody else started hiking. When he saw he would have to play alone, Morley grabbed his booty and joined the retreat.

There was no respite. The tunnel was one place the night people could escape the light. And once free of its maddening influence they became rabid, terrible enemies again.

Nevertheless, we outran them to the mouth of the world.

49

"What the hell is this stuff?" Morley growled as we struggled through the webbing or netting or wire that had materialized in the mouth of the cave during our time below.

"How the hell should I know? Just get through it." I was fussing over Kayean. She hadn't spoken a word yet. But she was whining like a baby. At first I thought it was fear of going out into a world she hadn't seen in years. Then I realized it was because the tangle we were in was wire and the metal's touch hurt.

Who put it there?

My money was on Zeck Zack. But where had he gotten the wire? And what did its presence mean to us?

We broke out. It was broiling, summer hot out there.

"Midnight," Morley groaned. "We were down there longer than I thought."

"Keep moving. Lots to do yet."

We were halfway down to the desert floor when the screaming started behind us. There was pain in it, but it was mostly frustration and rage.

Dojango gasped. "They say those things can recover from almost anything. You think any of the masters will come around?"

I told the truth. "I don't know. We'll tell the army first chance we get."

We hustled across to our camp. There was a three-quarter moon, so the going was quick, though Kayean kept whimpering at the brightness. So did Morley's prisoners. As we climbed to our camp, Dotes said,

"We'll have to pack them in moist earth and wrap them up good to protect them from the sun."

"We have to do some talking, too."

"I suppose so."

"What happened to the major? Tinnie, do you know?"

She was sticking as close to me as Kayean was. "The one who arrested us? I don't know. I guess he got killed when the vampires attacked."

"Vasco. Did you see what happened to him?"

"I was too busy."

"Anybody?"

Rose said, "I thought I saw them carry him away. But maybe I was wrong. He wasn't in the cages when you showed up."

"Maybe they ate him," Dojango suggested.

"We have the right number of bodies," Morley said. Then he gave me a sudden, odd look, as though he suspected me of knowing something I hadn't shared.

I did, but I hadn't shared it only because it had hit me just minutes before. I whispered, "That name that kept turning up on those have-you-heard-of lists. The one I'd heard but couldn't remember? I remembered."

"And?"

"A legendary Venageti agent. Supposedly a shape-shifter. Also supposedly caught and killed. But if he was, why are some folks—with Venageti connections—so interested in him?"

"I don't know and I don't think I want to know. All I'm interested in now is moving myself from this godforsaken here to there where I can sit down to my first healthy meal in a month. But I suppose we have to protect ourselves. You think we rescued him?"

"There's a chance."

"Which one?"

"Take your pick."

"Not the women?"

"No. One would know the other had changed. I'd vote for someone about his size."

"Always assuming he's still with us."

"Always assuming that."

We were pleasantly surprised to find our camp as

we had left it, unplundered and the horses uneaten and patiently waiting. Morley sent Marsha off for a load of moist earth. He assumed the job of sentinel. The rest of us doctored one another. When I was satisfied that I wouldn't succumb to the disease through my wounds, I hunted for Dotes. He was perched on a boulder contemplating the desert between our camp and the mesa. He said, "You haven't said a word to her."

"I'll talk to her when she wants to talk. For now I'm satisfied with her letting me bring her out after what you did to Clement. It's time you explained the latest moves in Morley's Game."

"I suppose. Otherwise you'll badger me incessantly. You knew that six years ago the kingpin's number one walked with half his plunder."

"Old news. I also heard that he and his brother ran off to Full Harbor."

"It took them a couple of years to find that out. The kingpin sent some men down. They must have stirred things up the same way we did. Something happened to them. They only got one report back. It said Valentine wasn't in Full Harbor anymore, and that after a fast romance, his brother had married a local girl named Kronk. She had gone off with her husband when he followed his brother wherever."

"Then you knew all along who she married."

"Yeah. But telling you wouldn't have helped you find her. His trail was already covered."

I controlled my anger. "So the kingpin sent you down here."

"Not exactly. I volunteered. When you asked me to join up with you, it was like the answer to a virgin's prayer. An honest-to-god miracle. The kingpin was ready to list my name with those sleeping among the fishes. It was an out. I went and told him the story and said I would get Valentine if we could call it even. He bought it. He wants Valentine a lot worse than he ever wanted me. So I went ahead and hooked up with you, betting the longest odds I ever played, hoping you could find the woman and she would have lasted longer with Clement than she did with you or your buddy."

For a while we stared at the desert. Shapes moved there, but none came our way. They didn't have the fully developed senses of their masters. Finally, Morley started talking again.

"I didn't have the foggiest where it was going till we walked into that place of Zeck Zack's and found those vampires waiting. Then it clicked. The evidence was there all along. I knew Valentine back when. He was dying a slow death and he had no more conscience than a shark. For him it was the logical way to dodge death. He probably took the money in case he needed to buy his way in. Knowing him, he probably figured on being bloodmaster within fifty years."

"So. The loose ends begin to come together. But there's still one big one hanging out. Who were the people on that ship with the striped sail? What were they doing? Why were they interested in us?"

I had an idea and I thought Morley's confessions lent it strong circumstantial support. But I meant to reserve that. It might prove useful. I wasn't convinced that those people were out of the game.

"Why take Valentine back?" I asked.

"For the kingpin's peace of mind. And mine. I don't want him doubting for a minute."

I glanced out at the desert. "What are they doing?" Those who had come out of the nest behind us were scampering around like blind mice.

"I don't know. But I'll give you another loose end. Zeck Zack."

"Not much we can do about him."

"I should have cut his throat.'"

"And you criticize me for what red meat does to me?"

"Marsha's back. Let's pack our prizes."

"What are we going to feed them?"

"Let them get hungry. They'll eat what we give them." He dropped off his boulder. "Where do we go now?"

"Back to Full Harbor. Take a peek through the centaur's tunnel. See how much excitement there is about us. I hate to leave our stuff if we don't have to. Buying new would stretch the budget too far."

"That innkeeper probably sold everything already."

"We'll see. Keep a watch on our friends. Just in case the major is with us." I had a couple tricks up my sleeve yet, one of which would probably give me the major, but I didn't want to use them if I didn't have to. Magics of the sort I had gotten from the Old Witch were too precious to squander.

We packed our prizes, as Morley dubbed them, in the earth Marsha brought, wet them down, bundled them up, and loaded them on the wagon. Tired though we were, I wanted to be traveling with first light.

Before I folded my blanket over Kayean's face, she met my gaze directly for the first time and rewarded me with a feeble smile.

The nineteen-year-old Marine was still alive. He could be touched.

50

Vasco and Saucerhead also went into the wagon, with a moderately carved-up soldier on the driver's seat. Doris insisted he was capable of helping Marsha pull. Fine. Let him if he wanted. Let him bleed to death. I wasn't his mother.

Mrs. Garrett taught her boys never to argue with grolls.

We put the women on horseback. Everyone else would walk, like it or not.

We were ready to head out when Morley summoned me to his boulder. "Bring the spyglass."

When I got there I heard it. It came from the direction of the cave. I trained the glass. There was barely enough light. "The ones who came out can't get back inside."

"Oh, my. Isn't that sad." Then he muttered something else, and pointed.

"Oh, my twice or thrice," I said. "I guess this means we slip out the back door."

"Yep. Papa's coming home. Jodie goes out the window and keeps moving fast. It won't take him long to figure we got out again."

I could hear them now as well as see them. "I never saw so many in one mob before. He must have rounded up his whole tribe." I guessed there were at least five hundred centaurs. Their advance was a movement of precision to be envied by any cavalry commander. They changed directions and formations as easily and quickly as a flock of birds, and with no more apparent signaling.

"Let's not sit here talking about it while they just prance up and grab us."

"Good thinking." We got moving.

Zeck Zack and his people didn't interfere with us at all, though I'm certain their scouts knew where we were. We hastened eastward as fast as we could hoof it, with me sort of hanging around the rear, staring at backs, wondering which, if any, was the major.

News of Glory Mooncalled's adventure had reached every cranny of the Cantard. The land was coming to life. Three times we went into hiding while soldiers passed. They were all headed south. The smallest lot were Venageti rangers. No telling what they were up to when they heard and decided to head home. I didn't care as long as they didn't want to include me in their game of kings.

Morley and I both watched our companions more closely than we did the rangers. The major, if he was with us, didn't give himself away. Not that I expected him to, but I wasn't missing any chances.

We kept on until everyone was stumbling, and kept on still. What Zeck Zack might want to do with us we had no idea, but he had no cause to be friendly. And there were the other perils of the Cantard, which Glory Mooncalled had conjured to life like a shower livens the plants of the desert. It seemed we couldn't go five miles without some sort of alarm. The nights were more friendly than the days.

We reached the abandoned mill without falling into misfortune. I began to feel optimistic. "We'll rest here a day or two," I announced.

Some of my comrades by circumstance wanted to argue. I told them, "Take it up with the grolls. If you can whip them, go do what you want." I wasn't feeling a bit democratic.

The only would-be sneak-off was Rose.

I had to give the little witch credit for being stubborn and determined. No matter what, she was going to keep after Denny's legacy until she got it. She worked on Morley, but he had reached a state where he had nothing on his mind but watercress sandwiches. She worked on Saucerhead, but he had signed on with my squad and the gods themselves couldn't have moved him until I released him. She worked on Vasco, but he was completely introspective, interested only in going home. She worked on Spiney Prevallet, but he said he'd had his fill of pie in the sky by and by and told her to go to hell.

She decided to take the future by the horns herself.

I caught her with a sharpened piece of firewood trying to decide the best place to stick it into the bundle containing Kayean. I'm afraid I lost my temper. I sprawled her across my lap and applied the stick to her posterior.

Morley said, "You should have left her with her spiritual family."

She gave him a look to sear steel.

I think his remark hurt her more than the spanking, though a person of her temperament was the sort to turn the thrashing into a grudge worth nursing for years. It sent her off to sit alone and reweave her skein of self-justification. Come the next night, while we were waiting for Dojango to come back with a report on our standing in the city, she decided to go her own way.

Morley reported her defection. "Shall we let her go?"

"I guess not. Chances are she'd get herself enslaved or killed, and I have an obligation to her family. We know she won't learn from experience, so there's no point letting her suffer for education's sake. And if she did get through, she'd just set us up for something unpleasant."

Tinnie was sitting beside me, her shoulder half an inch from mine. We'd been rehashing those things men and women talk about when they have other things on their minds.

"You really ought to ditch her, Garrett." Morley sighed.

Tinnie said, "His conscience wouldn't let him. And neither would yours, Morley Dotes."

He laughed. "Conscience? What conscience? I'm too sophisticated to have one and Garrett is too simple."

I said, "Go get her, Morley. And put hobbles on her."

Once he had gone, Tinnie asked, "Would he really let her . . . ?"

"Pay him no nevermind, Red. We talk that way. But it's just talk."

Rose was not fighting when Marsha lugged her back into the circle of light cast by our fire. The fight was out of her. Morley came to report, "She ran into something out there. We scared it off. She won't say what it was, but you might consider a double watch and maybe a prayer for Dojango."

"Right." I took care of it and resumed my seat, considering Rose across the fire, feeling moody.

Tinnie touched my arm and said, "Garrett, when we get home . . ."

"If we get home is soon enough to talk about when we get home." It came out more curt than I'd intended. She fell into a silence as sullen as my own.

51

Dojango waited until afternoon to return. His report was exactly what I wanted to hear. Nobody in Full Harbor was the least interested in a band of nosies from TunFaire. Nothing unusual had taken place while we were away. All the talk was about Glory Mooncalled and the epic dust-up taking shape down south. Our things were still at the inn, being preserved by an innkeeper who felt kindly disposed because we had left him the clothing and possessions of those thugs we'd thrown into the streets mother-naked.

"Or so he says," Dojango editorialized. "Actually."

"We'll watch him. Let's get it packed up. I want to hit that tunnel as soon after dark as we can. Did you make the other arrangements?"

"No trouble. They'll be delivered to the back door of the inn. They should be waiting when we get there."

"What about shipping complications?"

"Shouldn't be any, actually. It's done all the time. Every ship headed north carries a few for families that can afford it. Strictly routine, actually."

"Good. Morley. One problem left, and tonight would be the time for it to make itself apparent." We wandered away from the others slowly, keeping our backs toward them.

"You have any candidate in mind?" he asked.

"Pressed, I'd have to call Vasco's name. But he's the only one I know well enough to know he's not acting normal. And he's got good enough reasons."

"You have a move in mind? A test?"

226

"Right after we come out of the tunnel. I want Dojango, Marsha, and Saucerhead to go through first. You and me and Doris will bring up the rear. If we load the rest down with what has to be carried, they'll be surrounded and have their hands full when it happens."

"You could go to work for the kingpin, scheming like that."

"I've got to bring it off before it's any good. This isn't some stupid kid we can pluck like some ripe pear. He's going to have moves and plans of his own."

"We wouldn't have it any other way, would we?"

We ventured back. During the afternoon's course we passed the word on the night's festivities. Though some were not pleased with my dispositions, they were all realistic enough to understand that I would put people I trusted most where they would do the most good.

That was the disposition we assumed when we broke camp, except for having the grolls take turns pulling the wagon. I told Saucerhead he could ride until we neared the wall, but he insisted that he had healed enough to hike. Vasco and the wounded soldier also hoofed it, saying they wanted to keep loose. Morley and I trudged along eating everybody's dust.

A time or two I moved up to make sure Kayean's wrappings were holding. After the second check I dropped back and said, "I've noticed you haven't done anything to keep your prize from starving."

Kayean threw up almost everything I gave her. When I unwrapped her, I had to make certain her hands and feet were bound. I had clipped her claws first chance after we had come out of the nest. She still had her teeth and the hunger was upon her, though when she was rational she was game enough in battling the disease.

"You also notice he's gone into the long sleep that gets them when they're starving. He'll last till we make TunFaire. And that's all I need."

Much as I disliked the deed itself, I now suspected

that Morley had done the best thing by killing Clement. Clement's death had freed Kayean.

Without a word having been exchanged I somehow understood that she had marched through the doorway to hell only because that was the pathway her husband had taken and she was a wither-thou-goest kind of lady. For his part, I think Clement made his move sixty percent out of conscience and remorse, forty percent out of spite. Kayean wasn't wearing white because she was his bride. One of the masters had taken her from him.

I hoped she hadn't been forced to bear one of their soulless brats. I didn't believe any woman could recover from that.

It all went perfectly, with rescuees carrying our prizes into the tunnel. It was spacious enough for the wagon, but I didn't want to be found roaming the streets with army property I couldn't explain having. We could hire something on the other side.

Morley and I were fifty feet from the tunnel's end, with Doris behind us, when it happened.

Up ahead Marsha started booming his lungs out.

"Damn it!" Morley swore. He translated, "Ambush. Nine men, one woman. Striped-sail bunch. They must have made Dojango while he was in town."

"I wanted to hold on to this forever," I said, dipping into a boot. "Grab on to me. Tell Doris, too."

Beyond the tunnel's end Rose started yelling. "Garrett! Help! Morley!"

Morley muttered, "Shut up, you stupid bitch."

"Stupid? She figures she just solved her whole problem for nothing."

Rose's yelling stopped with a smack so loud we heard it back in the tunnel.

"Against the wall," I said. They held onto me. I ripped the paper spell open. Two seconds later four guys with swords galloped into the tunnel, ready for anything. They looked around and didn't find it.

One yelled, "Ain't nothing in here."

I didn't hear the reply. They withdrew.

"What now?" Morley breathed.

"As long as we move slowly and don't make any noise or any sudden moves, they won't see us or know where we are. We'll slide out and see what's going on."

What was going on was that the two thugs I knew from the striped-sail ship, with a woman who appeared to be in charge, and seven other men, had my folks lined up against a wall in the storage basement where the tunnel began. Marsha they kept contained with a ballista almost as heavy as a field piece.

In half a minute their questions made it obvious they were after a specific person, but didn't mind trampling a few others along the way. My folks just looked at them, baffled, except Rose, who put on a great crying act. I gathered that Tinnie's was the hand that had reddened her cheek.

"Well?" Morley whispered. "We can take them if Doris gets that ballista."

"We don't need any blood in it. We'll bluff. You go over there and yell for everybody to freeze when Doris busts up the ballista. I'll put a knife to the lady's throat. Take these." I gave him a couple of throwing stars from my collection of un-Garrett-like weapons.

He needed no further explanation. He told Doris what to do. We parted. I drifted toward the lady commander, no doubt the woman about whom Master Arbanos had been so dubious. Dojango had begun yammering at her, explaining that everyone else in the several parties that had gone out of the city had been killed by unicorns or vampires.

"What the hell was that?" asked one of the men at the ballista, whirling around. "Skipper, is this place haunted?"

A ballista went up in the air and shattered against the joists supporting the floor above.

Morley yelled, "Everybody freeze!"

I laid the edge of my knife on the woman's throat and whispered, "This is your friendly spook. Don't even breathe fast. Good. Now, I suggest you have your boys put down their tools."

Doris pounded three or four men out of sheer youthful exuberance. Morley tripped and head-kicked Ugly One when he took a notion to turn on me.

The lady gave the order. And added, "You're interfering with royal business. I'll have your—"

"Not at all. I have a damned good idea what you're looking for and I'll be happy to help you find it. I just don't want my people getting chewed up while you're getting your man. Do you have some way to pick him out of a crowd?"

"Pick who out?" Oh, she wanted to play coy.

"Are you the only person ever born with a brain? This is your stalking horse talking. I figured your crowd out a month ago," I lied. I backed her up a careful five steps and in plain voice vented the moment's inspiration. "I also figured out that Big One there is on the other side. He tried to kill me in Leifmold, which would have just ruined your whole scheme."

Big One started moving toward the nearest weapon.

Two throwing stars hit him, followed in an instant by a grollish fist.

The woman said, "That explains one hell of a lot. I thought we were snakebit. All right. What do you want, Garrett?"

"For me and mine to be left the hell alone. Take your man if you can pick him out. I'm all for that because I don't like what he's got planned for me. Hell. I'll narrow it down for you. I've been working on it. I know who he's not. If he's anybody. He could have been killed out there. A lot of men were."

I gave orders. The women, Saucerhead, Dojango, and Marsha, the latter three lugging Kayean and Valentine, moved to one side. I said, "Do your shopping among what's left."

"Will you let me go?"

"Why not? You don't seem to be a suicidal lady."

"You're going to find out if you call me lady one more time."

Morley snickered. "You've made a friend for life, Garrett."

What she had to say to him does not bear repetition. She asked me, "What's in those bundles?"

"What I came after." I turned her loose.

Morley was flickering around the edges because of too many hasty movements. So was Doris. I had stayed slow, though, so I figured I was still good. I tiptoed after the woman who was not a lady.

She examined the crop, dipped a hand into a pocket, brought out an amulet built around a piece of amber with an insect embedded.

Spiney Prevallet went from somnolent indifference to explosive fury so suddenly I would have been astounded if I'd had time. He knocked the amulet away with one hand and seized the woman's throat with the other.

I pricked the wrist of that hand with my knife, sliced his cheek, then got back out of the way because that—pardon the expression—lady was going to work.

I found a part of me glad the villain had not been Vasco.

Spiney ran for it. The woman snagged her amulet and raced after him. Her minions—those still upright—did nothing because they weren't sure what we would let them do.

"Fade," Morley suggested.

"Yes."

Dojango was many things, some of them things I didn't like, but he was not stupid. The moment he saw some folks preoccupied, he started getting other people out of there.

Spiney tried for the exit himself and ran head-on into a grollish fist. The woman jumped him immediately, forced the amulet into his mouth while he was still groggy.

He began to *change.*

I have heard that a shapeshifter has no true shape of its own. That it does not even have a sex as we know it, but just splits into unequal masses when it comes time to reproduce. I don't know.

Spiney changed into the major, then into a character who looked vaguely piratical, then into a woman vaguely familiar, apparently regressing through identities assumed in the past.

Everyone else was out. I wasn't curious enough to stay and see the ultimate form the Venageti agent assumed. I had no reason to presume any excess of good will on the part of the striped-sail people.

52

It was a dawn-threatening hour when we reached the inn. I had let the soldiers go their ways, betting they would be so happy to get back alive that they'd cause no immediate grief. Morley and I had an argument. He thought we should have fed them to the striped-sail gang, who would have kept them busy answering questions while we got out of town.

A brief interview with the innkeeper confirmed my suspicions in that direction. He had kept our quarters open and had maintained our gear intact at the behest of the striped-sail crowd, who had hoped we would come back so they could catch our trail again. Which they had done with Dojango's visit.

I slept like the dead for five hours, then went out looking for transportation home. My luck was limited. I went back and announced, "First ship with room enough for all of us doesn't leave till day after tomorrow. The Glory Mooncalled situation has the fainter-hearted civilians heading north. The scow I did find is a garbage pail, but the next best chance means waiting more than a week." I did not mention that even this sleaziest of transports had stretched my remaining expense money to its limit. We'd all get hungry if it was a very long passage home.

I sat beside Morley. "I'll never take another job that takes me out of TunFaire, even if there's a hundred thousand in it for me."

"Speaking of money, when are we going to get paid? It's not critical to me because I didn't sign on for the pay. But the triplets did and they're starting to wonder."

"It'll have to wait till I can corner Tate and gouge him again. I committed what I had left to getting us home."

"They're trusting you, Garrett. Don't disappoint them."

"You know me better. I'll get my money out of Tate, one way or another, and you guys will get yours. Dojango! Where are those boxes?" He'd just come in. "You didn't drink up that money I gave you, did you?"

"Actually, I just came to tell you they're here, on a wagon out back. The landlord is having a fit that they might upset his customers if we bring them inside."

Morley grumbled, "I'll go have a fit of dancing on his head."

We put our prizes into their caskets that night. They were the standard, cheap shipper coffins folks from up north bought to bring their sons home from the war. Dojango admitted that he had gotten some drinking done. He had gotten a buy on the coffins because the long quiet spell in the Cantard had caused a depression in the Full Harbor casket industry.

I was irritated but didn't press.

After dark I took my prize out and got her cleaned up before I installed her in her coffin. Tinnie helped with the trickier parts and Kayean wasn't too much trouble. She didn't do any screaming.

I wondered what sorcery went into the creation of those white gowns. Kayean's refused to be damaged and soil would not cling.

Morley was less fastidious. He put some fresh dirt in the other box, unwrapped his prize, dumped it in, began nailing the lid down. He had to ask Marsha's help when the pounding wakened Valentine and he started screaming and trying to break out.

We'd just gotten him quieted down and the landlord off our backs again when Zeck Zack came calling.

The centaur came alone and started out friendly enough. He pranced in, looked us over, asked, "Did you bring her out, Mr. Garrett?"

"Yes."

"May I see her? I haven't seen her since she followed her idiot husband into shadow. Her and her
damned twisted sense of what is right. I should have
stopped her somehow."

"Might have been nice."

Morley and Saucerhead gave him ferocious scowls.
Tharpe didn't know him at all. I feared there would be
sparks. But he disarmed them by saying, "I never laid
a hand on her and I never would. Despite my reputation. And not just because her father was a friend of
mine."

As Morley had observed before, another one.

I opened the casket. She was sleeping. The centaur
looked for a while, then backed off. "That's enough.
Close it. Can she be cured, Mr. Garrett?"

"I think we reached her in time. She fought it all the
way. I think she's got enough left."

"Good. Then we can get down to business. Someone among you took something from the nest that
rightfully belongs to my people."

That drew some puzzled looks.

"The bloodmaster's amulet. His symbol of power.
The nest's bloodstone."

I don't know who started laughing first.

He gathered his dignity like a cloak. "Gentlemen, I
went through years of hell and humiliation in order to
find that gateway so my folk could cleanse that nest
and gain enough booty and bounty money to migrate
out of the Cantard. You can have your two bloodslaves.
One of them I owe, and the other isn't worth enough
to make a difference. But everything else in that hole
is mine!"

We exchanged looks. Dojango was getting nervous.
I didn't want to start anything, but I wasn't going to
tolerate the centaur's tone, either. "You've got more
balls than brains if you think you can walk in here
talking like that. You could get yourself hurt."

"I don't have any swords hanging over my head
now, Mr. Garrett. And I have friends in town who will
be happy to help me recover my property."

"Now that's an interesting coincidence," I said. "Just yesterday I made a new friend, a lady down from TunFaire rounding up the Venageti priest's friends. I wasn't going to mention your name."

He stared at me a moment, decided my bluff needed calling. "Go ahead. Meantime, get that bloodstone out to my place before sundown tomorrow or find Kayean a new guardian."

"He's insane," Morley said. "You should have let me kill him when I wanted to. It's going to be trickier doing it here."

Zeck Zack said, "A large group of my friends are waiting in the street. They'd rather not disturb anything in such a public place, but they will come in if I'm not out in a reasonable time."

"Go on," I said. "Get out. Before I call *your* bluff."

He went, but left an admonition to get the bloodstone to him by next sundown. Or else.

Dojango asked, "You're not going to give it to him, are you, Garrett?"

Morley snarled, "We're going to give it to him, all right. Only it ain't going to be what he wants."

I said, "Take it easy, Morley. Think. He's trying to set us up."

"I know. And it's going to be a shame to abort his scheme because it's a wowser for a creature as mentally handicapped as a centaur. We've got plenty of time. Let's get some sleep and worry about it tomorrow."

53

I woke up very late, and what dragged me from dreamland was Saucerhead Tharpe and the grolls stomping in. I popped up. I'd been left alone with the women and Vasco. I checked myself for knife wounds.

"Where're Morley and Dojango? What have you guys been up to?"

"Around somewhere," Saucerhead said in his slow way. "I think Morley said something about getting something decent to eat. We took the coffins and most of our stuff down to the ship so we'd be ready to go tomorrow morning."

I grumbled a bit and went for a breakfast of my own. I didn't worry much until afternoon rolled around and still there was no sign of Morley or Dojango. I started fisheying Saucerhead, who had something on his conscience and was doing a poor job of hiding it. Then I found the bodies.

Actually, they weren't bodies. They were Kayean and Valentine, bundled up and concealed under some odds and ends and junk and straw left from when the place had been a stable. Then I knew what Morley had done.

Saucerhead looked relieved. He told me, "He said just sit tight and pretend they're around somewhere if anybody asks."

Two minutes later I noticed that my last paper spell fold was missing. I couldn't guess what Morley planned to do with it since there was no way he could know what would happen when he opened it. I tried fifty lines of reasoning but fixed on none of them. There was no predicting a darkelfin breed like Morley.

When afternoon gave way to evening I started prowling. The grolls got restless, too, and might have gone off if they hadn't the strictest of orders. My game of tease with Tinnie lost its savor. Rose got nervous because everyone else was, though she didn't know what was going on. Only Saucerhead was able to relax. I have to fight the temptation to say that it was because he wasn't smart enough.

Nothing happened until just before midnight, when one of Zeck Zack's "friends" came to chide us for not having delivered. I told him, "We're right here waiting whenever he wants a piece of us. Tell him he'd better bring a box lunch because it's going to take awhile to get the job done."

The messenger departed a little flustered.

I wondered how the centaur's nerves were doing, out in the graveyard or wherever he was planning to take us when we tried sneaking up on him. I was willing to bet he'd planned for every contingency but us sitting tight. I hoped Morley hadn't walked into any of his plans.

Two hours later the handful of people left in the common room began buzzing. I went to find out why. Rumors were flying about a large fire out in the Narrows Hills. One of the mansions there.

Morley's opening move, I presumed.

There was nothing more for another three hours, then Dojango stumbled in, wounded, pale, barking in grollish. He flopped down as Doris and Marsha stamped out.

"Well?" I demanded.

"They're going to pick up the coffins."

I looked him over. Tinnie helped. She had a fair touch with wounds.

"That all you have to tell me?"

"Morley sent me back 'cause I got hurt, actually. He's still out there working them. If that critter gets out of this alive, it sure won't be on the cheap." And that was all he would say.

Awhile later the grolls came tramping back in with the coffins. The landlord was right behind them raising hell about our bunch stomping back and forth through the common room during quiet hours. "I'm never leaving TunFaire again," I promised myself once more, and snarled. "Quit your bitching. You've made a bundle because of us, playing all the sides, and we'll be out of your hair in an hour anyway. Do us all a favor and make yourself disappear."

I looked so nasty he had no trouble getting the hint.

We refilled and sealed the coffins and gathered what remained of our possessions. For Tinnie and Rose and Vasco and Saucerhead Tharpe that meant no work at all. Their adventures had left them with nothing but the clothing on their backs. I wondered if I ought to put a burr under Dojango's saddle, recalling how meticulously he had gone over the ruins of their last encampment, salvaging coins and jewelry the night people had discarded. I decided the wiser course was to keep everyone dependent upon my charity.

We marched out to the sighs of the landlord and his crew.

We reached and boarded our ship without suffering misadventure.

Time passed. The tide turned. The sailors prepared to cast off. And still there was no sign of Morley.

"Where the hell is he, Dojango?"

"He said don't worry. He said go ahead. He said don't hold up anything on his account." Dojango said it, but he didn't feel it. He wanted to do something.

I didn't believe it. Morley Dotes wouldn't sacrifice himself for anyone.

"Here he comes," Saucerhead said. The deck crew was paying out the last lines, fore and aft.

He was coming for sure, in that sort of wild sprint only elfin can manage. Zeck Zack was thirty yards behind and gaining fast.

"Perfect," Dojango whispered.

Perfect, like hell. Morley wasn't going to make it without help. I looked around for a weapon and couldn't find anything.

"Now!" Dojango said. And, "Actually!"

The striped-sail woman and her crew materialized

from amid the freight on the pier. They all carried ready crossbows. Morley whipped past. Zeck Zack skidded to a halt, stood there shuddering. Morley leaped from the pier to the ship, teeth glistening in a grin.

"Is this the one?" the woman called.

"The very one, darling," Morley gasped.

The gang closed in on the centaur.

"You damned fool!" I yelled at Morley. "You could have been killed."

"But, if you'll notice, I wasn't."

54

The passage north was slower than it had been going south. The winds were less friendly. But it was almost as eventless. There was a spot of trouble one night when Rose tried pushing Kayean over the side, but she collected only bruises for her trouble. There were no encounters with pirates, privateers, Venageti, or even Karentine naval vessels. We made Leifmold and I almost believed the gods had decided to lay off me for a while.

Rose's assault on Kayean was due to my lack of foresight.

I was taking her out of her box at night, giving her the chance to breathe real air and face the real light of the stars. Foodwise I had gotten her to where she could keep down small amounts of lightly browned chicken flesh. I'd left her on deck to fetch some, and had gotten into an argument with Tinnie, who felt I should be apportioning my time somewhat differently. Rose made her move and took her lumps in my absence. I found out what was happening only when one of the ship's night watch told me Rose needed saving.

I got there in time, though Kayean almost crossed the line and surrendered to the hunger. Rose crawled away, into the comforting arms of a Morley getting back to his cynical ways.

I calmed and fed Kayean and we sat in the starlight awhile, watching the wake luminesce and the flying fish leap. She finally spoke. "Where are you taking me?"

Her words were barely intelligible. Down in the nests, it is said, they don't allow their brides to talk. She was rusty.

No one had told her what was going on. I'd just snatched her and dragged her along, giving her as much control of her destiny as she'd had while she was in the pit.

So I told her the story, and I wound up saying, "I think you ought to grab it. Denny wanted you to have it, and right now it's the only thing you've got going in this whole world."

She gave me a look that took me back in time. I had to take her down and put her away before I did something foolish. I returned to the deck to watch the sea unscramble my brain.

Morley came out of the darkness and settled beside me. After a while, he said, "I have a statistic I want you to consider, Garrett. Of all the guys who have loved her, only one is still alive." Then he was gone. The superstitious half-breed.

Later I took advantage of Tinnie's conciliatory mood to lay my haunts for a while.

Fate had us overhaul *Binkey's Sequin* running up the Leifmold channel and I cut a deal with Master Arbanos even before we made the quay. He was vastly amused to see me saddled with Rose and Tinnie again.

We laid over three days in Leifmold, waiting for Master Arbanos to offload a cargo of army supplies and take on twenty-five tons of smoked cod. Morley split his time between getting fat eating green leafies and keeping Rose too busy to get into trouble. The triplets sold one of their unicorn horns and went on a toot. I think Vasco spent his time thinking about doing himself in. The rest of us just waited, with me lending a thought or ten to my routine once we reached TunFaire.

I still had to get myself and my associates paid.

55

We tied up at *Sequin's* place on the TunFaire waterfront late in the afternoon, which pleased me to no end. Eager as we were to escape the smell of fish and visit old haunts, there were things Morley and I had to get done before our return became known. Keeping control until sunset was less difficult because it was only for a short time.

After hard dark fell, we all trooped off and slithered around the city's back ways to the back door of Morley's place, where everyone and everything, willing and unwilling, went into temporary hiding. I sneaked off to get some advice from the Dead Man while Morley worried about how he was going to consummate his arrangement with the kingpin.

He had asked Saucerhead and me to be his bodyguards when the meet went down, for which he would "gladly pay your standard fees—as soon as Garrett delivers me my wages for the last couple of months." I figured he had delivered above and beyond the call, if mainly to save his own hide, and I could do him a favor in return. Saucerhead signed on because he'll do any damned fool thing as long as he's getting paid.

I swear I did *not* know what he was going to pull.

The Dead Man acted like I'd just stepped out half an hour ago and had just given him time to work into a comfortable snooze before I came clanging and banging. After having fulfilled his reputation for being cranky, he asked for my story. For five hours I gave it to him. He didn't interrupt often as he didn't need more information for anything. He thought my precautions against getting stiffed by Willard Tate would prove needless, but supposed they would hurt nothing.

We talked tough at each other a little while I cleaned up around there, then I hightailed it back to Morley's to grab thirteen winks before I walked into the Tates' den.

News from the Cantard was all the talk when I got back. You miss a lot when you're traveling.

It seemed that when all the armies and half armies and whatnots had turned up at Indigo Springs for the big soirée that would determine who kept the water hole, Glory Mooncalled was gone. Without a trace except a friendly note to the Venageti warlords on his list.

I liked the guy's style.

I was grinning when I went to work on the Tate gate by dawn's early light. "I'll get a little of my own back here."

A sleepy apprentice finally opened up. He was too addled to recognize me.

"How's the arm? Looks good. I need to see the old man."

"It's you!"

"I think so. Last time I looked it was world-famous me, back with the goods from the wars."

He dashed away, which is something people don't ordinarily do, yelling all the way. I closed the gate behind me and waited.

I have to admit that Willard Tate was a lot sharper at that hour than I will ever be. By the time the kid led me in, there were steaming cups of tea set out. His first words were, "Sit down. Breakfast will be ready in ten minutes." He looked at me expectantly.

I set my accounts down beside my tea, got comfortable, took me a sip, and said, "I've got her. Tinnie and Rose, too. If you want them."

That old man was downright spooky. He glanced at what I'd placed on the table, considered my choice of words, gave a nod that said he understood the situation, and asked, "What is she like?"

"Like nothing you ever imagined. Like nothing I ever dreamed, either, even in a nightmare."

He reached for the accounts. "May I?"

I pushed them toward him.

"Tell me about it while I'm looking at these."

The version I gave him was more tightly edited than the one the Dead Man had gotten, but I didn't leave out anything he needed to know. To say he was surprised would be putting it mildly. To say he took it all well would be understating. The short version took two hours and skirted the worst behavior of females surnamed Tate. I think he caught wind of what I left out, though.

When I finished, he said, "I've checked and you have a reputation for being honest with your expenses. Bizarre and substantial as these are, I suppose they're justified. Considering."

"The advance covered almost everything but salaries," I informed him. "Between us we're maybe a hundred out of pocket, mainly because of the cost of bringing the girls home."

Tate grunted, shoved the accounts back. "You'll have the balance before you leave."

"And my executor's fees?"

"That's in the hands of the probate. When can I expect delivery?"

"Tonight. But very late. Probably after midnight. I have to help Morley with something first." Morley's business had gotten lost in the editing.

"All right. I guess it will have to do." Then he let me in on why he was being so understanding. "Would you be interested in taking another job? After you've recuperated from this one?"

I raised an eyebrow.

"You know the major portion of our business is army boots. The most expensive component of a boot is sole leather. Army specs require thunder-lizard hide for soles. We have our own contract hunters and tanners, trustworthy men all. I thought. But of late the shipments have been short."

I saw where he was going and shut him out. I had turned out to be crazy enough to go into the Cantard, but I will never be the screaming sort of psychotic who goes into thunder-lizard country. Besides, I'd made myself a promise never to leave TunFaire again and I never break a promise to myself without my self's prior permission.

I let him talk. When he ran dry I said I would give it a think and got the hell out with my expense money, knowing I would shriek a big "No!" the second I had my executor's fees in hand.

56

Morley had set his meet on wooded creekside ground at the boundary between the real world and the high city of the dukes and barons and stormwardens and whatnot. It was a place often employed for such encounters. Any uproar, as might be caused by treachery, would bring an army of high city protectors down on everyone.

Over the years the formula and etiquette of a "brookside" have become fixed. As proposer, Morley set the time of the meet and the size of each party. He picked an hour after sundown and four people. It would take four of us to lug Valentine's coffin. Dojango, Saucerhead, and I would back him.

The kingpin, on agreeing, got to pick which end of brookside was his, and could come early if he wanted, to check the grounds for signs of treachery. Morley was not permitted an early survey.

The kingpin agreed to meet. An hour after sunset I was helping carry a coffin uphill, into a situation that seemed to me to be of no special value to either of the principals. The kingpin's reputation said he was good for his word. If he'd made promises to Morley, he would keep them. I couldn't understand why he had agreed to the meet—unless his hatred for Valentine had overcome his good sense.

Morley Dotes was a tough and tricky independent, known to be in need of money, and TunFaire boasted a dozen men willing to pay large sums for the kingpin's life.

We went up with Morley and Dojango in front, me and Saucerhead in back, so we bigger guys got most of the weight. We parked the coffin carefully. Morley stayed beside it. The rest of us fell back ten steps and kept our hands in plain sight.

After a while a shadow left the poplars opposite us and came over to Morley. "He's in the box?"

"Yes."

"Open it."

Morley lifted the lid carefully from the foot end.

"Looks like it could be him. Hard to tell in this light."

Morley slammed the lid shut. "Go get a torch, then." He kicked the coffin. "This guy isn't going anywhere."

The kingpin's man went away. I hoped Saucerhead and I were back far enough not to be recognized. I was getting a bad, bad feeling.

There was some talk in the woods. Then somebody struck a spark. A torch flared.

Saucerhead said, "Let's get out of here, Garrett," and began backing up. I noted that Dojango had already vanished. Morley was easing away from the coffin. I drifted with Saucerhead, got myself behind a nice bush. Tharpe kept going. Morley held up about five feet from my side of the box.

The kingpin and his troops marched up. "Open it," said the boss of bosses. One of his boys got the job done.

"Gods. He looks weird," another said.

The kingpin asked, "What did you do to him, Dotes?"

Morley replied, "Nothing. He did it to himself."

"Right." The kingpin tossed Morley a bag. Major gold, from the sound when it hit Morley's hand. "We're quits, Dotes." And then the boss of bosses just had to do it. He just had to bend down for a closer look.

"You're right," Morley said. "You're absolutely right."

A bone white arm shot up. Unclipped claws closed in the flesh of an exposed throat. A fanged mouth rose to feed, the smell of blood bringing the fever on the monster so powerfully it could think of nothing for the hunger.

The kingpin's bodyguards started to do their jobs.

I started to make tracks.

Morley passed me before I'd gone a hundred yards. He was chuckling, which made me even angrier.

We had one hell of a blowout about it, and it might have gotten violent if Saucerhead hadn't been there agreeing with everything I said.

It was the talk of the morning, the vampire found surrounded by four dead men, feeding, so gorged it couldn't defend itself when the uphill protectors arrived. They hacked it to pieces, then burned the pieces and coffin on the spot. They threw the victims into the fire, too, just to make certain the infection didn't spread.

We were in the clear. But that didn't alter my attitude toward Morley.

Meanwhile . . .

57

Meanwhile I made a delivery of females to the Tate compound, as fine-looking a set as ever I have seen. A pity they had so many nonvisual defects between them—though I meant to see Tinnie again.

Tate at the gate, mate. Actually, as Dojango would say, Tates at the gates, mates. About fifteen of them, including the old man himself. Such huggings and kissings and tear-sheddings and backpattings. "I am amazed, Red," I said when a lull in the action gave me a chance to get a word in to Tinnie. "You'd think they were glad to see you guys." Tinnie was getting two-thirds of the attention, but that left plenty for Rose.

Only the old man remained aloof. When the crest of the storm passed, he forced his way to me and asked, "Where is she, Mr. Garrett?"

"On the wagon."

He looked. He saw nothing but the box. "You've got her in a *coffin*?"

"Did you pay any attention at all last night? She can't go wandering around in her condition."

"All right. All right." Suddenly he was a very nervous, irresolute little man.

"Come on, Pop. You're doing all right. Get some muscle to do something useful. You did get a place ready?"

"Yes." Now he was my old aunt, wringing hands. Kayean had become an important bridge to the son he had lost.

When you looked at it up close, you kind of had to feel for Rose, the living child whose return he hadn't

250

bothered to acknowledge. Maybe she thought if she got her hands on all that money he would notice her.

"Don't expect a lot, Pop. She can't do much but sit and stare at things nobody else sees. And probably just as well." He didn't know about Kayean and me before Kayean and Denny. I was not the boy to clue him, but I did admit, "I've got an emotional investment here, too. I want you to know something. You try any fanciness, you treat this woman less than perfectly, and you won't have to worry about boot soles and thunder-lizard hides anymore."

I got a little too intense. He backed off and gave me the look you give the nut on the corner preaching that pixies are the secret masters and if we don't do something they're going to run off with our sisters and daughters. Then he formed a crew of cousins and apprentices and got the coffin moving.

He had done a room, all right. Nary a window, and as light-proof as you could get. One very pale, consecrated candle burned on a mantel over a fireplace before a large mirror. A very black, very huge, very fat, very wrinkled and very old woman sat to one side, the tools of her trade on a table beside her. I recognized her. The Mojo Woman. Mama Doll. TunFaire's leading authority on the diseases of the undead.

Maybe I owed somebody an apology.

A couple of the boys got in ahead with sawhorses. The pallbearers deposited the coffin. Mama Doll moved her bulk like it was all the work in the universe. First this part of her, then that, then another, got under way, like the sailing of a ship of a thousand parts. Before anyone could mess with the coffin lid, she slapped a hand down right above where Kayean's would be folded over her heart. She rolled her eyes and mumbled to herself for a minute, then backed away and nodded.

While the boys unfixed the lid, she grabbed protective amulets from the table. A big lead-up to a big anticlimax. When they lifted the lid, Kayean did nothing but keep on sleeping.

I had to go shake her to wake her up.

*   *   *

It was evident Kayean was in control and safe to be near.

"Out!" Willard Tate ordered. "Everybody get out!"

Relatives and apprentices hurried. Mama Doll moved at her usual lugubrious drift. Garrett stayed where he was.

The boss turned on me. "Out!"

"Move me, Pop."

"I can call the boys."

"I can break both your legs before they get here."

"That's enough," Kayean said, her voice little more than a whisper. She touched my arm. "Wait outside." A ghost of a smile touched her lips, light as a moth's kiss. "I can break his legs if he asks for it." Her touch was slightly heavier, her voice softer. "Thank you for still caring."

And the boy Marine was alive again.

Only two things you can do in a situation like that. Be a goof or get the hell out.

I got.

There was light outside when Tate left. He was a wrung-out, exhausted old man. He found me blocking his path. In a hurried mumble meant to get it over, he told me things.

Kayean was going to stay where she was for a while. Part of her inheritance would be used to buy a home and part invested to create a living so she would be free of worries when Mama Doll declared her cured. Of the rest of the fortune she wanted ten thousand given to Vasco and the remainder divided among Denny's other heirs.

So Rose would make out after all.

"She is in and of the family, Mr. Garrett, by virtue of my son's love for her. You need not be concerned for her. We Tates take care of our own."

"I guess you're all right, Mr. Tate. Thanks." I stepped aside.

He limped off to his bed.

*   *   *

She was lying on the bed, cold and corpselike in the light of the lonesome candle. But at least she was in a proper bed and not laid out in that goddamned coffin. I collected the room's only chair and positioned it silently.

I stared at her for a long time, wrestling with the kid Marine. I touched her hair, which had begun to show a hint of color. When I could stand no more, I rose, bent, and brushed those cold lips with mine for the last time.

I headed for the door.

I heard a sigh. When I glanced back, she said, "Good-bye, Garrett." And smiled a real smile.

I never slowed down.

I went and wrapped myself around a barrel of beer.

Each year, on the anniversary of the day I brought her out of the nest, a courier brings a package. The gift is never niggardly.

I know where she lives. I never go up that way.

58

The probate coughed up my fees four days after I delivered Denny Tate's heir. I got in touch with Tinnie. The redhead and I did some celebrating. She was along when I went to visit the Dead Man.

She invited herself and she made it stick. Redheads are stubborn witches.

She looked at his place and said, "It's a dump, Garrett."

"It's his home."

"It's still a dump. How do you feel?"

"Almost broke. And kind of good about myself."

"Smug self-satisfaction, I'd call it."

"Come on. Try your witchcraft on him. See how far it gets you."

He woke up the way he always wakes up. Cranky. *Garrett. Again. I demand that you cease your infernal pestering.* Then he noticed Tinnie. *What is that creature doing here?* He has no use whatsoever for females of any age or species, an attitude I find too parochial. But there's no convincing him, and I doubt there would be even if he was still alive.

I tolerate too much from you, Garrett. I reap the gall-ridden harvest of my indulgence.

"You're going to have to indulge me a lot more now, Old Bones. Or you might find yourself camped in the street. You're talking to your new landlord here."

After half a minute, he asked, *You bought this place? You spent the money from the Tate business on it?*

Ah. That genius still worked. "Yes. Call it an investment in my future. The pestering has just begun."

For the first time in our acquaintance I had caught him without a comeback. The silence stretched.

I started the housekeeping while he stewed.

ABOUT THE AUTHOR

Glen Cook was born in 1944 in New York City. He has lived in Columbus, Indiana; Rocklin, California; and Columbia, Missouri, where he attended the state university. He attended the Clarion Writers Workshop in 1970, where he met his wife, Carol. "Unlike most writers, I have not had strange jobs like chicken plucking and swamping out health bars. Only full-time employer I've ever had is General Motors, where I am currently doing assembly work in a light duty truck plant. Hobbies include stamp collecting, and wishing my wife would let me bring home an electric guitar so my sons and I could terrorize the neighbors with our own home-grown head-banging rock and roll."